SECRETS IN THE

Thea Slocombe is struggling to entertain her step-children through the long summer holiday while her husband Drew works, so she keenly accepts a new job house-sitting in Barnsley, near Bibury. However, her commission proves to be far from relaxing when she stumbles across a woman hiding among some bushes. The woman's story is thin and incoherent, but Thea agrees to offer her sanctuary for the night. When her guest is found dead the next morning, Thea turns to the police for help, but their preoccupation with a major animal trafficking investigation means she is effectively on her own. As she digs deeper into the deceased's background, she discovers a tangled web of lies, secrets, and at least three very likely suspects . . .

SPECIAL MESSAGE TO READERS

THE ULVERSCROFT FOUNDATION
(registered UK charity number 264873)
was established in 1972 to provide funds for
research, diagnosis and treatment of eye diseases.
Examples of major projects funded by
the Ulverscroft Foundation are:-

- The Children's Eye Unit at Moorfields Eye Hospital, London
- The Ulverscroft Children's Eye Unit at Great Ormond Street Hospital for Sick Children
- Funding research into eye diseases and treatment at the Department of Ophthalmology, University of Leicester
- The Ulverscroft Vision Research Group, Institute of Child Health
- Twin operating theatres at the Western Ophthalmic Hospital, London
- The Chair of Ophthalmology at the Royal Australian College of Ophthalmologists

You can help further the work of the Foundation
by making a donation or leaving a legacy.
Every contribution is gratefully received. If you
would like to help support the Foundation or
require further information, please contact:

THE ULVERSCROFT FOUNDATION
The Green, Bradgate Road, Anstey
Leicester LE7 7FU, England
Tel: (0116) 236 4325

website: www.ulverscroft-foundation.org.uk

SECRETS IN THE COTSWOLDS

REBECCA TOPE

ISIS
LARGE
PRINT

First published in Great Britain 2019
by
Allison & Busby Limited

First Isis Edition
published 2020
by arrangement with
Allison & Busby Limited

A catalogue record for this book is available
from the British Library.

ISBN 978–1–78541–913–3

Published by
Ulverscroft Limited
Anstey, Leicestershire

Set by Words & Graphics Ltd.
Anstey, Leicestershire
Printed and bound in Great Britain by
T. J. International Ltd., Padstow, Cornwall

This book is printed on acid-free paper

This one's for Esther and Leonie

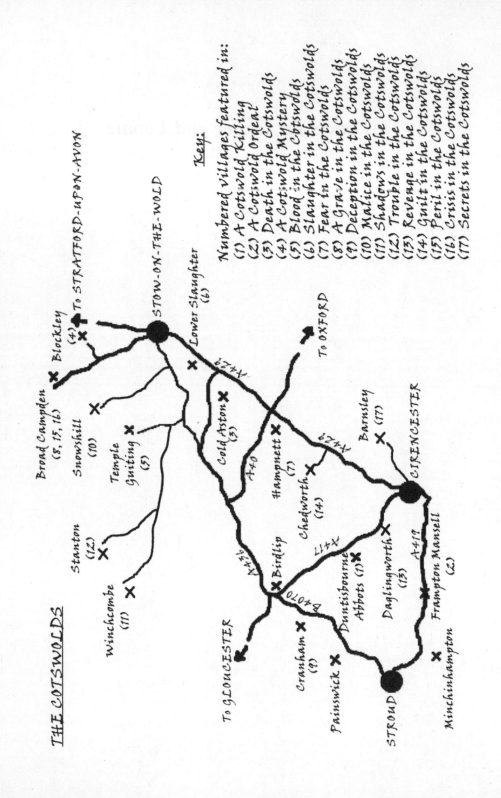

THE COTSWOLDS

To STRATFORD-UPON-AVON

Blockley (4)

Broad Campden (8, 15, 16)

STOW-ON-THE-WOLD

Snowshill (10)

Lower Slaughter (6)

Temple Guiting (5)

Stanton (12)

Cold Aston (3)

A40

A429

To OXFORD

Hampnett (7)

Winchcombe (11)

Barnsley (17)

Chedworth (14)

A436

CIRENCESTER

Birdlip

A417

A070

Frampton Mansell (2)

A429

Daglingworth (13)

A419

Duntisbourne Abbots (1)

To GLOUCESTER

Cranham (9)

Painswick

STROUD

Minchinhampton

Key:

Numbered villages featured in:
(1) A Cotswold Killing
(2) A Cotswold Ordeal
(3) Death in the Cotswolds
(4) A Cotswold Mystery
(5) Blood in the Cotswolds
(6) Slaughter in the Cotswolds
(7) Fear in the Cotswolds
(8) A Grave in the Cotswolds
(9) Deception in the Cotswolds
(10) Malice in the Cotswolds
(11) Shadows in the Cotswolds
(12) Trouble in the Cotswolds
(13) Revenge in the Cotswolds
(14) Guilt in the Cotswolds
(15) Peril in the Cotswolds
(16) Crisis in the Cotswolds
(17) Secrets in the Cotswolds

Author's Note

As with all the titles in this series, the setting here is a real village. Liberties have, however, been taken with the barn and the business park, and individual private houses have been invented.

CHAPTER
ONE

"I thought you said you were going to Bibury," said Drew, shaking his head in confusion. "What's this about Barnsley? Isn't that in Yorkshire?"

"Yes, but there's a little village in Gloucestershire of the same name, and that's where I'll be staying. It's near Bibury. All very upmarket over there."

"As opposed to the poverty-stricken hovels we live amongst down here in Broad Campden, you mean?"

Thea laughed briefly. She had been trying to reconcile her husband to her forthcoming absence for a whole week of the summer, and still he seemed to think it wouldn't really happen. She was leaving him in charge of his two children and his alternative funeral business, with the assistance of his colleague, Andrew. The school holiday was almost halfway through, during which Thea had conscientiously entertained Stephanie and Tim day after day. "Why can't we go to the seaside for a bit, as a family?" Drew had asked three days into the holiday. "Wouldn't that be nice?"

Thea had shaken her head impatiently, without really hearing the tone behind the words. "We can, if you organise it," she said. "I can't do that for you, can I? You'll have to clear the diary, let the nursing homes know — and all sorts of other things." Thinking back on it later, her words sounded cold in her own ears, but they were nonetheless true. People did not die to a schedule, and the small-scale operation in Broad Campden had no facilities for embalming or long-term storage of more than two bodies. To close down even for a week would risk disappointing people who were relying on having one of Drew's burials. Thea had gone on to say, "I think it's a bit late now. Everything will be booked up already."

For some days Drew had carried a thwarted look, which Thea belatedly supposed had to do with his own desire for a holiday. There was a subtext, which said, *Most wives would have made sure something got done in good time. I've got enough to think about without arranging family holidays.* But he knew what her answer to this would be: "If you want a family holiday, Drew — you fix it. Because for myself, I'm not sure it's something I'd enjoy." She didn't say that out loud, but they both heard it anyway. The unpredictable nature of Drew's work really did preclude any prolonged absences. He did, however, frequently find himself with very little to do for three or four days in a row. He had become adept at using these periods for relaxation, guiltlessly watching old films, reading biographies or walking the local footpaths with Thea and her dog. But he seldom involved himself in household minutiae. He was a reluctant cook and inefficient cleaner. He would play board games with his children and hang washing on the line in the small back garden, but increasingly he left domestic matters to his under-occupied new wife.

Again, there was a definite subtext that said, *If you're not going out to work, then surely it's obvious that your job is to run the house and family.* Thea could never find a persuasive argument against this assumption. She knew she had boxed herself in by having little desire to get herself an outside job, while finding the daily grind of basic survival increasingly tedious.

The suggestion that she abandon her husband and stepchildren for a short while had come a few months earlier from Detective Superintendent Sonia Gladwin, who had observed something of the reality in the Slocombe household in recent times. Her relationship with Thea had broadened and deepened over the years since they were first brought together in a village crime. Thea had found a body and Gladwin, newly transferred from the North-East, had been happy to make use of her, regardless of her amateur status. Now Thea was firmly established in a hard-to-define role that gave her an unusual level of access to police matters. Drew's profession clearly helped to make them both acceptable as semi-official assistants in murder enquiries.

Gladwin, it turned out, had a friend by the name of Tabitha Ibbotson in possession of an old Cotswold house in need of renovation. The builders had to be supervised, the contents safeguarded, and the friend was temporarily unavailable. Thea would be paid to take charge, staying on the premises day and night. It was something she had done many times before, in the company of her spaniel Hepzibah. Only since marrying Drew had she abandoned her house-sitting career, and she found herself missing it.

But this time, Hepzie was to stay behind. Stephanie had insisted, with Drew's somewhat surprising support. Thea was at first distraught at the prospect of a house-sit without her faithful companion, as well as doubtful as to how Hepzie would cope with the separation. "She's never spent more than three days without me," she protested. Those three days had been the minimal honeymoon that she and Drew had awarded themselves, a year earlier. They had gone to the Scilly Isles, while Thea's mother looked after the dog and Drew's colleague Maggs had accommodated the children. The spaniel had sat attentively at their feet, aware of being at the centre of the discussion. Thea bent down and fondled the long ears, in an excessive demonstration of her love.

"She won't even notice you've gone," said Drew heartlessly.

While the argument was still raging, Gladwin had mentioned that her friend had vetoed the presence of a dog anyway. "It'll get under the builders' feet, and there's quite a busy road through the village," she said. "And I don't think there's a proper door at the back. They've knocked a wall down, and it's open to the world."

Thea had gone to view the property at the beginning of July and hadn't been back since. "There was a perfectly good door when I saw it," she grumbled.

The distance between Barnsley and Bibury was barely more than three miles, which accounted for Drew's bewilderment over their names. Initially Gladwin had cited Bibury as the location of the property, and somehow nobody had bothered to correct her to name the smaller village, which boasted a pub, a church and a hotel that called itself a spa. In a random piece of research, Thea had learnt that it was on an old drove road, which had been replaced by the B4425 two centuries earlier, shifting the focus to the south, and causing the hotel's frontage to become its back. There was considerably more history going back to Roman times, which she resolved to investigate during the dull days of house-sitting.

And now it was only one more day until she took up residence there, and she was again reassuring Drew that he'd manage quite well without her. Stephanie was eleven, and Timmy almost nine; they could be left in the house for an hour or so while Drew conducted a burial. Thus far, he only had three funerals in the diary, but "There are bound to be at least another three before you come back," he said.

"So? If you're as worried as all that, you can ask one of their little friends' mothers to have them."

It was an unforgivably blithe response, as she well knew. Stephanie had two or three classmates she counted as friends, but they had made no plans to meet during the summer. They were all going to the same secondary school in September, and would undoubtedly regard the presence of Timmy as an intrusion, being a mere "Junior". In any case, he would resist all attempts by adults to park him at some girl's house, even for an hour.

"I can't," said Drew, listing several of these good reasons.

"Well, you could hold it over them as a threat if they don't behave."

"You mean if they burn the house down, or one of them falls out of a window and cracks its skull?"

"Oh, stop it," she snapped. "You're only trying to make me feel guilty."

"No, no. If I wanted to do that, I'd develop some psychosomatic illness and take to my bed. Then you'd tell me to pull myself together, and go off anyway."

"Like Emily's Bruce used to do," said Thea. "He was a genius at it, until she realised what was going on. I think Damien can be a bit prone to it as well."

Damien and Bruce were Thea's brother and brother-in-law respectively. Damien was experiencing parenthood for the first time in his late forties. The resulting anxiety was bordering on the pathological. One of Drew's many virtues was that he kept any tendency to worry under strict control. "My father worried enough for us all, when I was small," he said. "I grew up determined not to go the same way. Other people's neuroses are such a blight. I wouldn't inflict that on anybody who chose to live with me."

Now he said, "If I get like Bruce or Damien, you have my permission to shoot me." This was followed by a sigh, which Thea chose to ignore.

"That's more like it," she said. "So stop agonising about the kids, okay? And don't let them bully you. A bit of boredom will do them good. Stephanie's quite

6

happy with all her YouTube stuff, and Tim's got that canal map to finish. Just leave them to get on with it."

Drew sighed again at this brisk advice, but made no further objections.

The logistics of getting to Barnsley had not been considered until the last minute. The Slocombes only had one car and there was no question of Thea taking that. "I can drive you there," said Drew. "But then you'll be stranded without any transport."

"I don't suppose that matters," she said doubtfully. "I expect there's a bus into Cirencester, so I can go and do some shopping. And I can walk to Bibury and other places. There's a trout farm — I can live on fish, if necessary."

"You can order food online with your phone," said Stephanie, as if delivering a piece of wholly new information. "And a person brings it to your door in a van."

Thea groaned. "That sounds terrible," she said. "Probably more hassle than finding a convenient bus."

Drew was in complete agreement with this. "Take some provisions, then. Tea and coffee, beans and bread. Is there a freezer at the house?"

"I don't think so. The kitchen's being gutted. I can just about boil a kettle, and I think there's a microwave."

"Can you microwave trout?"

"Probably," she said.

Stephanie, Tim and Hepzibah went with them on the Saturday morning, the car full of Thea's luggage.

Clothes, books, her laptop (although she had forgotten to ask whether there would be Wi-Fi at the house and it seemed unlikely), a sketchpad and several coloured pencils, the large-scale Ordnance Survey map, boots, phone, some DVDs — there was a small television and DVD player provided — and a grubby piece of needlepoint that she had started years ago and never finished. It had been sitting patiently in her house in Witney, which was now sold and forgotten. She had wanted to throw the needlework away, but Drew wouldn't let her. "It'll be lovely when it's finished," he assured her. The picture was far from the usual cottage with garden and little stream: instead it depicted an urban scene with a crane, several high-rise blocks and cars in the foreground. Her first husband Carl had bought it for her as a joke, having found it in a charity shop, wool and needles included.

"It's never going to be lovely," Thea argued. "But it might keep me amused for a few evenings."

Hepzie could not believe her senses when her mistress got out of the car, unloaded all her bags and then told her to stay where she was. She scrabbled at the window and whined, convinced that there had been an oversight. Stephanie clutched her to her chest and repeated, "You're staying with us, Heps. It's okay — your Mumma's coming back soon."

Thea waved them off, once Drew had checked she could get into the house, and advised her with all due humility to do something to barricade herself in at night. There were tears in her eyes at her own multiple betrayal as the car disappeared from sight. "Selfish —

8

that's what I am," she muttered, before adding a mental note that surely she was allowed to have at least some time and space of her own. They were Drew's children — it was only reasonable that he should share the responsibility of looking after them. Any feminist would agree with her; but feminists seemed to be sadly thin on the ground these days.

She looked around, standing in the short driveway. At the side of the house there was a cement mixer, daubed with misshapen lumps of grey cement, its cable draped untidily around its legs. Exploring down towards the back, she found a small skip that must have been delivered on a truck squeezing through the space between the house and the hedge that separated it from a wooded area to the north-east. Whether or not there was a neighbouring house beyond the woods had yet to be discovered. So far, the only other house she'd noticed was across the road from the front gate. The skip was piled with cardboard, glass and rubble. The latter must be the ruins of the stretch of wall that had been knocked down, she realised. There was a hole into the kitchen, scantily covered with a plastic sheet. Peering inside, Thea could see rough walls where cupboards must have been torn down, and gaps waiting for new installations. There were no worktops, but the floor-level cupboards were in place. It seemed to Thea that there was a good deal of work still to be done.

She went round to the front, where she'd left the door ajar, and embarked on a quick exploration of the ground floor. The house was sparsely furnished, with no carpets in the hallway or dining room and no pictures on the walls. Her footsteps echoed along the hallway. When she opened doors, there were smells of fresh plaster, new wood, and the sharp tang of some kind of adhesive, but the main rooms did not appear to have been structurally altered. The work was all concentrated on the kitchen and what appeared to be a brand-new downstairs lavatory.

She felt much more alone than on previous house-sits. The absence of the dog went a long way to explaining this, but the ravaged condition of the house added to it. It lacked the essentials for comfortable existence — nowhere to sit with your feet up, reading a book. There was a table in the dining room, pushed against the wall, where she could put her laptop. There were two upholstered chairs in the living room, and a small television, but again, they were awkwardly positioned, as if placed there reluctantly for Thea's use, without any thought. Everything felt temporary and indecisive. The owner of the house had lived there for only a few weeks, she remembered, having bought the house not very long ago. Presumably she had spent those weeks planning the renovations, and scattering furniture more or less at random. The fitted carpet in the main living room was clearly old and unloved. One corner had been pulled up and left loose.

A brief tour of the upper floor revealed a functioning bathroom, which she knew was also due for modernisation, a back bedroom that had been reserved for her, two further empty rooms and a locked door that had to be Tabitha's private domain. Thea's room contained a single bed, chest of drawers and chair. A narrow flight of stairs led up to an attic.

It was all perfectly bearable, she assured herself. On Monday morning, builders would arrive, and Thea would have all the company she could handle. There was a list of jobs to be done by the end of the week, and if everything went to plan, she would then be free to leave. There should be secure doors by that time, as well as new flooring in the hall and a set of modern appliances in the kitchen and bathroom. With a healthy dash of efficiency and forward planning, it had to be achievable.

She went back to the wreckage of the rear wall, to examine it from the inside. It would be quite easy for an intruder to get into the kitchen if he or she realised what was going on. The biggest risk, Thea supposed, was from unauthorised squatters — but the days had long gone when they could make free with an empty house, the law impotent to eject them. She had raised the question with Gladwin, who could speak for the owner of the house on every topic, apparently. "I'm pretty brave," Thea said, "but even I might feel a bit nervous about sleeping in a house with no back door. And Drew's really agitated about it."

"Don't worry — we thought of that. The builders have made a temporary thing between the kitchen and the rest of the house. You'll see. It's almost medieval in design." Now Thea had a look, and found two stout brackets fixed to the door frame halfway up, and a plank to slot into them. It was ugly and clunky, but it worked.

The conversation with Gladwin had taken place the week before, over a quick drink in the Broad Campden pub. Thea had been full of questions, characteristically. "I'm not really worried," she said, once answers had been comprehensively supplied. "The crime rate around here is pretty minimal, after all."

"Give or take the occasional murder," Gladwin smiled. "But I wouldn't have suggested the house-sit if I thought you were in any danger. Mind you, there's been a spate of pop-up brothels."

Thea had assumed this was a joke, until the police detective enlightened her.

"No, they're perfectly real," Gladwin insisted. "Mostly people from the Far East, with girls who thought they were coming to respectable lives and jobs. Trafficking, in a word. They move into an empty house, set up shop for a while, and then melt away if somebody starts to show any concern. My friend Tabitha would not like that at all."

"No," said Thea faintly. "I don't suppose they tidy up after themselves."

"Right."

Thea had acquired a minimum of background information about Tabitha Ibbotson. In her sixties, and already earning decent money as a professional pianist, she had been left a considerable sum by her mother, two or three years earlier. The mother, it seemed, had inherited it in turn from a husband, who had been big in lawnmowers. Months before dying, he had sold the enterprise for three million pounds, and then left it equally to his son and second wife. Even after inheritance tax, they were both very much the richer. "He was a nice old chap," said Gladwin. "I knew him before I knew Tabitha and her mum, actually. He used to play bridge with my neighbour, and I sometimes made up a four with them."

"You play bridge? You never said." The game had been a factor in a recent investigation, which had drawn Thea in to an uncomfortable extent.

"Well, I've lapsed lately. I don't think I was ever very good at it, but it was a refreshing change when I was a stressed-out Tyneside rookie."

Tabitha Ibbotson, stepdaughter to the lawnmower man, found herself in possession of almost all her mother's inheritance, because the old lady died barely six months after her husband. Before long, much of the money had been spent on this house, and Tabitha was expecting to part with another fifty thousand on the renovations. "At least," said Gladwin.

There were five bedrooms, counting the one in the attic, a large bathroom, a lovely dining room and living room, both with decorated ceilings, and a garden approaching half an acre in size. Built of the usual mellow Cotswold stone, it was old and solid and beautiful. "It'd make a perfect brothel," Thea thought to herself with a smile.

CHAPTER
TWO

Managing without a car was a new experience, and Thea began to worry about it halfway through her first day. Bibury, which boasted a big hotel, several very famous old buildings, a river and a trout farm, was three miles away. The round trip would be quite a long way on foot. She also realised that she had hardly taken a walk without her dog in the past seven years. There would be something very weird about doing so now.

In the other direction from Bibury were the three Ampneys, which she was eager to explore. Ampney Crucis, Ampney St Peter and Ampney St Mary formed a cluster around their three venerable churches and would occupy a whole day quite easily. But there was also Quenington, about five miles distant, which she would have liked to visit. "I should have brought a bike," she muttered, annoyed that this had never occurred to her or Drew. While it would have been scary to set out on an open road on two wheels for the first time in over thirty years, she could in theory do it, if it was true that you never forgot how to balance and pedal at the same time. Perhaps she could borrow one from somewhere, she thought vaguely. As for shopping, she supposed she might have to accept Stephanie's suggestion and do it online. The prospect chafed her, as did most activities connected to her phone. Often the ghost of Carl, her first husband, was conjured when modern technology raised its annoying head. Since his death, the world had thrown itself wholesale into all the delights that a hand-held gadget could provide, and Thea regularly acknowledged how much he would have deplored it. Drew was hardly more enthusiastic, and between them they waged a low-level little war against the whole intrusive business. They tried never to send each other texts, much to Stephanie's bewilderment. They were scarcely more willing to communicate by actual telephone. "Will you want me to call you every day?" she asked him before leaving for Barnsley.

"Perhaps you should," he said. "Just to make sure everybody's still alive."

They'd both looked at the dog, knowing that her survival was, if not the most important, the most likely to be jeopardised. "Okay, then," Thea agreed.

She found the Barnsley kitchen to be completely unusable, since its electric supply had been cut off. Instead there was a microwave and electric kettle in the big dining room, on the oak table sitting at one side of the room. Plates, mugs, cutlery and a plastic washing-up bowl were also provided, along with a sheet of paper with the advice on it to "get water for washing up from the downstairs loo in the jug that's in there. Food can be kept in the cool box in the hall. Sorry it's all so uncivilised. You can always eat at The Pub. It's open every day." It was signed by Gladwin, but must have been dictated by Tabitha Ibbotson. Thea had already ascertained that the pub was officially entitled The Village Pub, and was uncomfortably expensive. It would make a substantial hole in the hundred pounds a day that she was being paid, if she ate there each day.

She continued to explore, finding that there was at least Wi-Fi provision, rather to her surprise. The password was taped to the router box in a small back room evidently destined to be an office, and her laptop placidly connected to the great wide world without demur. The presence of a small amount of furniture indicated that Tabitha had taken up residence here herself, to some extent, before being forced to go abroad for her job. "Which is what, exactly?" Thea had asked Gladwin.

"She's a professional pianist — surely I told you that?"

"You did not. Not a word. Will there be a piano at the house, then?"

"Bound to be — but you probably shouldn't touch it." And there was. In the main living room at the front of the house, with its tall mullioned windows and decorated marble fireplace, there was a grand piano. It was shiny and black and important-looking. What a peculiar way to live, Thea mused — always needing something like this close at hand, and what a business it must surely be to transport it from one place to another.

Tabitha Ibbotson's lifestyle was becoming increasingly hard to grasp, as the exploration went on. Did she have some other home in Britain somewhere? A flat in London or a modest townhouse in Bristol or

16

Manchester? After all, Gladwin had implied that she had been more than averagely well off even before her inheritance. Had she sold up and adopted the barely habitable Barnsley house as her sole base? How much did a professional pianist earn? Was she part of an orchestra or a solo performer? None of these questions had seemed remotely urgent until now, compared to the task of keeping Drew happy and reconciling herself to the separation from her dog.

It was midday and she was hungry. The cool box held milk, bread and some sliced ham, so she made coffee and a somewhat dry sandwich. By the evening, she would be ready for a much more substantial meal — provided presumably by the packets and tins she'd stacked on the floor. "Think of it as a camping trip," she muttered to herself. Beans on toast, cuppa soup, fruit cake, more ham. "Oops — no toaster," she realised. And no butter or any kind of spread. It was all much more irritating than she had anticipated, with the result that she decided there and then to go and eat at the Village Pub, regardless of the expense. At least it might be a way of meeting some local people. Which was another reason for resisting the idea of ordering a boxful of provisions from a Cirencester supermarket and waiting for a man in a van to bring it to her. She liked strolling around well-stocked aisles, seizing impulsively at random packs of exotic foods she would never have thought of while sitting at her laptop. And it would be good to find herself surrounded by people for a little while — if she could find a way to get there.

But before eating anything, she should go outside into the warm August sunshine and get her bearings. The house was at the northern end of the village, close to a junction with a small lane that ran westwards, and shortly before the road veered sharply to the east. Barnsley was on a kink in the Roman road known as Akeman Street (which was a lot more kinky than most Roman roads), presumably created in response to some long-forgotten exigencies arising from village life. A scrutiny of the map showed the little lane linked to another that ran in a nearly straight line from the A417 to the A429, with some zigzagging at its northern end. There was no shortage of minor roads in all directions, and without the dog to worry about, she could amble contentedly up and down them, even stopping to try her hand at a sketch or two if she felt so inclined.

So she set out to walk the bounds of the village, in a square route that added up to barely a mile in total. She went southwards, passing the usual handsome houses, the church and a particularly attractive village hall set back from the road. There were no other people travelling on foot, no dogs and no residents enjoying the sunshine in their front gardens. A small group could be glimpsed outside the church, and a pair of cyclists sailed past, smiling at her as they did so. *Gosh*, she thought, *friendly cyclists. There's a surprise.* On a recent trip to the outskirts of Bristol by car, she had three times been treated to rude hand gestures from cyclists.

Turning off the main street, she quickly found herself in a leafy country lane, bordering fields. There were no long views, and only a single farmhouse was visible. Two cars passed her before she turned again, into the lane that led back to the house. The whole walk took barely half an hour, and had taught her very little about the nature of the place. She was back again in the house on the corner — which she realised had no visible name. This omission was concerning — how did the postman find it? And all those delivery vans filling the minor roads across the land, reliant on satnavs and clearly displayed house names: where did they leave their parcels? Gladwin had mentioned that it was known locally simply as the Corner House.

The quiet of the place bordered on desolation, and Thea experienced a flash of panic at the prospect of several more days like this. At least there would be builders to talk to, she reminded herself. By the end of the week, she would probably be craving some peace and solitude after their depredations. Would they have Radio One blaring, shout to each other through the house and demand regular mugs of tea? "Having the builders in" was not something she had ever really experienced. Her Witney house had been in good order, with no need for alterations, and the one Drew had been left in Broad Campden was equally satisfactory as it was. Any decorating was done by themselves, and the occasional minor job needing a professional could be accomplished in a day.

Meanwhile there was still half of Saturday and all of Sunday to get through. Thank goodness Tabitha's living room did at least provide the television and dusty-looking DVD player. That was a major brownie point for Tabitha, given that most people "streamed" their films nowadays, if their broadband was equal to it. But Thea, always a technophobe, had no idea how such a process was to be implemented.

The sudden absence of people (and dog) was uncomfortably difficult to adjust to. Although Broad Campden was no more vibrant or populous than Barnsley appeared to be, she did at least have Drew and one or two neighbours to chat to while the children were at school. And she had the use of the family car more or less any time she wanted.

All she could think of now was to explore the top floor of the house, and then sit out in the garden with a book and some tea. And a slice of cake. But none of that held much appeal. *Make something happen*, a voice insisted at the back of her head. She could send emails, make phone calls, even invite somebody to come and join her. She could stand in the little village street and try to thumb a lift to Cirencester from a passing stranger. She could hang around the church and accost people who turned up for a look at it.

She did at least carry her bag of clothes up to the bedroom she was to use, and then went further up to look at the attic. Thea liked attics for their potential to expose secrets. There had been one in Cold Aston, especially, which had been quite a revelation, and another in Chedworth. This one, she now discovered, was surprisingly clean, had a good-quality rug laid over most of the floor, and was entirely devoid of furniture. It had a dormer window overlooking the back garden and beyond. "No secrets, then," she murmured to herself. Except for its strangely pristine condition, perhaps. The whole inspection lasted barely two minutes, before she went down the little staircase again and out into the furthest end of the garden, beyond the piles of building materials.

She stood as far back as she could, inspecting the old house. It had obviously been added to at various periods, so there was no attempt at symmetry from this angle. The frontage had been left unchanged, while the back had been thoroughly interfered with, leading to an impression of two quite different buildings, depending on where you stood. A whole extra section had been attached to the back wall, fitting cleverly to the existing roof and rising above most of it to accommodate the attic space. It had a fairy-tale quality that Thea was only just starting to appreciate. She guessed the oldest part had to be eighteenth century at least, witness to the ancient droving road, and all the waxing and waning of fortunes that Barnsley had experienced.

And through it all, she could not ignore the little voice that kept asking, *What are you doing?* Why had she so violently and uncompromisingly escaped from her family, despite their obvious need of her? It had been Gladwin's idea, and coming with such an endorsement, it had been irresistible. Thea had missed the novelty and unpredictability of her house-sitting years. She disliked routine and familiarity and tedious domestic chores. She had complained to the detective about it and hinted that she might be available for more official police work than the entirely unorthodox and disorganised help she currently gave them. "I could be some sort of consultant," she had suggested. "After all, I know my way around the Cotswolds better than most, by now." She had looked after houses in a dozen different villages, unearthing old secrets and making intelligent connections that had very often assisted police enquiries into violent crimes. Gladwin had ducked the question and come up with her own temporary solution to Thea's lack of purposeful activity. "After all, they're not your children," she had said, which had felt to Thea rather a dangerous remark. By marrying Drew, they had in effect become her children, surely? She loved them and was grateful to them for the easy way they had accepted her as a replacement mother. But there was something inescapably relentless about their very existence. She had raised her own daughter without really thinking about it. Carl had done a good share of the cooking, for a start — which Drew seldom did. Somehow, even ten years ago, life had felt simpler than it did now. Or perhaps it was merely that Thea felt under much greater scrutiny in her current role. Married to a well-known alternative undertaker, as well as being almost notorious in her own right, she could never shake free of the sense of being watched. Perhaps it was this that Gladwin — who was at heart such a very good friend — had noticed, and tried to help her to evade. And having successfully accomplished the evasion, she owed it to all concerned to make the most of it.

It was still only mid afternoon. Perhaps, she decided, she should go out again and take a different direction, getting as full a picture of the village as she could. She might even make a start on working out how all the footpaths connected, preparatory to devising a route to Bibury that did not require a risky march along a road that made no provision for pedestrians. According to the map, a path ran northwards for a short distance, then veered to the east and eventually connected to a small track that emerged shortly before Bibury itself. It looked an easy walk, provided the signs were adequate. A patch of green along the way was labelled "Barnsley Park" — not to be confused with Barnsley House. "Not very original in their naming," Thea muttered, before setting out to have a look.

It was frustratingly difficult to locate the path and took some time. Finally discovering that it began at a point behind the church, she was immediately confronted by a kind of stile she had seldom seen before. It was a solid slab of stone set into the wall, with chunky steps up to it on both sides. A dog would have to be lifted over unless it was extremely agile. She climbed over and found herself in a field liberally covered with cow pats, but no sign of any cows. The path was a thin thread of slightly browner ground, passing a tantalisingly secluded little cottage with roses growing up its back wall. Two large trees turned out to be walnuts on closer inspection.

By the time she'd crossed the field, she had almost forgotten her purpose. There was more than enough to look at and enjoy for its own sake. Another two stiles took her over the road and into a long straight track that bore all the signs of having once been a handsome avenue approaching a substantial property. When she finally noticed the property itself, it was with a small shock. On her right, behind a wrought-iron gate, stood a lovely Georgian mansion, which appeared to be the main component of the tucked-away Barnsley Business Park. A sign on the gate said, "Proceed By Invitation Only", which she thought must be the politest way of saying "No Entry" she'd ever seen.

Still wondering about the business park, she pursued the path, and found herself in a time warp. To the left was a large Elizabethan-style garden, full of roses, herbs, privet hedging in geometric patterns and generally exuberant vegetation. To the right was a huddle of old stone buildings that must comprise the workshops and commercial units she had read about on the computer. There were also small houses, and parking areas. Between Thea and the big house was an overgrown ha-ha to catch unwary intruders. There was no sign of movement. No voices or engines or barking dogs. In that respect it was familiar Cotswold territory, but here the silence seemed deeper and less easy to explain.

Creeping closer, she could just see several cars neatly parked around a central yard. The whole enclave seemed secretive and unwelcoming. She had not yet located the road by which vehicles could access it. There was something deeply ambivalent about the notion of business people pursuing their twenty-first-century careers in this particular spot. They could be doing absolutely anything, tucked away from the public gaze, no doubt minding their own business where their neighbours were concerned. Asking no questions, turning blind eyes. Thea's mind began to toy with a range of hypothetical activities going on within those solid stone walls.

There were undoubtedly other similar enterprises across the region, out of sight up small lanes. It was as if the old stone houses in the villages, with their handsome churches and upmarket pubs, were the false facade on something much more contemporary and businesslike. Had it taken her all these years to finally recognise this reality? Had she failed to notice that there was actually a great deal more going on than first appeared? Even living in the Cotswolds, she had been slow to appreciate the fact that not everybody commuted to Oxford or Stratford for their work. She regularly passed a small industrial complex right outside her own home village of Broad Campden, after all. But it was still startling to find here, in little Barnsley, that there was a fully-fledged business park, where people were not only employed, but obviously lived as well.

She consulted her map and tentatively followed a small path beside a wall that seemed to be going in the right direction. A man was coming towards her with a brown dog on a lead. Neither looked particularly friendly, and as they drew level, the man gave Thea a hard stare that made her flinch. She wanted to protest that she was on a public footpath, minding her own business, and he had no right to behave in such a hostile fashion. But she simply returned his stare with defiance and walked on. The dog had kept its head down, but there had been a slow tail-wag that suggested an inclination to make friends.

Ahead of her was another field containing sheep and several large trees, which she found to be mature beeches. The path was yet again ill-defined, and without the map she would have quickly become lost. Just one more stile, she decided, and then she would either turn back, or construct a circular path that led back to the house. There was something slightly bleak about walking in the countryside without a dog. Hepzie would have tried to befriend the one with the man she'd met and forced some sort of exchange with the hostile person. All sorts of things might have gone differently, in fact.

The final stile turned out to be the high point of the walk so far, in more senses than one. It loomed above her, at least seven feet in height, providing the only way over the equally high wall bordering the field. Thea's feeling for history left her in no doubt that here were the remnants of a large and important estate, its boundaries constructed with great emphasis three or four hundred years ago. The wall was in good condition, unambiguously designed to repel invaders. The "stile" was plainly a reluctant concession to the occasional need to get over the wall. There was no way of seeing over it, the estate concealed from view, at least from this direction.

She climbed the stone steps, each one at least eighteen inches high. No dog could have managed it, and many children would be confounded. Anyone with stiff hips or a delicate back would have to turn away and retrace their steps. But Thea scrambled up without any real difficulty, and was immediately dumbstruck by what lay on the other side.

The map showed a track, named Cadmoor Lane, which had led her to expect an easy path, possibly even navigable by cars — or at the least, horses and bikes. Instead there was a virtually impenetrable mass of vegetation. She could just discern an official way-marker pointing northwards, but more clearly visible was a printed laminated sign saying FOOTPATH, indicating that walkers should turn either right or left, heading west or east. Either would involve pushing through long grass, wild flowers, brambles and bracken. She decided at that point that she had definitely gone far enough. But then she saw something that made her pause and think again.

CHAPTER
THREE

Emerging from the dense undergrowth only ten or fifteen feet away, crouching like a wild animal and almost as wary, came a person. A female in some sort of difficulty, evidently. One shoulder looked lopsided, and the black hair was in disarray.

"Are you all right?" Thea asked.

"Hmm, umm, ohh," came the inarticulate reply.

"You've hurt your shoulder, have you?" Now fully face-to-face, Thea found herself looking at a woman of roughly her own age, with features that seemed Chinese or possibly Japanese. There were signs of suffering on her face. The body language heightened this impression. One hand was clutched to the opposite shoulder and the whole stance was bowed in pain.

"I think it might be dislocated," came the reply. "I fell off that . . . thing." She pointed at the monumental stile. The accent was slight, the English perfect, rather to Thea's relief. "But I was already hurt, before that," the woman added, as an afterthought.

"Gosh — you poor thing! That must be horribly painful. Can I get you to a doctor or something? Have you got a car anywhere near?"

"No. No." The woman was breathless, but was clearly making an effort to seem less damaged. "I'll be all right. I can walk." She kept glancing from side to side, as if expecting to be jumped on by something large and dangerous.

"Well, I can't just leave you here, can I? The trouble is, I've got no transport, either, so I'm not sure how useful I can be. We could go back to the business park and ask for help. Have you got a phone on you?"

The woman began to shake her head, before realising that this was likely to exacerbate the pain. Again she said, "No," and then added, "Sorry."

Fighting against a growing sense of helplessness, Thea tried to assess the options. She looked more closely at the injury. "You know — I'm not sure it is dislocated," she said. "Your arm's still at a fairly normal angle. From what I've heard, it would be dangling horribly if it was out of its socket. What exactly happened to it? I mean — did you land right on it? Did you fall from the top?"

"I wrenched it. I tried to save myself from falling and it got twisted." There was a clear avoidance of Thea's eye at these words, oddly suggesting the presence of an untruth. "That thing is an outrage." She glared at the stile.

"Did you hear any popping sound? Have you put it out of joint before?" Thea was frantically dredging up everything she had ever known about dislocations. Her father had had a brother who did it, making a famous family story that had been told fifty times. "There's dreadful pain, for a start," she went on. "I can see yours hurts, but you're not exactly rolling on the ground in agony, are you?"

This brisk attitude had an obviously bracing effect. "But it really hurts. It's burning right down to my elbow." An undertone of indignation roused Thea's innate curiosity. Who *was* this woman? Surely she had a whole lot of explaining to do?

"Where do you live? Where were you going? I assume you must be local, if you're out without a car."

Again the aborted head-shake, but no eye contact. "No. Not local at all. I was brought here." An expression more of emotional than physical pain crossed her face. "I ran away."

A host of thoughts filled Thea's head. People trafficking. An irate husband. An effort to evade detection after committing a crime. Immigration difficulties. One by one, she dismissed them as unlikely. The woman was surely too old to be a reluctant prostitute, and too assertive to be afraid of a husband. This was no retiring violet; despite her suffering she had an air of competence. An aura of assurance and automatic assumption of equality emanated from her. "Well, we'll sort it out somehow. My name's Thea Slocombe. What's yours?" asked Thea.

"Grace. I'm Grace."

"And where are you from?"

The woman briefly closed her eyes and exhaled slowly. Thea groaned inwardly, hearing herself ask that age-old unthinking, viscerally prejudiced question. Was it only the Brits who challenged anyone of alien appearance as to their right to be on their precious island? "I'm sorry," she said quickly. "That sounds rude. I don't mean what country. Just whereabouts in Britain?"

She was making it worse, probably. But then Grace answered with no sign of having taken offence. "My father was British and my mother's Chinese. I lived there for much of my early life, but since then I have been here. The past twenty years, anyway."

It was a carefully delivered summary, revealing nothing that Thea regarded as relevant. Neither did it answer the question she had actually wanted to ask.

"But where do you *live?* Have you got family here?"

"No, not really." The words emerged as a whisper, vaguely regretful. "My father died."

Thea did not waste breath on empty platitudes about loss. Instead she stuck to the same line of questioning, intent on getting hold of something relevant. "You say you ran away? Who from? What's going on?"

Grace swallowed, and adopted a different tone. If anything, she became even more assertive. "You don't need to know the details," she said with finality. "Are *you* local?"

Thea shook her head, aware of her supple neck and wholesale good health. "I'm looking after a house in the village. I could take you there, if you like. We should call the police, if you've been attacked in some way. Held against your will. Whatever it is that happened to you."

Grace looked up with a complicated expression that seemed to involve making a decision to trust her rescuer. "I would be grateful for somewhere to sit down," she smiled. "But there's no sense in involving the police. There's nothing they can do." The smile was fleeting, replaced by a much harder look. "I'm sure they must have better things to do," she added. "Which way is your house?"

Already Thea knew she ought to be regretting the offer of hospitality. There was something profoundly unsettling about this person. The scrappy story in itself would be a worry, but the demeanour of the woman added to the sense of venturing into something unsavoury. But Thea Slocombe, formerly Osborne, was no shrinking violet either. She was almost eager for something challenging; it could be as dodgy as it liked, if only it gave her something to focus on — it was the answer to a prayer. Drew would groan and her daughter Jessica would be horrified. Gladwin would sigh and roll her eyes — but with an understanding smile. This Grace was deeply intriguing. Small like Thea herself, and full of energy. Complicated, too. "You'll have to tell me more about what's going on," she stipulated. "I promise not to judge you," she added rashly.

"Judge me? Why would you say that? Do I look like a criminal to you?"

They were still standing on the tiny pathway leading through the overgrown semi-jungle, while shadows lengthened. It had to be after five, Thea realised, feeling hungry. She was not inclined to answer the irritable question thrown at her. No human beings were anywhere in sight. "Do you know anyone at that business park?" she asked, following one of many possible threads.

32

"Will we have to go past it to get to your house?" This was another oblique answer, but Thea assumed it meant, *Yes and I don't want to meet them.*

"Let me have a look." She unfolded the unwieldy map, and found an alternative route. "It's a bit further," she warned. "And it involves walking through all this overgrown prickly stuff and then along a road. It's very quiet, though. Is somebody looking for you?"

"Possibly. I was hiding here all afternoon. They might have given up by now."

"Who are 'they'?"

"I'll explain — perhaps. It's not a very nice story." Her lips were then pressed tightly together, giving Thea to understand that no further information was to be forthcoming just then.

"Come on, then. I'm hungry, although there's not much food in the house. I'm more or less camping there."

"How strange."

"Not really."

"I won't stay long. If you could find something to put on my shoulder, that would be really helpful."

"Is it hurting horribly? Have you been like that for long? Let's hope it's not dislocated, then — you're supposed to get it dealt with as quickly as possible. The ligaments get tighter or something, and it's a lot more difficult to put it back, if you leave it." She wasn't altogether certain of her medical facts, but it sounded right. "I don't think I have got anything for it, though. Possibly an Ibuprofen in my bag."

"You're probably right that it's less serious than I thought. Just a pulled muscle." She rubbed it gently. "I must admit I'm quite hungry and thirsty, as well. It's been a hot day."

They began to push their way along the path, in single file, Thea leading. They were going in a westerly direction, destined to meet the small road that formed the western edge of the village. It was all perfectly plain on the map, including something labelled a "field system" on their left. "What's a field system?" Thea wondered aloud, thinking Grace might be ready to be distracted. But no answer was forthcoming, and when she glanced back at her companion, she could see that walking was proving uncomfortable. Her hand was once again gripping the damaged shoulder, as if to hold the joint in place.

"Actually, I know this," Thea went on, aware that she was prattling to no good effect. "It means you can see furrows or lines where walls have been, if you know where to look. There are all sorts of Neolithic and Roman remains around here. I've always been keen on history, but I prefer something a bit more recent. Canals and old barns, for a start. And really old houses." She knew the woman wasn't listening, but she kept on talking in a forlorn hope that the walk might seem shorter if they were engaged in conversation. Grace did not seem to share this optimism. She walked with a plodding determination that Thea found painful.

"Have you been in the Cotswolds before?" she asked.

Again a sigh that struck Thea as impatience with the questioning. Then she answered in a flat voice. "Never. They brought me here from Manchester."

"Manchester? What — the airport, do you mean? Have you been away somewhere?"

The woman frowned fleetingly and then nodded. "That's right," she said.

"And you were brought here against your will? But where's your luggage?"

"In the car. Everything's in the car."

Thea tried to envisage the scenario. A terrified woman, small and powerless, threatened by criminals of some description, seizing a momentary opportunity to escape and make a run for it across unfamiliar fields and stiles with only the clothes she stood up in. The drama of it was undeniably thrilling.

"You poor thing," she said. "Were they threatening you? Have they got your passport?"

Again, there was a silence, in which some sort of internal debate was plainly being conducted. "Please don't ask any more questions. I very much appreciate your helping me like this. I could tell you were going to be kind, and capable, the moment I saw you. But I won't stay long. You don't have to worry about me, or bother with knowing all about me. My problems are mostly of my own making, if I'm honest. All I need is somewhere to stay out of sight until the danger's past." She was speaking to Thea's back, as they kept on walking. "I don't want to make any trouble for you."

"All right," Thea threw the words over her shoulder. "I can't force you to tell me if you don't want to."

"Please believe me when I say it's in your own interest. All I need is somewhere to rest, and a bit of food, if you can spare it. I'll leave early tomorrow morning. Perhaps we can call a taxi or something."

The prospect of having to find food for another mouth was starting to worry Thea. In any other country there would at least be a source of bread in a village the size of Barnsley — although possibly not on a Saturday afternoon. The shop attached to the Bibury trout farm would perhaps be open the next morning, to satisfy the many summer tourists, but that required a lengthy walk, there and back. Even Stephanie's much-lauded online deliveries would hardly manage to bring provisions at a moment's notice. "I'm afraid I haven't very much to offer you," she warned. "I only arrived today, and it's still very disorganised." For the first time she realised that her companion had no possessions whatever. No bag or coat, and her tight cotton jeans did not reveal the outline of a passport or purse. "Have you got any money on you?" she asked with her usual directness.

"No. I told you — I left everything in the car. I knew I could be found if I brought my phone with me. And no way could I use a bank card."

"Why not? Unless the police are after you, it would be safe enough. Ordinary people can't just track you by your card — or your phone, come to that."

"Before long, my people at home will ask the police to find me."

"So? Are you hiding from them as well?"

"That remains to be seen."

Thea was flooded with a mixture of frustration and excitement. It was turning into a veritable James Bond adventure. She imagined helicopters appearing out of nowhere, or perhaps a malign drone, filming them and then dropping a bomb on them. She had seen *Eye in the Sky* and knew what was possible.

They finally reached the road after what felt like an epic trek worthy of Doctor Livingstone, and turned left. "It's about half a mile down here," said Thea, peering again at the map. "Maybe a bit more. Can you manage that?"

"If a car comes, I will have to hide." They both eyed the barely existing verge and the thick summer hedge above it.

"That might be difficult."

"Perhaps if we walk close together, they will not think . . . we will not seem remarkable."

"If we hear a car, we can pretend to be picking flowers," Thea suggested, before adding, "Except you're not supposed to do that these days. They might stop and harangue us about it."

"'Harangue'? What does that mean?"

"It means giving a bossy sort of lecture. Sorry — it's a favourite word of my mother's. She says my brother does it all the time. It's true. He does."

"Does your mother live here? And your brother?" She looked around as if expecting relatives to jump over a hedge at them. "Do you have a husband?" The woman eyed Thea's wedding ring. Thea noted that Grace's hand had no matching adornment.

"No, no. My family are miles away. Yes, I do have a husband, but he's quite a distance, as well. I don't know anybody here. I've almost never been here before — just Bibury once or twice. I had no idea that business park existed, for a start. I was very surprised to find it."

"And I did not expect to be brought here, either."

"It's a long way from Manchester. I still can't really understand what happened. Did they tie you up, or what? Couldn't you have attracted attention somehow, and got somebody to notice you were in need of help?"

Grace gave her a long serious look. "You sound as if you think this is just a game," she reproached.

"Sorry. I suppose I do. It's difficult not to, actually. I mean — none of this feels very real. Even your dislocated shoulder is nowhere near as bad as you said. You haven't told me anything that sounds true. And I can tell you I've been involved in some very bizarre happenings not a million miles from here. People have died. Terrible crimes have been committed. And none of that was remotely as weird as what you've been saying. I still can't really believe the things you've told me." She paused, conscious of the hostility behind her words. It had been a defensive reaction to Grace's accusation of flippancy. And she was annoyed at the withholding of any real information. "And if you won't tell me anything, then that really *does* feel as if you're playing a game with me."

"I understand," said Grace stiffly. "Has it not occurred to you that I might be *ashamed* of myself? That the story would reflect very badly on me, and I

38

really don't want you to see me as someone to despise or condemn? All I can say is that I made a very stupid mistake, which was based on greed. The whole thing is based on greed, in fact. Now, please let's not talk any more until we get to the house. I am genuinely in pain, as well as possibly still being hunted. You have to believe that, if nothing else."

An engine was heard before Thea could respond, approaching from behind them. "Just walk normally, if you don't want to be noticed," Thea said. "Don't look at the driver. Keep right into the side." They were walking on the left side of the road, contrary to the Highway Code's advice. Drew had informed her that it was safer to face the oncoming traffic, because a driver was less likely to kill you if he could see your eyes. It was sheer human instinct, he insisted.

But if you were a refugee escaping from some nameless threat, you might well be safer to show only your back. Two women strolling along at the end of a summer's day were unlikely to be remarkable, anyway. Grace did as instructed, walking steadily, her head bowed. The vehicle slowed behind them, and then passed giving them a wide berth. Thea could see at least four heads in the silver-grey car. "They've been for a family day out," Thea said. "They won't have any spare attention for us."

"Oohhh," moaned the woman at her side.

"What's the matter?"

Grace was swaying on her feet, her eyes almost closed. "I was so terrified," she breathed. "I thought I was going to faint. Is it much further to your house?"

"Well, we've got to turn left again in a bit, and that's the last stretch. We did have to take a detour to avoid the business park, you know. Just keep on walking, okay? One step at a time and all that." There were ripe blackberries in the hedge, she noticed with regret. They'd have made a useful contribution to the meagre food supplies at the house. But she not only had to keep Grace walking, but she didn't have anything to put them in. *This is silly*, an inner voice insisted. Silly to come here without a car; silly to exchange one sort of bored isolation for another; and *extremely* silly to adopt this strange woman whose every action was suspicious.

She said nothing, wrestling with feelings of remorse at her persistent questions and sceptical reaction to those few answers she'd been given. Wasn't every crime, on some level, based on greed? Traffickers, whether of people or animals, made very good money. Betrayals and deceptions were generally motivated by a desire for something unobtainable by legal methods.

"Please don't be annoyed with me," Grace said, after a few minutes. "I just want to rest for a while. Your kindness is deeply appreciated. Tomorrow — tomorrow I'll go."

"You'll need clothes. A toothbrush. All sorts of things."

"Oh, no. Just food and drink and somewhere to lie down where I won't be found. Like an animal."

She was like a frightened rabbit, Thea realised. Or rather — a fox, escaping the hunt by means of cunning. Hiding in a thicket; taking a roundabout route to safety, driven by fear and determination to survive. All her life, Thea had sided with the fox against the bloodthirsty huntsmen and their slavering dogs.

The turning and the village roofs beyond were now visible. Talking had helped to propel them along. Another car swept past without slowing. Two people were in it, the passenger holding a phone to his ear. Grace shuddered and drooped, but less so than before. "They didn't even glance at us," Thea assured her.

At last they reached the house. It stood serene and solid, the upper windows like eyes, gazing across the distant wolds and dreaming of past glories. The front door scraped as it opened, which made Grace wince. "Another job for the builders," said Thea. "The whole place is being renovated — modernised. It's been neglected, poor thing."

"You are doing the work?"

"Gosh, no. I'm just here to supervise, basically. And to keep intruders out. In theory, anyway. The owner is usually here, but she's had to go abroad. I've never met her, actually. It's all been arranged by a mutual friend." Even to her own ears, this explanation sounded almost as garbled as Grace's story had. And wasn't this peculiar woman an intruder herself, potentially? Wasn't Thea breaking an agreement by allowing her into the house? She hesitated in the hallway, suddenly apprehensive. What on earth was she *doing*?

"I don't really understand," sighed Grace. "Where can I sit down?"

"Through there. The living room. There isn't much furniture." She followed her visitor into the room, where Grace slumped onto one of the chairs. "I'll make tea," said Thea. "The kettle's in the next room. I'll go and fetch it." She noted the surprise when she came back with the makings of tea on a tray and took it all to the side of the room, where she switched on the kettle. "I told you — it's all rather chaotic. The kitchen's out of bounds, so the basics are all in here and the dining room. Do you take milk? There's no sugar, I'm afraid."

"Black, please."

In a different world, Thea would perhaps have offered China tea, or Earl Grey. As it was, there was a box of Tetley's teabags and nothing else. The milk would soon go off, as well. "There are some biscuits, luckily," she announced. "And I've got a tin of soup and some fruit for later. We won't starve — quite."

The kettle was making a breathless sound, which Thea realised meant that there was hardly any water in it. "Oops!" she said. "Better not burn out the element." She switched it off again and took it to the downstairs toilet, where she awkwardly filled it from the cold tap of the basin. "This gets more like camping by the hour," she muttered to herself.

"How can you be here without a car?" Grace gazed up at her, the question clearly confounding her. She took the mug of tea with one hand, the injured shoulder still obviously causing pain if she moved it. "It makes no sense."

"I agree. It's ridiculous. But I thought I'd be fine just pottering about on foot, having a few meals at the pub, doing a bit of sketching. It's only for a week or so. The weather's going to be quite nice, I think." She looked out of the window at the road outside, where there was no sign whatever of any human activity. "I thought I might find somebody who'd give me a lift now and then, perhaps. It all sounds terribly vague, I know. Really, I just needed to be by myself for a bit, somewhere different." She was feeling more normal now they were indoors. Grace's obvious fear had been more contagious than she'd realised. There had been a tightness in her chest that was only noticed now that it had almost gone.

"And now I'm here to spoil it for you."

"Don't worry about it. So, what are we going to do about that shoulder? It ought to be X-rayed, and strapped up, even if it isn't dislocated. You could have torn a tendon. They take ages to heal up, if so."

"You can strap it up for me as well as a doctor, I expect."

"I doubt that. Besides, I can't see that it would be of much help."

"You're probably right. So have you anything I can put on it? A gel that might ease the inflammation? Did you say you'd got some Ibuprofen?"

Thea went to find her bag and upended it on the table. "Sorry — doesn't look as if I have." Helplessness swept through her. "I'm almost entirely useless to you."

"You've been kind and concerned. That counts for a lot. And nobody's going to find me here."

"That's true. I'm not expecting any visitors. Although there will be builders here on Monday," she remembered. "They'll see you. So you'd better be gone by then, like you said."

Grace settled herself more deeply into the sofa, looking pale but determined. "I'll have to consider my options and find some money somehow. And you're right, of course. I should have spare clothes and a toothbrush. I just wish I knew if those . . . people have stopped chasing me." She gave Thea a narrow look, her black eyes suddenly suspicious. "I can trust you, can't I, not to call the police?"

"I suppose so. What were you saying about being ashamed of yourself? Do you mean you've done something illegal?"

Grace attempted a lopsided little shrug. "That's my secret," she said. "I can't tell you."

"You're in some kind of gang, then? And your friends, or whatever they are, don't like something you've done. Or they're scared you're going to get them into trouble somehow? You've obviously upset them in a big way."

"Close enough," Grace nodded, with signs of relief. "You know the saying 'We fear those we hurt'? Well, it's a bit like that. In a way." She frowned. "Except —" She stopped herself. "No, I'm not saying any more. I need to have a proper think about it all before it makes much sense, anyway."

"All right," said Thea reluctantly, still not inclined to trust this very odd person, who virtually admitted to having at least some criminal tendencies. "But I really don't want you to stay more than one night. That's what you said. You can't foist yourself on me for any more than that." She took a long breath, and bit back any further words. It was all her own fault, after all, and there was no real reason to throw her visitor out at this stage. She could easily call Gladwin if necessary. Grace presented no physical threat, with her injured shoulder. Even if she was a karate expert or something of the sort, Thea was confident she could defend herself. Besides, what good would it do the woman to render her host incapacitated? Looked at logically, there seemed little to fear other than considerable inconvenience and perhaps embarrassment. On the plus side, she could see she wasn't going to be bored.

"Please don't worry," Grace urged her. "Nothing's going to happen to either of us now. If I can just have a bit of something to eat, I'll go and lie down somewhere and not bother you any more. Where can I sleep?"

Thea spent ten minutes warming soup, making a banana sandwich and refreshing the tea. Grace ate everything she was given, and then repeated her wish to lie down.

Here was another unforeseen difficulty. Only two of the rooms had beds in them — Tabitha's and the one Thea was using. Tabitha's was locked and explicitly stated as out of bounds; no way was Thea going to share or give up hers.

"Perhaps we can make some sort of nest for you in one of the bedrooms, but they're not at all cosy. Actually, you might be better up in the attic," she said. "It's got a rug on the floor, and we can find cushions and probably a blanket somewhere." Visions of Anne Frank floated up, adding a range of new emotions to the situation.

"An attic would be perfect," Grace enthused. "It will keep me out of your way, and I can have a long quiet sleep."

"Okay, then," said Thea.

CHAPTER
FOUR

Gathering cushions, a sheet from the airing cupboard and a blanket from a shelf in Thea's room, they slowly climbed the steep stairway to the top storey of the house. It was clean and light, but uncomfortably hot. Thea managed to push the dormer window open. The room was small and completely empty, but the rug on the floor made it a tolerable place to sleep. "Will you be all right?" Thea asked doubtfully. "It's very hot up here." It seemed perverse and unkind to banish Grace like this, when she could curl up on the sofa far more comfortably. But that would leave Thea herself with nowhere to spend the evening, having to keep quiet and still — which would be annoying. Besides, Grace herself obviously wanted somewhere private. "At least nobody would ever think to look for you up here," Thea said, as much to reassure herself as her guest. Again, she imagined Anne Frank, and other terrified fugitives from hostile forces. There was a romantic kind of heroism to the providing of sanctuary like this. She just hoped the woman was a worthy recipient of her benevolence.

Grace evidently read at least some of these thoughts. "I would be in your way downstairs," she acknowledged.

"And I am not too worried about the heat — and I suppose it will be cooler in the night. It is actually quite perfect," she said with apparent sincerity.

Still Thea had no notion of what this woman's life had been. What were her qualifications, her career? Did she have any close family? Was she actually a criminal of some kind? Was she perhaps insane? Would it be wise to barricade the way to the attic, to prevent herself from being murdered in her bed? Again, the damaged shoulder swung the argument. "Will you manage to get down to the loo?" she wondered. "I'll leave the landing light on for you, so you can find the bathroom."

"I can wait until morning," said Grace with a very oriental serenity. "I'll be more myself tomorrow."

"Good — because I still don't understand what's going on. I'm trusting you, okay?" Somewhere at the back of her mind, Thea had the idea that to mention trust was to reduce its force. People said *Trust me* when they were at their most unreliable and dishonest. Too late now, she thought.

"I understand. I really am grateful. And actually, I haven't told you any lies." Grace finished with a direct look.

The words only served to increase Thea's doubts. "Okay," she said. "Although . . ."

"You will be calling your husband this evening, I expect?"

Thea nodded.

"Can I ask you not to say anything about me? Is that completely unreasonable? Is it too much to ask? It's because he'd obviously worry about you. He might even come to see for himself. And then people might notice something unusual. It's probably silly, but I think there's a chance that they might still be watching out for me — somewhere out there. Do you understand?"

Thea found the emotion behind these words difficult to assess. Everything sounded formal and calculated, on the one hand, but why should the woman bother to say these things at all if she wasn't genuinely frightened? "Just for this evening," Thea conceded. "But after that, I'm not making any promises." Again, she felt tendrils of apprehension that this mysterious woman might actually attack her in the night. She wondered whether she could block her bedroom door somehow.

When she finally went back downstairs it was half past eight. The sun had set and an owl was hooting loudly somewhere close by. An owl! Thea thought ruefully that she would have found this exciting before she'd raised the bar on thrill levels by admitting an extremely strange woman into a house that did not belong to her. What was wrong with her, she asked herself fiercely. Nobody else would have done as she had — except she *did* have good reasons. Grace was so helpless, with no car or phone. In the face of such evident need, there really had been nothing else to do. Perhaps if Thea had taken her own phone with her on the walk, everything would have been different.

She called Drew, once she'd tracked her mobile to the pocket of her light jacket, slung over the back of a chair.

His first words made her feel that things were even more complicated than before. "Gladwin called at five with a message for you. She couldn't get you to answer your own phone — as usual. She says there are two new investigations since yesterday, and she won't have time to come and see you. She won't even be able to talk to you, the way things are going. And she's sorry."

"That's the way it goes in her job," said Thea, both philosophical and anxious at the same time.

"So — how's it going with you? Are you missing me? Us?"

"I am. It all feels a bit silly, actually. But I'm committed now. It's awkward not having a car."

"I could bring you a box of food. You didn't take much this morning."

"I might hold you to that, on Monday or Tuesday. I might equally well have something worked out by then. It's not very far to Bibury, and there's a shop there. I should have had the sense to borrow a bike from someone."

"You might even bite the bullet and sign up with Tesco for home deliveries," he said lightly. "Stephanie would be proud of you."

"I will if I'm desperate," she said, knowing the chances were extremely small.

"We haven't got used to managing without you yet," Drew said forlornly. "We've all got embarrassingly dependent."

"You're trying to tell me I'm doing something therapeutic, are you? Something that's going to be good for you."

50

"I'm trying to tell *myself* that. But it doesn't feel right. It's never going to feel right. I thought you'd finished with house-sitting for ever. It's weird to have you revert to your old self."

"I haven't done that. Maybe I just needed this last one to get it out of my system. I'm remembering how glad I was to give it up — how boring it can be. Except when things happen."

"And things always do happen. That's probably what scares me most."

She swallowed hard. How was she going to avoid telling him about Grace? How could she tell such a large lie by omission? There was no possible justification for keeping it from him, other than knowing that a secret was only a secret if nobody talked about it. "Well, this is only the first day. I'm determined to do some sketching. It's been on my to-do list for ages. I was good at drawing at school. And there's so much material around here."

"Good," he said listlessly.

"How's Hepzie?"

"Miserable."

"Oh dear." Thea felt an echoing misery on behalf of her abandoned pet.

"She'll survive. It's not the first time."

"She thinks it is. She's forgotten last year."

"We'll take her for long walks and wear her out." He coughed briefly. "Tim says she's got to go to the poodle parlour. Her lumps are a disgrace."

"Feel free," said Thea recklessly. She hated to see dogs all shorn of their natural coats. But it was true that as the spaniel got older, her hair became more matted and in urgent need of daily brushing. Nobody in the family had acquired the habit of giving her so much attention — not even her devoted mistress.

"It costs thirty quid," Drew complained.

"Shop around. There might be cheaper places in Gloucester. We don't always have to pay Cotswold prices."

The conversation smoothly diverted into domestic details, followed by a few words about the forthcoming funerals. It lasted another fifteen minutes and successfully dodged any awkward moments where Thea had to choose how honest to be. She finished the call with sincere expressions of marital commitment and dedication, which Drew accepted a trifle coolly. "I'll phone again tomorrow," she said.

Tomorrow would be Sunday, and Drew would take the children and dog out somewhere. There had been talk of Dudley Zoo, as an attraction so far unvisited. But they couldn't take Hepzie there, which left it near the bottom of the list. Thea had deliberately avoided asking her husband what he was planning. It was not her business. Entertaining the children was a relentless task that she had adamantly refused to undertake for the next week. She didn't even want to think about it.

But she was not at all satisfied or contented for the rest of the evening. She had landed herself in a pickle, as her mother would say, and not even Gladwin was available to help her out of it. In fact, it was tempting to blame Gladwin for it happening in the first place. She had urged Thea to take this job, and then dropped her into a situation that was barely tenable. Not having a car was ridiculous. Everybody had a car. It was like another limb — or a whole set of extremely necessary limbs. Now there was another woman in the house with her, also in urgent need of transport. The damaged shoulder had gone untreated, which was almost a crime in itself. Given the nature of little Barnsley, there was every chance that a doctor lived two hundred yards away, if they only knew it — although Grace would never have agreed to go looking for such a person.

The thought, however, sent Thea to her laptop. *If in doubt, do some googling* had become something of a mantra over recent years. To that extent at least she had cheerfully overcome her aversion to modern technology. She started with another look at the website featuring Barnsley Park and found it provided accommodation for numerous people in cottages scattered around the village. Units were available for a wide range of small enterprises. How easy it would be to set up something innocent-seeming, and then carry on a much less wholesome business behind that front. The set-up seemed almost to demand such behaviour. Tucked away behind rolling wolds and age-old hedgerows, never even suspected by passing tourist traffic and readily ignored by the locals, anything could be going on.

Informative as the Internet was, though, there was far more direct information to be had from Grace herself — if she could be induced to reveal it. Thinking back over everything she had said, Thea realised there was virtually nothing of any significance. The woman had come from Manchester with an indeterminate number of people, and somehow during the journey — presumably in a car — she had become alarmed, perhaps even afraid for her life. Arriving in or near Barnsley, she had run away, leaving all her possessions behind. At some point she had wrenched her shoulder and then further damaged it by falling off the big stile. Then she spent several hours hiding amongst the undergrowth and scrubby little trees, not knowing whether or not there was still a search for her going on. Yet when Thea had approached, the fugitive had deliberately emerged into full view. The implication of that was that Grace had seen a lone woman coming towards her and decided to appeal for help. Perhaps carefully staging the way she would appear, she had moaned miserably, clasping her shoulder, the picture of destitution. Anyone would have stopped to ask if she needed assistance. But she would have had to work fast — nobody could see over that impossibly high wall. Thea had not come into view until she was at the top of the stile, perhaps only about twenty seconds before Grace had crawled out of her secret lair.

The very elaborateness of the scene now made Thea suspicious. Had Grace waited all afternoon for the ideal rescuer to come along? Had she kept her eyes fixed on the stile, alert for a likely rescuer? Someone she could trust not to be associated with the gang or whoever it was that was hunting for her. Someone who looked easy to manipulate. Had Thea matched this specification in an instant, she wondered. And had she subsequently been found wanting? The lack of a car

54

must have been a blow. Or was it, she slowly started to ask herself, even more sinister than that? Had Grace somehow known about the house-sitting, the lone woman in the insecure building, with no local attachments? Had she, Thea, been deliberately set up, not just by this one woman, but by a whole group of malefactors? Should she be afraid — or was it enough to simply feel very foolish?

Every word of what she'd been told could easily be fabrication. The shoulder wasn't dislocated, for a start. It might actually be perfectly sound, the whole thing a pretence. The secrecy was alarming too, of course. People did not go into hiding, as a general rule. Battered wives, perhaps. Runaway teenagers. And criminals. All along, from the first words of the vague and shadowy story, Thea had understood, somewhere in the depths of her mind, that Grace had to be evading the forces of the law. This did not rule out the possibility that she was also being pursued by fellow felons, of course. But it now seemed glaringly obvious that she, Thea, was harbouring a wrongdoer of some description — with absolutely no good reason. There was no justification for remaining silent. And yet — perhaps there was. Perhaps Grace was a minor player, in genuine danger from more violent and ruthless crooks. Perhaps she intended to betray them to the police. Perhaps her shoulder had been wrenched by a large man grabbing her, intent on stifling her.

She took herself to bed, missing her dog as much as her husband, finding the bedding to be uncomfortably heavy for August, the water in the bathroom sadly tepid, the window impossible to open. The house itself seemed old and exhausted, reluctant to co-operate with the efforts to bring it back to life. There was a musty smell throughout the upstairs floor, with a hint of mice. There seemed little need for a house-sitter, anyway, given the absence of any valuables except for the piano. The fact that she had jumped at the offer, that she had rushed all too willingly back to her former habits, meant that everything that now happened was her own stupid fault.

With this unnerving thought, she firmly fitted a chair under the door handle, in the time-honoured manner so popular in films. It worked exceedingly well, she discovered when she tested it.

Sunday morning dawned bright and cheerful, sunshine flooding the bedroom. "Must face east, then," she murmured to herself. Which meant the attic window looked west, the room much less light. That might mean that Grace was still asleep — there were certainly no sounds issuing from the attic. Thea hoped so, for no reason she could explain. She found herself filled with resentment — blaming the woman for the poor night's sleep she'd endured, the shortage of food, the need to make decisions and ask questions. She wanted to be rid of her, to have a nice dull day with her sketchpad or a book in the garden, or a pleasant stroll around the lanes. Somehow all her curiosity had evaporated during the night, leaving only a residue of irritation and worse.

In a deliberately soft voice, she called "Hello?" up the attic stairs, more than half hoping the woman would not be awake yet. When there was no response, she hurriedly went downstairs.

"To hell with it," she said aloud. "I'm going out."

It was ten to eight, the village wrapped in a Sunday silence. With no sense of purpose other than to shake off dark feelings, Thea crossed the road to a point where the street widened to provide a short stretch apparently designed to offer parking space. There were two or three vehicles on it. She then walked towards the church and the village hall. Shortly after the church there was a side road, which she decided to explore. Within a few yards she found herself staring at an image from a fairy tale. An old barn was barely visible behind a dense screen of small trees, nettles, brambles and long dusty grass. Ivy grew up the peaked roof facing her. It was totally inaccessible to anyone not wearing protective clothing and carrying a billhook or scythe. There was a farm of some sort up to the left, presumably claiming the barn as part of its outbuildings — but why let it get so derelict? She had passed another barn closer to the church, without really giving it any attention — but this one was far more arresting.

There had also been a barn in Chedworth, much bigger than this one, but similarly unused. When first exploring the Cotswolds, she had come to the conclusion that virtually every stone-built barn in the region had been converted into a house years ago. If a farmer wanted somewhere to keep his hay, he erected a steel and concrete monster of no aesthetic appeal, and certainly no mystery. But now she had to revise that conclusion. There were still a number of these handsome, historic empty spaces, home to birds and spiders and small scuttling creatures. Here was an example so tucked away and secret that it made Thea's heart skip to see it. Remembering the grim discovery that she and Drew had made in Chedworth, she felt no desire to push through the undergrowth for further investigation. It was enough just to know it was here, in this modern world of business parks and computers and far too many cars. Had it seen the days when the old drove road was the only way through Barnsley? Was it under the protection of some kind of preservation order? Had the farm gone out of business, with everybody too distraught to give an old barn any attention? Or was something hidden in it behind all these weeds? Something that had been there for decades, carefully wrapped against moss and rust and bird droppings?

Perhaps Sleeping Beauty was in there. That had been Thea's first childish thought. An unembellished photograph of this forgotten scene would perfectly illustrate that particular fairy tale.

She followed the lane round to the right, where she could glimpse the side of the barn with more ivy climbing over the tiled roof. A little way further, and she found herself in a car park attached to the smart Barnsley House Hotel. She could see the gardens and main entrance, through a gateway in a wall, before turning back the way she'd come. She paused again by the old barn, listening to birdsong and wondering where to go next.

In the main street again, she saw people starting the day. She drifted along to the short approach road leading to the church and observed three or four people standing amongst the headstones. It was Sunday — they were probably preparing for a morning service. Not wanting to get involved, she turned back towards the Corner House. Two cars passed and a woman came out of her front door, locking it behind her. Thea knew she should go and tend to her guest. She'd been gone ten or fifteen minutes already. Ancient rules of hospitality might never have been as strong in Britain as elsewhere, but vestiges remained. She should make tea and produce some scraps of food. Under more normal circumstances, the two of them could have enjoyed an early lunch at the Village Pub — but Grace would never agree to an appearance in public — and besides, Thea wanted her gone before then. The irritation and resentment were coming back. She was more and more certain that she had been "played". Deceived, exploited, made a fool of. She would have to insist the woman left. She might even give the wretched creature some money, if it helped to get rid of her. In fact, she thought crossly, she could scarcely *avoid* giving her money for a taxi or a bus, or whatever transport Grace could find. That in itself was going to raise a host of difficulties, especially on a Sunday. With a sigh, she turned back the way she'd come, walking slowly like a reluctant schoolgirl, knowing she had no choice.

The house showed no signs of life. Thea had left the front door unlocked, and pushed it open impatiently. It still scraped on the floor. Perhaps, she thought hopefully, the sound would be enough to rouse Grace if she was still asleep. She went down the hallway, glancing into the living room and then the dining room, wondering whether Grace had come down. She then found herself wondering what she had failed to do to acquire properly hot water. The boiler must have been turned right down, or put on a very intermittent time switch. Gladwin's lengthy list of instructions had omitted that vital detail, probably because it was deemed to be self-explanatory. There had to be a temperature control somewhere that could be turned up. It was sure to be a clunky old-fashioned system, like everything else in the house. Nothing had been upgraded since the nineteen seventies.

The door into the kitchen did at least have its stout bar in place. After the many brushes with extreme violence that she had experienced, she had finally learnt to take more care. Except in this instance she had barred the back, but left the front unlocked. Most people might see this as careless, if not downright irrational, while to Thea it seemed perfectly sensible. The door had been closed, after all. And to lock her visitor in would have seemed quite wrong.

She found herself actively looking forward to the arrival of the builders next day. That, if nothing else, would probably send Grace away. The men might well need to go upstairs, for ill-defined reasons. Turning water on and off, perhaps. They were installing a range of modern equipment in the kitchen, with wholesale disruption to be expected, not least to the plumbing. Thea was required to remain on-site, dealing with any unforeseen crises — quite how, she didn't know, but it was pleasing to think she could be useful. She could take notes, perhaps, or offer sympathy. And she had to make sure nobody hurt the grand piano.

It was nine o'clock. She set the kettle boiling and went upstairs. "Grace!" she called, much more loudly than the previous attempt, at the bottom of the flight to the attic. "Are you awake?"

There was no response. *Oh well*, thought Thea. *She must have been very tired*. And she decided to leave her a bit longer. She went into her own bedroom and tidied the rumpled duvet. Again, she missed her dog. Hepzie had always given shape to the day, needing to go out, wanting a walk, having to be fed. The gap she left was alarmingly large, and Thea felt a pang of dread against the day when the dog would die. She would get another one, of course. Perhaps it would be sensible to get a puppy soon, so there would be a generous overlap. Hepzie was only eight, with perhaps six or seven years still to go. But it would be unfair to introduce a new dog when the spaniel was old and set in her ways. Now, it would keep her young and active. The idea was appealing and boosted Thea's mood considerably. She made a note to mention it to Drew when she phoned that evening.

She went down again and made tea, discovering that the milk had gone sour overnight, with no fridge to keep it cool. The so-called cool box was a poor substitute in August. There was no avoiding the necessity to do some shopping. There had to be buses in and out of Cirencester, even on a Sunday. That would be the main task for the morning, then. It would be a good diversion from the problem of Grace, who could huddle in her attic as much as she liked. The laptop would find a timetable, and location of the nearest bus stop. But when she turned on the computer, a quick consultation revealed the shocking news that buses did not run on a Sunday. She sat back in disbelief. The problem could only be solved by walking to Bibury and back, or asking Drew to bring more supplies. Why had she been such a fool as to not bring enough food in the first place? She had not thought past Saturday evening — and neither had Drew. Unless, she thought cynically, he had planned all along to pay regular visits with food boxes, as a way of keeping an eye on her.

Well, the day could not be allowed to run away like this. She went back upstairs and shouted, even more loudly than before, "Grace!!"

When there was still no reply, she stomped up the steep stairs, and banged on the door at the top. Then she pushed it open and went in.

The woman was lying on the pile of blankets, one arm flung out. Her legs were bent and splayed in an unnatural, graceless position. Her face was very white and still, the eyes open.

"Oh, God," said Thea.

CHAPTER
FIVE

The body was warm when Thea put a trembling finger to the neck, but there was no sign of life. *How?* came the question repeatedly. And *When?* And shamefully, there was also a thread of selfish panic that she, Thea, would be blamed for this. She had been stupid, dishonest, gullible. She had kept her visitor secret when she should immediately have told Drew, and probably Gladwin, of her existence. She had left the door unlocked and gone for a self-indulgent walk for no good reason at all.

Now she had to tell the world about it. She had to attract the attention of the people of Barnsley, and admit to Tabitha Ibbotson that she had seriously messed up. What would happen next? Would the police forbid the builders entry to the house? Would they send Thea home to her rightful place at her husband's side, feeding and entertaining his children?

She swallowed and looked again at the body. Police? Was this a deliberate killing, then? Given her substantial previous experience, that had been her immediate assumption. There was no blood, no visible wounds. Grace was wearing a T-shirt and pants, lacking any sort of nightwear. Again, Thea reproached herself for failing to offer anything of the sort. Not that she had a spare nightie with her anyway. The pale legs looked pathetically vulnerable, and the outflung arm suggested at least some feeble effort at self-defence. If the cause had been heart failure or a brain haemorrhage, would there have been less movement?

Numbly she went downstairs for her phone and keyed in Gladwin's number. But her call went straight to voicemail, which Thea supposed was meant to convey that this was Sunday, a day of rest, and even detective superintendents did take time off from work now and then. But hadn't Drew said Gladwin was fully occupied with two separate investigations? That she was too busy to enquire after Thea's welfare? So, didn't that mean she ought to answer her phone? She left a brief message, saying somebody had died, and she was expecting trouble.

The prospect of dialling 999 and having strange uncomprehending police officers turn up was grim, but there was no alternative. She resisted the powerful urge to call Drew for advice. What could the poor man say? Far kinder to leave that until the worst was over and she could report it all in relative tranquillity. She had brought this disaster entirely onto herself, and she ought to deal with it on her own, if that was what it came to.

So she made the call and forced herself to explain patiently to the woman, who asked a long list of questions that felt entirely irrelevant. There was a predictable moment when it was assumed she was speaking from Yorkshire. "No, it's a small village in

Gloucestershire," Thea insisted. "A few miles east of Cirencester."

"Do you know the postcode?"

"No. Sorry. I only got here yesterday. It's not my house."

Thea could visualise the woman scanning her crib sheet for this eventuality. Was it acceptable to take a call about a dead body from somebody other than the official resident of the property? Had anybody foreseen this particular scenario, and if so, what had they decided to do about it? "Can I give you directions? It's not very difficult," said Thea.

Apparently this old-fashioned idea was no longer tenable. Without precise programmable digits and letters, the responders would be lost. "Well, it's all the same to me," said Thea impatiently. "I've done my duty in calling you. If you can't process the information I've given you, that's your problem, not mine." It gave her immense satisfaction, she discovered, to turn everything around like this.

"Thank you, madam," said the woman stiffly. "Someone will be with you from Cirencester in a few minutes."

"So I should hope," said Thea.

And they were. It had to be less than ten minutes later that a car pulled up outside the house and two women got out. Two women was a first, and Thea savoured the moment. It was obviously ridiculous to suppose that they would be any more intelligent or patient than men, but there was at least a glimmer of hope that they might be slightly more human.

The hope was in vain. Something about the uniform, perhaps, rendered them every bit as robotic and cautious as all the other uniformed officers Thea had encountered. *Nearly* all, she corrected herself. There had been one or two honourable exceptions over the years. She led them up to the attic, where they stared at Grace for a minute or less, then called in the team that would deal with a sudden and suspicious death. They asked Thea for a name, time last seen alive, and brief explanation of her relationship to the deceased. Her answers were obviously unsatisfactory. "I know it sounds strange," she said with a deep sigh. "It makes hardly any sense to me, either. I don't even know for sure that her name really is Grace. She hasn't got anything with her to say who she is — was." Thea had not even tried to tell the whole story, as Grace had told it. The escape from nameless and numberless individuals; the Manchester mention; the wrenched shoulder; the hint at her own guilt. "She didn't seem ill at all — just tired and scared."

"Human trafficking?" muttered one officer.

"Seems a bit old for that," judged the other. "Can't see any signs of violence. Could be natural causes. Heart or something."

They all knew the procedure: wait for a police doctor, photographer, somebody from CID. Don't touch anything. Keep the witnesses calm and the bystanders at a distance. But Thea knew better than to reveal just how accurately she could predict what happened next. She wanted Gladwin, more than she wanted Drew or Hepzie or any member of her family. This house belonged to Gladwin's friend, after all. She would be forced to show up at some stage.

But it was another two hours before that happened. Late in the morning, when the small village had become invaded by a convoy of official vehicles, which came and went with no attempt at discretion. Local people came for a look — more inquisitively than Thea could recall from any other Cotswold incident. Perhaps they were more concerned for appearances here in Barnsley, so close to Bibury, where everyone seemed rich and important and flocks of tourists came every day to admire the old houses there. In Blockley, they had taken a murder very calmly, barely breaking a step to find out what was going on. In Snowshill and Stanton and Winchcombe, they'd been almost as uninvolved. But this one was different. Three separate people came right up to the front door, eyeing the police tape with horror, shouting for information.

"Sorry, sir. There's nothing to worry about. Everything's under control. There'll be a statement in due course."

Gladwin, when she came, was impatient to the point of meltdown. The body was still in the attic and the detective superintendent went to see. When she came down, she was pale and angry. "I haven't got time for this," she snarled at Thea. "What on earth happened? Who *is* this person? What's *wrong* with you, that this always seems to happen?"

"Nothing's wrong with me," said Thea with a rigid dignity that was the only way she could stave off sudden tears. If Gladwin was going to be furious with her, what hope was there for Drew's response? "I think I was set up, if you want to know the truth."

"Of course I want to know the truth. But I'm in the middle of something else, and it won't wait. There's a ghastly media circus, because some pest found pangolin scales in a lock-up in Cheltenham, and it's all leave cancelled, all hands to the pump." She slumped against the banisters at the bottom of the stairs. "And now you've got some illegal migrant that's gone and died on you."

"Who said she's an illegal migrant?"

"I don't know. Isn't it obvious? No papers. Foreign-looking. Unwashed as well, I suppose. I didn't look that closely."

Thea smiled wanly. "She's perfectly clean, as it happens. And I think she could just as easily have been some high-powered businesswoman from Greater London. More likely, actually, the way she came across."

"Well, I hope there's still a shadow of a chance that it was natural causes, but I have to say it looks highly unlikely. Luckily the uniforms are going by the book, just in case."

Thea gave a tentative shrug. "I don't think it can have been natural. She was pretty healthy last night, apart from a sore shoulder. Why would she just *die* like that?"

"People do," said Gladwin impatiently. "She could have had a thrombosis. What if she'd just come off a long-haul flight? Or there might have been all kinds of underlying conditions that didn't show — heart problems or something. She's not that young, is she?"

"She's not old, either. Don't get me wrong — I'd be extremely relieved if it was something like that, the same as you. But I just can't believe it. Except I can't believe somebody just walked calmly in and went upstairs and murdered her, either. I mean, I was only out for twenty minutes — that's insane. Isn't it?"

Gladwin merely groaned. Then she slapped a hand to her cheek. "What'm I going to tell Tabitha? She'll be furious if the kitchen isn't done by next week. Everything with her is always on a ruthlessly tight schedule."

"You too, from the sound of it. What changed since Friday?"

"I told you — pangolin scales. It's the most endangered animal on the planet, apparently. Chinese medicine uses it, so there's big money to be had from buying and selling the poor things. They bring them here in cars across the Channel and then sell them on. It's a huge network — almost impossible to track their movements."

"Chinese . . . ?" said Thea thoughtfully.

"So? What do you mean?"

"The dead woman — didn't they tell you? She's half-Chinese. Didn't you notice just now?"

Gladwin stared at her, then huffed a sceptical laugh. "Come on! That would be too much of a coincidence.

69

Bibury's full of Chinese this time of year, for a start. Coachloads of them, looking at that row of old houses. She's most likely one of them. Running away from a husband, or defecting or something. Do they still defect from China?"

"I don't know. Probably."

"Listen, Thea. I *really* can't stop. There's still a chance it'll turn out to be heart failure or something, and there'll be no more to be said. Except we'll have to try and identify her, of course. Let's hope she's been reported missing. Oh — and phone your husband. He sounded very low when I spoke to him yesterday. It made me think this whole exercise was a bad idea. He's trying to be brave about it, but I could tell he really hates you going off like this. And he's much too nice to blame me for it, even if it was my fault."

"I'll phone him," said Thea distractedly. "When all these people have gone. Will Tabitha want me to stay here, do you think?"

"Why wouldn't she? The builders will be back again tomorrow, and she's desperate for that kitchen to be finished. Plus, you'll be handy for the bods from Cirencester. They'll have a whole lot of questions for you. Obviously."

"Even if she died of heart failure?"

"'Fraid so. It's a bit unusual, picking up stray Chinese people and shutting them in an attic room with no bed. She was sleeping on the floor, for God's sake. What was that all about?" Then the detective put up a hand. "No, don't tell me. I haven't got time. But if it was murder, you'll have to show somebody where you

70

found her yesterday — the exact spot. Can you find it again?"

"Yes. Easily. So you're not going to be around, then?"

"That's right — I'm not. It's not just the rare species business. There's been some trouble in a farmhouse, this side of Northleach. Why in the world did I ever sign up for a job in such a place? I spend half my life driving from one remote little village to another."

Thea knew Northleach, with its big old church and unusually useful shops. If she had been staying there, she'd be able to buy all the bread and milk she wanted, she reflected gloomily. "It's not very nice here without a car," she said. "We didn't think that through very well, did we? There aren't even any buses on a Sunday."

"Why? Where do you want to go? Is this some kind of displacement activity, to take your mind off what's happened here?"

"Not really. I need to get to a shop. I didn't bring enough food with me. And don't tell me to order it online, because that's even more hassle than getting to a shop."

"Only you would think that," Gladwin sighed. "Well, I suppose I can drive you to the supermarket in Cirencester, if you come now. But you'll have to get a taxi or something back again. Although . . ." She eyed one of the uniformed policewomen, who had still not left the house. "Hi!" she called. "Sorry — I don't know your name. Do you think you could drive Mrs Slocombe back from Waitrose in about half an hour's time? She's got to get some urgent shopping."

The officer looked pained, but compliant. "Okay," she said.

"There you are. Sorted. Come on then, if you're coming."

Thea threw a few words at the reluctant chauffeur, as to where she could be found with her shopping, and scrambled after Gladwin.

CHAPTER
SIX

It was a ten-minute drive at most. On the way, Thea was treated to a monologue about the ease with which a person could order up a selection of unlimited diversity from any one of three or four supermarkets without leaving the house. "Even on a Sunday," the detective added.

"So they tell me," said Thea. "But this is still going to be quicker."

"Hasn't hit you yet, has it? Someone dying in the house while you were asleep. That's quite a thing, you know, even if it wasn't murder."

"Yes. No. I mean — I do feel rather numb about it. She was so *mysterious*. I've got a hundred questions I still want to ask her. It's like running into a brick wall, to think she's never going to answer them now. And it's so weird to think she was right to be scared. Somebody really was after her. We both thought she'd be safe in the attic — that nobody would ever find her. It's terribly sad. And everyone's going to think I was a total idiot to leave her there with the door unlocked."

"They might well think that," said Gladwin with scant sympathy. "Although I realise there's a lot more to the story than you've told me."

The supermarket was only moderately busy and Thea was amused that the detective had assumed they should go to Waitrose, as opposed to Tesco or the Co-op. Gladwin was evidently mutating steadily from a Geordie to a proper middle-class Cotswold resident.

Then the illusion was shattered. "I hope this is all right. It's the only one I know around here. I don't suppose it matters if you only want some basics. I wouldn't be seen dead here as a rule."

"You're an inverted snob," Thea told her.

They returned to the subject of Grace's death, Gladwin repeating that it looked ominously like foul play to her, and if so, she would not be the investigating officer. "Apart from anything else, I'm personally involved," she said. "It would be a conflict of interest. If it turns out that you killed the woman, I'd be seriously compromised. Not to mention that it happened in a house belonging to a friend of mine."

Thea's attempt at a laugh fell sadly flat. "I didn't kill her," she said weakly.

"Well, I certainly hope you didn't. We'll know the cause before long, at least. From the bits I've gleaned, it sounds like strangulation to me. Pressure on the carotid. It causes heart failure, if you get the right spot. The face goes very pale."

"Could it be self-inflicted?"

"Easily — but there'd be a ligature still in place. I didn't observe anything like that."

"No," said Thea. "There was nothing like that."

"Well, here we are. Don't rely on me, okay? I know it's bad of me, but it's beyond my control. The job has

74

to come first — which I realise is not ideal. It's not just you — I was supposed to take my boys out today. To be fair, I haven't let them down too often this year, so far. But they only remember the disappointments, don't they?" She was speaking in agitated jerky sentences, waving at Thea to hurry. "I'll call you," she said. "Sometime. Keep your phone on." And she drove off like a pig escaping from the slaughterhouse.

The shopping took less than twenty minutes. She snatched at packets of instant soup, ready-made microwavable meals, milk, bread, squash, biscuits, fruit, cheese and a few salad ingredients. Her thoughts were only sporadically on the food. Grace's dead face insistently imposed itself on the tomatoes and apples. A sense of guilt at her own folly weighed heavily on her chest. Why was she stocking up so lavishly when she was surely not expected to stay in Barnsley all week? Tabitha would be summoned, the builders put on hold, questions endlessly asked. Not least, of course, by Drew, who had yet to be told what had happened.

It was half past twelve when the police car came into view, stopping when she waved at it. She pulled open the passenger door, sitting with her shopping arranged around her feet. "This is very nice of you," she said, despite knowing the woman had no choice but to do as the superintendent commanded.

"Makes a change," she said briefly. "I gather you've got a special pass with Superintendent Gladwin. We'd heard about you, even over here in Cirencester." She deftly manoeuvred the car and was soon on the road back to Barnsley. Thea did not recognise the road, feeling alien and vulnerable. Rather like Grace, in fact. This part of the Cotswolds was unfamiliar to her, with Bibury almost entirely unknown. She was even more helpless without a car than she had first thought. Now it seemed vital that she should be able to get away from Barnsley at a moment's notice. Without Gladwin's stalwart support, she was alarmingly alone. The closer they came to the house, the more she panicked. "Will there be police people here all day, do you think?" She wasn't sure what she hoped the answer would be.

"I doubt it. Once they've removed the body, that might be it."

"Oh. Don't you think it was suspicious, then? The death, I mean?"

"Not for me to say. No signs of disturbance, though. Or resistance. Just lying there — but they'll not waste any time in finding out."

"Even on a Sunday?"

"That could be an issue, maybe." The woman shrugged. Thea gave her a closer look, for want of anything else to divert her. Aged about thirty, with the rank of sergeant, she was not so different from where Thea's own daughter was likely to be in six or seven years' time. Ready for anything; trained to manage a host of difficult situations; bound by the shackles of inclusivity, tolerance, rigid politeness, so that any self-proclaimed victim must be taken seriously, and any leaping to conclusions firmly suppressed. All good in theory, but often leading to inefficiencies in practice. Gladwin's scant respect even for some of the more exigent and insistent rules was the main source of Thea's liking and admiration.

"I think somebody killed her," she said boldly. "I think it's a bit slack of the police doctor not to flag it up right away as a murder, in fact. So there should be a SOCO team, and photographer and the whole works. Even on a Sunday," she added crossly.

The policewoman did not take umbrage. "We'll seal off that room until we know. Normally we probably would have got the whole team in, just in case, but they've all gone off to some farm in the wilds up near Northleach or somewhere. They can't be everywhere at once, and I gather there might be two fatalities up there. It all kicked off at the same time as your woman."

Somewhere inside, Thea felt a faint glow of satisfaction that other people got into horrible pickles besides her. She imagined a farmer shooting his overworked wife, and then himself, because the crops had failed or the bank had cancelled their loan, or their EU subsidy had evaporated. Then she chastised herself for such an unworthy feeling. "Sounds pretty awful," she said. "Poor people."

"Yeah."

There didn't seem to be much more to say. They were almost back at the Barnsley house, where Thea would have to get through the rest of the day somehow. She would be told which rooms she could use, and be interrupted at unpredictable intervals by various branches of the police. Already she had been told to stay where she could be easily found, and to call a specific number if she thought of any more useful information.

"Who is the SIO, then?" she asked the officer as they got out of the car.

The woman sighed. "There isn't one, is there, until we know if there's been a crime. Everything hinges on that. You brought a strange woman back here — she might have been seriously ill all along, for all you know. That sore shoulder you talked about — that might have been a symptom of something really bad — a blockage or something. It's not fair to accuse the doctor of incompetence. If he's not sure, then he has to say so. *Actually*," she went on with heavy emphasis, "all he has to do is declare life extinct. It's not his job to say what caused the death."

"Oh," said Thea. "I don't think I knew that."

"Look — you're going to be needed. Someone will phone you later today or tomorrow with an update, and probably a summons to be properly and comprehensively questioned — okay? You'll be all right now, won't you? Make sure all the doors and windows are securely locked before you go to bed. You've got a good friend in DS Gladwin. Pity she's so busy, but she won't forget about you. Just . . . sit out in the garden or something. Have an early night."

"Right. Thanks. You've been great," said Thea sincerely. "And yes, I'll be fine. The first thing I'm going to do is make myself some lunch."

Which is what she did, because she suddenly remembered that she hadn't eaten anything all day.

78

★ ★ ★

All the police people had gone, and the house was eerily quiet. Grace had been taken away and the locals had drifted back to their own concerns. Nobody had spoken directly to Thea, but there had been several very curious glances. "But this is Mrs Ibbotson's house," one woman had said loudly. "Who's that woman, then?" But nobody had provided an answer. The house itself, with the piles of building materials and overflowing skip, was apparently viewed by the villagers with a degree of distaste.

Would she be all right, she asked herself. A lot of people wouldn't, given the circumstances. If Grace had been murdered by a stealthy intruder who came and went in the short time Thea was strolling around the village, that had the most alarming implications. Somebody watching for an opportunity, perhaps waiting all night just a few yards away. A figure from a fairy tale, a bogeyman with evil intent.

Such thoughts were best banished quickly. A good way to do that might be to phone her husband, and tell the story as lightly and humorously as possible. He might express mild concern, but he wouldn't overdo it. He'd offer to come and see her, perhaps, and accuse Gladwin of recklessness in landing Thea in such a situation.

She called him on his mobile, and was surprised when a little voice breathed "Hello?" into it. "Is that Thea?"

"Stephanie? Why've you got Dad's phone?"

"It was on the bed."

"What? Which bed? Where are you? Where's Dad?"

"Your bed. He's here as well. He's feeling a bit —"

The phone suddenly went silent for a few seconds, and then Drew's voice replaced Stephanie's. "Hey, Thea! You're phoning early. We were just having a little Sunday zizz."

"Wasting the sunshine? Surely not? I thought you'd be going out somewhere. That's why I called the mobile."

"We decided to just stay at home, after all. We're reading, actually."

"Even you?"

"Why is that so surprising?"

His voice sounded strained, as if every word was an effort. At the same time there was an underlying urgency, a need to keep talking at all costs. "You sound funny," she said. "Has something happened?"

"No, no. Absolutely nothing. What about you? I spoke to Gladwin yesterday — did I tell you? She's ridiculously busy."

"Yes, you told me. I saw her today, actually. Busy isn't really the word. She's like a whirling dervish."

"So why did you see her? Where was she?"

Thea took a deep breath. "Listen, Drew. It's all gone a bit crazy here. Can I tell you a long story without you interrupting?"

"Try me."

She imagined him lying back on the bed, having his lazy Sunday zizz like someone from an earlier age. Even the word *zizz* came from many decades ago. Thea's grandmother had used it. "Here goes, then," she said,

80

and launched into an account of the past twenty-four hours.

At the conclusion, Drew's tone was reproachful. "You never told me a word of this last night. I didn't suspect a thing. You're scarily good at keeping secrets, when you want to."

"I know. It's a terrible fault. Not like you. You're a hopeless liar."

"So what's going to happen next? Are you staying there as planned, or what?"

"I've no idea. It depends, I suppose, on what the post-mortem shows. If Grace was murdered, that has all sorts of implications. The police will be back with a thousand questions. I'll have to go over every tiny detail about yesterday. But it won't be Gladwin. I don't expect I'll see Caz Barkley, either. Pity — I like Caz."

"She scares me," said Drew.

Caz Barkley was a new member of the local CID team, a young woman thoroughly dedicated to her job, with sharp wits and extensive personal experience of the murkier depths of British society. Thea and Drew had met her once, a few months earlier, and seen her in action.

"Anyway — everything's up in the air at the moment. I'll be sure to lock myself in tonight. Tomorrow the builders will show up — even if the police decide to send them away again."

"Why would they do that?"

"Good question. They probably won't. I'll be glad of the company. You wouldn't believe how much I miss Hepzibah. It's pathetic, but I feel as if I've got a limb missing, here without her. I keep looking for her. Going for a walk without a dog seems utterly futile."

"And . . .?" he prompted.

"And I miss my beloved husband, of course." She used a gushing, over-sentimental tone that she hoped masked the slight exasperation she felt at his neediness.

"And I miss you. So do the kids. But we'll survive. Just make sure you do as well." Again he sounded strained, and slightly breathless.

"Don't worry about me," she breezed. "At least I've got some food now. And the weather's really good."

"All of life's needs satisfied, then," he said. If it had been anybody but Drew Slocombe speaking, she might have thought there was a hint of sarcasm in his words.

CHAPTER
SEVEN

Sunday evening closed down early, with thick cloud rolling in from the west. Thea barred the door into the kitchen at seven o'clock, and yet again wished she'd insisted on bringing the spaniel with her, in spite of Tabitha Ibbotson's refusal. For years she had taken the dog for granted, sometimes ignoring her for days at a time; but now she resolved never to be parted from her again. The mere fact of another living creature in the house with her would have made a tremendous difference. Instead there was the lingering presence of a dead woman, suddenly and violently gone with all her secrets unrevealed.

She sat in the living room with her needlework, silence all around her. There was no bird song outside and very little passing traffic. She had tried the television, but found it didn't work for some reason, which meant she wouldn't be able to watch DVDs either. Probably never been upgraded to digital, she thought crossly. She wanted to be quiet with her own thoughts, as well as able to hear any unusual sounds. What she felt was not exactly fear, but she was certainly on the alert for any threats. At some point since speaking to Drew she had become certain that Grace had been murdered. A person had come into the unguarded house, made his or her way up to the attic and somehow killed the sleeping woman. It was ludicrously unlikely, and yet far from impossible. Thea's imagination had always been fertile. Now she played with notions of implanted tracker devices, enabling Grace's enemies to find her with ease. Or perhaps Grace had come downstairs and used Thea's phone, calling a trusted friend who promptly betrayed her. Perhaps the two women had been observed walking through the lanes the previous afternoon and entering Tabitha Ibbotson's house. The front door was visible from at least one other property, and they had inescapably been seen by the occupants of two passing cars as they walked. If Grace's story was even half true, there could have been a concentrated search under way for her, with watchers reporting every movement she made.

She went back over every detail of the previous day, preparing herself for an inevitable police interview when the cause of Grace's death was eventually established. The strange lack of information, the obvious fear, the damaged shoulder — it was all clear in her mind, while at the same time not a very credible tale. Who else but Thea Slocombe would have so readily accepted the burden of an unknown fugitive and given her sanctuary in a house not her own? It was ridiculous to have done such a thing. And yet she could not see any moment when she had much of a choice. What else could she have done? She might, in fact, have done considerably more if she'd had a car at her disposal. She might have deposited Grace at an A&E somewhere, for a start. She might have driven them to a remote country pub and treated them both to a proper meal. And how odd that Grace had shown so little surprise at the absence of any such ordinary action.

Grace had known, of course, that there was no car available. Thea had told her that from the start. And she had been almost numb from fear or exhaustion or pain or trauma. The implication of her story seemed to be that she had flown in from some foreign place, landing at Manchester and being swiftly collected by people who turned out to be of malevolent intent. A simple story, if hard to credit in the smiling English countryside. While Thea knew there were people traffickers and drug smugglers and poachers of rare animal species — and many other extreme sorts of crime — all going on within a few miles of where she was sitting, she had very seldom been made directly aware of them. The many killings she had stumbled across since embarking on her role as a house-sitter had almost all had simple domestic explanations. Feuds, jealousies, old grievances and sudden flashes of rage had been more than enough to account for them. The idea that now there might be something much larger and nastier behind this particular sudden death was alarming. It felt fantastic, almost *unreasonable* — which she admitted to herself was foolish. But it took everything she knew about human behaviour to a different and much more threatening level. If there was some sort of ruthless gang operating from behind the bland facade of the Barnsley Business Park, then what hope did she have of evading them? If they thought Grace might have revealed a secret about them, they might well come after Thea herself.

With her mind full of unsettling thoughts, she firmly locked the front door and went up to bed. As on the previous night, she wedged the chair under the door handle before climbing into bed.

Monday morning was not only cloudy but damp. Light rain was falling, as it had done on and off for much of the summer. The weather had been a contributory factor to Thea's sense of imprisonment at home and exacerbated her restless mood with every passing week. That was why she'd accepted this unappealing commission, she reminded herself. That, and the money she was being paid, and the rampant curiosity she always felt in a new place.

But she shook off the inclination to revisit reasons and excuses, and tried to brace herself for whatever events might be in store for her over the coming day. Whatever happened, there would be people, voices, activity. After the silence of the previous evening, that in itself would be welcome.

And so it turned out. At precisely nine o'clock, a truck drew up just inside the front gate, disgorging two men. Thea met them on the doorstep, rapidly ascertaining that they knew nothing about the ructions of the day before. "Hi — I'm Sid and this is Dave," said the older man. "You must be the house-sitter. Not very comfy for you, with no kitchen. How've you been coping? Mrs Ibbotson knew where her best interests lay, didn't she? Soon as things got tricky, she found herself suddenly in great demand somewhere in Europe. Missed this weather, as well, lucky cow."

"Watch it, Sid," said Dave with an alarmed look. Then he smiled at Thea. "He don't mean nothing by it. Mrs I's a real star. Lovely lady. You'll be a friend of hers?"

"Friend of a friend, actually. The fact is, I've never met her. But listen — there's something you should know about before you get started. Come in for a minute."

She took them into the living room, and tried to give a brief account of the weekend. Sid interrupted every few seconds, horror ever more visible on his face. "Dead!" he repeated, as if the whole idea was new to him. "Up there in the attic? Blimey!"

"We should know today what she died of. If there's a full-scale police investigation, that might affect where you can go in the house — for a day or two, anyway. But it should be okay to be in the kitchen. I know Tabitha's got you on a deadline for that."

"End of the week, including the bathroom," nodded Dave. "Might need us to stay late once or twice, to get it all done. But we have to get into the roof, for the plumbing, see? The hot water tank's up there."

"Yes, well — we'll just have to take it a day at a time, and see what happens."

Sid was still numb with amazement. "But she can't have just *died*. People don't just die like that. And who *was* she? That's what I don't get. Not somebody you knew, at all?"

"No, I told you," said Thea, as patiently as she could. "She'd lost all her stuff and needed somewhere to sleep. I couldn't put her in Tabitha's room, because she's locked it, so we made a sort of nest in the attic. It can't have been very comfortable, but at least there was a rug on the floor. The other bedrooms are completely bare."

"Hot up there, as well," said Dave. "Maybe that's what did her in."

"Maybe," said Thea, who had withheld quite a lot of the finer details. "It was all very unlucky, and I was probably an idiot to bring her here in the first place."

"What does your 'usband think about it, then?" asked Sid with a glance at her wedding ring. "Must have something to say — nasty business like this."

She hesitated, torn between an indignant reply that it was no concern of her husband's, and an amused acknowledgement that men still believed that wives should remain under close scrutiny, and nothing but trouble came of letting them have too much independence. "He's not too worried," she said lightly.

"Hmm," said the man, clearly disapproving.

"Come on, Sid. Best get started," urged Dave. He led the way through the hall to the barred door. "I see you've made good use of this," he said to Thea, who was trailing after them.

She forestalled the next inevitable question by saying, "That's right. Very clever of you — although it's going to leave holes in the door frame."

"It's coming out anyhow," said Dave. "She wants an archway instead. Should look nice," he reflected,

88

staring at an imagined remodelling of the imperturbable old house. "The trick is not to do too much, see, with a house like this. Everything's all been thought out already, centuries past. All we've got to do is get it a bit more up to date, like. Can't change the outside, of course. Not in these parts. Perish the thought!"

"It's not listed, is it?"

"No, thank God. But there's all sorts of by-laws and neighbourhood agreements and I don't know what. Not that Mrs I would want to mess with any of that, anyhow. She just wants things to work a bit better, so it's not so cold in winter and sweltering in summer. She thinks there'll be better air flow without a door just here. And there was some damp needed fixing upstairs. We've got quite fond of the old place, eh, Sid?"

Sid nodded, still struggling with the morning's news. "Right," he mumbled. "Tiling first, we said, didn't we?"

"Once we've got the new sink in. Shame about the weather. We'll be out seeing to the drains later on."

"Drains?" Thea had an instant vision of the garden being ripped up by a mechanical digger.

"Nothing much. Just have to get the new pipes bedded in. Then we can start the new wall tomorrow. Got another couple of chaps coming out for that. Should go up in no time. Half of it's window, anyhow."

"Then we'll have a proper back door for you to lock," said Sid, reassuringly.

"Not tomorrow, surely?"

"Thursday morning, latest."

"Good, because that's mainly why I'm here — to guard the house while there's no proper security."

Dave treated her to a long thoughtful gaze. "Sounds to me as if you're not doing too great a job in that department, so far. Are you?"

She could do nothing but laugh ruefully and leave them to their work.

She sat in the living room again, with a mug of coffee and a portable radio she had found on a shelf. Assuming it to be defunct, she had been pleasantly surprised when it worked perfectly. Now she had it tuned to the blandness that was Radio Two, trying to adopt a matching mood. No sense in worrying, she told herself. Whatever happened next was out of her control. And even if she had felt able to do something, she would be wise to refrain. Gladwin and Drew would both agree on that point.

At ten-fifteen she received a text on her phone. "Still impossibly busy. Will try to send Barkley later today with update. Don't go anywhere till then. Might have found a car for you."

The promise of a visit from Detective Sergeant Caz Barkley gave Thea something to look forward to. The young woman had been transparently bemused by Thea and her ambivalent involvement in police murder investigations when they had first met a few months earlier. It would be good to see her again. Even more comforting was the suggestion of a car.

Don't go anywhere till then was rather an impertinent instruction, to Thea's mind. Where could she go, anyway? Well — she might walk to Bibury and catch a bus back. It was Monday — there were two or

90

three buses during the day. She was curious to have another look at the discreetly hidden Barnsley Park, and see how it looked on a working day. But even she could accept that this might not be a very good idea. Until the facts were known about Grace and how she might be connected to people who lived or worked at the park, it could be hazardous for Thea to venture there. And she'd be in trouble with Gladwin if she missed Barkley.

All the same, a whole day confined to the house was clearly unacceptable, even if it was raining. The rain looked as if it would soon stop, anyway. The bus could take her into Cirencester, where she could go to their famous museum, or browse the Oxfam bookshop. Ironically, now she had the promise of a car, she suddenly discovered that there was plenty she could manage to do without one. She wondered how it was that Gladwin could conjure up a vehicle, just like that. Had it been confiscated from some hapless drunk driver? Did the police keep a small stock of cars for a variety of purposes? Or what?

Sid and Dave were working quietly in the kitchen, and she wondered whether she should be showing a bit more interest in their progress. There was a cooker to install, and a dishwasher. Otherwise, as far as she could see, it was just a matter of slotting in a fridge and a freezer and getting the worktops in place, before tiling the new walls. She had to admit that she found the details of someone else's kitchen entirely uninteresting. Tabitha Ibbotson had not gone overboard on solid marble or smoked glass, as far as Thea could tell.

91

Everything she'd seen so far was more or less normal and unpretentious.

Radio Two had stopped its warbling to give listeners the ten o'clock news headlines. Second from the top was a piece about the trafficking of rare animal species, especially pangolins. Items had been found in a garage in Cheltenham, and a large-scale police operation was underway, to track down the criminals concerned. There were leads in Birmingham, Manchester and Leicester. "Uh-oh," said Thea. Gladwin's brief explanation of the previous day tallied exactly with the report on the radio, and amply accounted for her excessive busyness. What vile people these traffickers must be, she thought. And how short-sighted, the way they wiped out whole species for instant gain. But probably they didn't think like that. They came from desperate mean streets in places like the Philippines and survival was all they cared about. But however hard she tried to be tolerant and understanding, she found her sympathies remained firmly with the animals. She visualised herself working as a ranger, tracking down the criminals and shooting them as they tried to trap the unwary creatures. She thought she would rather enjoy that.

Such ferocious thoughts persisted through the next half hour or so. She had been sporadically enraged by elephant and rhino poachers, big-game hunters, with plenty of emotion to spare for tigers and orangutans. Her first husband Carl had been a committed environmentalist and much of his concern had transferred itself to Thea, even five years after his death.

She found herself wanting to rush off and join Gladwin in her hunt for the cruel characters who'd brought their trade all the way to Britain.

The association with Grace was inevitable for several reasons. The Chinese connection, mainly, of course. But the proximity in time between the Cheltenham discovery and Grace's death might also be significant. Had the woman been deceived into transporting pangolin scales, perhaps? And when she realised what was happening, she had threatened to expose the gang, and thereby got herself killed? It all seemed to fit very neatly. It made Grace into a good guy, rather than a willing participant in a gruesome trade.

Too much thinking, Thea decided. The only antidote was to get outside, and instinctively she looked round for the dog, intending to announce "Walkies!" Yet again the absence made itself felt with a sharp pang. She would make a point of asking Drew for assurances that the spaniel wasn't pining as much as her mistress was when she phoned him that evening. An evening that still seemed a long way in the future, with the rest of the morning and a whole afternoon still to fill.

With little conscious thought, she turned right outside the house, heading towards the centre of the village as she had the previous morning. The trees were gently dripping on her as she passed the church and noticed again a small group of people amongst the gravestones. They could almost be the very same people as had been there the day before. Were they ghosts, then, or very realistic statues? Intrigued, she went through the wooden gate, next to an unusual stone

93

arrangement that appeared to be designed to prevent sheep entering the churchyard. The people ignored her, as she strolled nonchalantly towards them, pausing to read headstones as she went.

Quite soon she realised that they were doing the same thing, with cameras and notepads, making the point that there was some serious researching going on. Family history, then, Thea concluded. Gleaning dates and names and sometimes other details from the lichened stone. There was a woman with a very straight-edged dark-brown fringe just above her eyes, and a man with a pronounced limp. They were working in pairs, moving from one grave to the next at a regular pace. The very intentness caught Thea's interest. There were muttered exchanges and a lot of note-taking.

"Excuse me — I've got to ask what you're doing," Thea said, as she came closer. "Are you recording every grave? Aren't they already in the church archives?"

The man with the bad leg paused in his note-taking and nodded at her. "We're researching family history."

"Oh?" Thea frowned. "Wouldn't it be easier to consult the records? Parish registers and so forth?"

"Normally, yes. But it so happens that our local records have been damaged. We've offered to try to fill the gaps, while we're working on our own project. There's often a lot of useful information on a headstone." He waved at a pair of slightly crooked monuments, lavishly filled with lettering. "Look at these, for example. The whole family's listed here. And there are sometimes little hints as to the people's trade." He turned to his left. "Over there, you can see

94

where the stone's got a sort of pie-crust topping. It means the man was a baker."

"Gosh," said Thea, who had heard of other instances where local records had come to grief through fire or flood or general neglect. "Must be fun."

"Oh, it is," said the man's partner, who was holding a professional-looking camera. "We're learning such a lot. You think you know your own village families, but it's been a *revelation*. Makes us want to delve much deeper and find out how all these people interconnect. It's mostly nineteenth century, of course, so not terribly far back." The woman appeared to be about seventy. On a quick calculation, Thea realised that her grandmother could easily have remembered the 1890s.

"I'm quite keen on history myself," said Thea, thinking of her abortive efforts to form a local group in Broad Campden to investigate some forgotten details of the Arts and Crafts Movement. "But how will you know where to stop? I mean — if you only researched the people buried here, it would take years of work. And the buildings . . . the drove road. I read about the drove road . . ." She tailed off, aware that she was attracting an uncomfortable level of scrutiny. "I'm just staying here for a bit," she added.

"You're not the woman in the Corner House, are you?" asked the person with the fringe. "Where somebody died? All those *police*. What a commotion!"

"That's me," Thea admitted. "And I suppose it was already a bit disruptive, with the builders and everything."

"That poor house won't know what's hit it. The old lady who was there before hadn't touched a single stone for fifty years or more. This new one — what's her name? — she seems all right in her way. Not that anybody's seen much of her yet. Comes and goes without any warning. And now there's you. A relative, are you?"

"Friend," said Thea with a smile. "Just keeping an eye on things, making sure the builders do what they're supposed to."

"So who died?" burst out the older woman. "That's what nobody can understand. Who in the world *was* she?" Her expression was a mixture of eager curiosity and apparent concern for Thea herself. "It must have been *dreadful* for you."

"Thank you." Thea found herself unreasonably grateful for even this crumb of sympathy. "The thing is, I'm not supposed to talk about it. It's all under police investigation, you see."

"No, we don't see at all," said the lame man, with a short laugh. "From the very few facts we can glean, it sounds as if you must be the prime suspect in a murder. That's what my young relative would say, anyhow. Sudden suspicious death of an unnamed woman. Our Ben would love it. As soon as he gets to hear about it, he's going to come dashing back down here, you see if he doesn't."

"Oh, Dick!" scolded his partner. "Don't make it sound as if that would be a bad thing. You know how you love having him."

"He's a bright boy, I'll say that for him," conceded the man.

The second man, who had said nothing so far, finally spoke up. "Pity he's at the other end of the country. We'd all like to see more of him — and the rest of his family. They've been the only ones who managed to keep the whole thing going." He pulled a rueful face. "Not one of the rest of you has done your bit."

"As you never tire of reminding me," said lame Dick.

"And it's no use accusing me of letting the side down," said the woman. "As far as Dick's concerned, females don't qualify. And I'm only a distant second cousin anyhow."

"Come on, Norma — that's not fair," Dick protested. "I never said any such thing."

"Well it's too late now," said Norma with a slightly uneasy laugh.

The second man joined in. "And it's none of my business anyway — as I'm sure you're itching to remind me. Even so, I'd be happy to have young Ben back again. He was invaluable when he was here last week, the way he helped us get a proper website up and running, and talked us through the mysteries of spreadsheets."

Both the men appeared to be in their seventies. Again, Thea performed her instinctive calculations as to generations and their relative ages. Since marrying Drew, the compulsion had only grown stronger. The most fascinating aspect of his funerals to her was the way the families were constructed. There would be devoted in-laws, committed cousins, second marriages

97

and teenage mothers. Aunts and uncles could be younger than their nieces and nephews, and it seemed that society abounded in step-relations. Thea loved to disentangle them with Drew at the end of the day.

It was a refreshing relief to be chatting to such normal people, pursuing such a wholesome activity. Even though they were understandably curious about the Grace business, they hadn't been especially persistent. They all seemed considerably more interested in their family history project.

"Well, I should get back," she said. "I'm meant to be keeping the builders happy."

"Keeping them at it, you mean," said the woman with the fringe. "I know how that goes."

"They seem very good, but there's quite a tight deadline."

"Good luck, then." That seemed to be a polite dismissal, and Thea started to drift away. It had killed about half an hour, at best, but she felt more grounded for the little outing. The very existence of these friendly villagers made a big difference to her mood.

The builders seemed to be hard at it when she returned to the house. She went round to the back garden and observed an obvious change in the stacked boxes and materials that had been there. As far as she could tell they were installing the dishwasher already. But there was no sign of the new window that had to be put in before the missing wall could be built and a new back door provided. She found herself impatient for better security, mentally rehearsing a whole new set of reassurances for Drew that evening.

For no reason at all, she decided to see if the online Scrabble website was still there. It had been four years or more since she last participated in a game and she supposed she would have to start again with a low ranking since there was no way she could remember the password she'd used. It was, though, still the same computer, and when she found the site buried in her lengthy "favourites" list, it sprang into life as if nothing had changed at all. Everything was exactly as it had always been, including her username (thewit, which was short for Thea and Witney) and the last place she'd achieved on the score chart.

With a sense of reverting to an earlier self, she clicked on someone called wozz0855 and was soon immersed in a fast game. She found herself recalling obscure words like *qoph* and *trez, baju* and *qanat* and cheerfully placed her tiles to spell *fulmine* on a triple word. When the game was over, and her ranking had jumped a few points up, she opted to observe a high-rating game, where almost every word was at least six letters in length, and the points scored were astronomical. It was hard to believe these were real human beings, rather than robots, but she admired their skill just the same. The idea that she might actually be learning something removed any lingering sense of guilt at indulging in such a time-wasting activity. What else should she be doing, anyway, she wondered. Nobody needed her to go anywhere, even if she could have done. A bus trip to Cirencester and back was the height of her ambition until released from this very ambivalent commission.

Her mobile came to life as she was still wondering what to do. "Mrs Slocombe? Cirencester constabulary here. We understand you're expecting us to call you about the fatality under your roof yesterday?"

"Not exactly my roof, but yes, I knew you were going to want to talk to me."

"Can you come in, then? Do you know where we are?"

"I do, yes. But I haven't got any transport. Do you want me to get the bus?"

"Urn . . . hang on a second . . ." There was a muttered exchange and then he came back. "We'll send somebody for you. Give us twenty minutes."

"All right, then."

But within ten minutes, the same person had called back to say they thought there would be more to be gained by Thea escorting a couple of officers to the place where she first met the deceased. That being so, it would have to wait a little while. "Can we say two o'clock?"

"No problem," said Thea.

And then it was noon, and she began to think about trying the pub for lunch. Another self-indulgence that her mildly puritanical husband would doubtless disapprove of, but she considered she'd earned it. She'd already established that the pub served food on Mondays, unlike some, and its somewhat pricey menu no longer felt like a deterrent. She resolved that she would limit herself to a maximum of two meals there

100

during her stay, with perhaps a third on the last day as celebration if the mystery of the dead woman had been solved by then.

She was wondering whether to change into a more respectable outfit when there was a knock on the door. She had an idea who it would be — an idea confirmed when she went to open it.

"Hello," she said. "I wasn't sure whether I should be expecting you. I was just off to the pub for lunch. We'd have to go now, because I've got to be back here by two."

CHAPTER
EIGHT

"I'll come with you, then," said Caz Barkley. "How far is it?"

"About three minutes' walk. Didn't you notice it when you came through the village?"

The detective sergeant shook her head. "I was too busy trying to find this house. I was sure Gladwin said the gate was green." They both looked at the wide wooden gate that was unambiguously brown. "Maybe it's just been painted."

"I doubt it," said Thea. "It doesn't look as if anyone's touched it for decades. The hinges are all wonky, so you can't really open or shut it. But you found me anyway, so that's all right."

"I've got the results of the post-mortem."

"That was quick." But then she realised that the revelations mined from Grace's body must be informing the Cirencester police, and would explain their need to speak to Thea.

"Not really. They start early. It was all done by ten, and they emailed the report right away." She waved her smartphone, to indicate that every pathological detail was securely lodged in its inner workings. "I can show you in the pub, if it won't put you off your food."

"Why? Is it very gruesome?"

Caz Barkley did not reply, throwing a cautious glance towards the kitchen, from where builder noise was issuing. "Better not say much here," she said.

"Okay. Come on, then. I expect I'm respectable enough, aren't I?"

Barkley eyed her baggy shirt and cut-off jeans and shrugged. "Shouldn't think it matters," she said.

During the short walk, it occurred to Thea that Caz was behaving oddly unprofessionally. She must surely be aware that Thea was officially "a person of interest", indeed, the only identifiable suspect in what was now looking very like a murder investigation. Yet here was Detective Sergeant Barkley intruding on a case that did not include her on its team, and about to reveal findings that certainly ought to be kept secret.

There were only a few people at the pub, scattered around the three distinct rooms. "Let's order the food and then sit outside," said Thea, who had developed the habit thanks to the almost constant presence of her dog. Caz quickly ordered a fruit juice and a cheese omelette, making a face at the price. Thea dithered before opting for fishcakes and a pint of Butty Bach ale. It seemed to her that she was getting better value for money than the young detective.

"Well?" she prompted, once they were settled at a table under a blue umbrella, in the company of one other small group of people. "Don't keep me in suspense."

The young detective answered almost too starkly. "It was murder. Pressure on both the carotid arteries by someone who knew what they were doing. It's not as easy as it looks on the movies, but it's not especially complicated, either. Your lady had pressure on both sides of her neck, cutting off blood flow to her brain very quickly. She actually died of heart failure, according to the pathologist."

"Oh, hell." The words were less forceful than they might have been, due to Thea's anticipation of just such a revelation. She felt wary and puzzled. "So — I must be a suspect, surely?"

"Well — on paper, perhaps. But anybody who knows you can see the idea's ludicrous. And just about everybody in the Gloucestershire police does know you, as far as I can tell."

"Okay. That's a relief." She paused, visualising the helpless woman, probably still barely awake, facing a determined killer looming over her. "She was right to be scared, then," she said. "All along, she was right. She said 'We fear those we hurt'. It sounded wise at the time, but I suppose it's obvious when you think about it."

"Someone out for revenge, then," said Barkley, with fresh animation. "That gives us something to go on."

"Only if you know who she was, surely?"

"We'll soon work out an identity for her. Everyone's so well documented these days, it can't take long."

Thea's mind had drifted sideways. "Oh Lord — what's *Drew* going to say?" Her abandoned husband loomed large in her thoughts. She could feel his exasperated concern from twenty miles away.

104

"Don't ask me. Wasn't he in something of a similar situation, a while back?"

"That's how we met, actually. I suppose it's good that he'll have an idea of how it feels. But what are the Cirencester people going to think? *They* don't know me, do they?"

"Gladwin's going to have a word with them, when she gets a minute."

Thea forced down a feeling of panic. It was irrational and distracting. There was nothing for her to worry about, she insisted to herself. But it certainly gave added force to the need to discover precisely who *did* kill Grace. And for that, she needed as much information as she could possibly get. "Do you have any idea what time it happened?" she asked.

"I imagine you know how that goes. She was warm, virtually nothing in her stomach, and a few other details that all point to only an hour or so from the time the police doctor got to her. That has to be a guess, of course. But it seems reasonably solid."

"Thank heaven for that, at least. I mean — that must make it less likely to have been me. If I was going to kill her, wouldn't I have done it in the night?"

Caz shook her head reprovingly. "Don't start thinking like that. You know you're going to have to go through every moment from when you met her on Saturday to when you called 999 yesterday. You *are* technically a person of interest, obviously. The *only* one, come to that. We're checking her teeth, clothes, DNA — anything that can identify her — but you're the only one who saw her alive."

"I realise that," sighed Thea. "So — are we doing that now? Here?"

"Of course not. It'll all be done formally in the interview room in Cirencester. I shouldn't be talking to you now, actually. You probably figured that out already. I'm nothing to do with this investigation. I've got no reason to be here, and if you quote anything I'm telling you, I'll be in serious doo-doo." She grimaced. "I'm not too pleased about it, to tell you the truth, but Gladwin says we can trust you, and we owe it to you to make it as easy as we can, after she got you to come here in the first place. But there's a limit to what we can do. All I'm saying is you'd better have a really good think about everything the woman said to you. Any tiny clue about her background, why she was here, who she might know in the area — the sooner we've got an identity for her, the better sense we might make of her death."

"So, I've only got myself to rely on to get me out of this mess," Thea summarised, feeling suddenly unafraid. If anything, there was a sliver of exhilaration somewhere inside her. Another murder mystery to pass the time was shamefully welcome. "It's almost as good as an old-fashioned locked-room puzzle, isn't it? Except the doors weren't actually locked," she added. "I do feel bad about that. If I'd behaved like a responsible house-sitter, the poor woman would still be alive. Maybe I should be charged as an accessory — if only an unwitting one."

Barkley gave her a severe look. "Don't go trying to make things worse than they already are. You're not like most people, Mrs Slocombe. On the one hand, you wander off, leaving the house completely insecure, and on the other, you invite a totally strange woman in and give her a bed for the night."

"Most people would think both those things were criminally careless. And I didn't give her a bed — just a room, and some cushions on the floor."

"Better than a ditch," said Barkley.

"Marginally." Thea agreed. "But I know Drew for one is going to say I brought all this on myself. I told him most of it last night, and he was fairly unimpressed. Didn't seem to want to talk about it, which I assume means he's cross with me."

"Superintendent Gladwin said he was a bit short with her, as well. Can't expect him to be happy, I guess. How long have you two been married — not long, I gather?"

"A year."

The word echoed inside her head. "A year exactly. Oh, my God — what date is it today?"

"The twelfth."

"No! Is it really? Yesterday was the eleventh, then? That was the date! Our anniversary. I forgot all about it. Never gave it one single thought for months. How idiotic of me — I *knew* we'd been married a year, but never associated it with an actual date. Does that make any sense? Lord help me — what's he going to think?"

"It's generally the man who forgets," said Barkley with a little smile.

"It's not funny," moaned Thea. "Why didn't he *say* something? Why didn't somebody remind me? I'll have to phone him. What am I going to tell him?"

"Don't ask me. It's not something I've ever had to think about. I guess you could send him a text right away if you don't want to phone him."

Thea shook her head. "No, that would be cowardly. I *do* want to phone him, but I daren't do it now. He might be in the middle of a funeral. I think he's got one today."

"Cowardly," Caz repeated thoughtfully. "I don't see that, to be honest."

"You'll have to take my word for it, then." She sighed. "Well, I deserve whatever I get," she decided. "I'm a rubbish wife, going off and leaving him like this and completely forgetting the date we got married. I can't imagine how I'll ever make it up to him."

"Well . . ." Barkley clearly didn't like the direction the conversation had taken. "I think we're done, aren't we? Didn't you say you had to be somewhere at two?"

"Oh — I should have told you. I've got to take some police people to the place where I first found Grace. You could come as well, I suppose. If you wanted to."

Caz shook her head. "No, I'd better not. No time, anyway. Now, let's see — how much was that omelette?"

Thea realised that she could not expect a free lunch courtesy of the Gloucestershire Constabulary. In fact, she got the impression that she might be expected to pay for both meals. She made a mental note to ask

Jessica what the protocol was for such a situation. "Don't worry about it," she said. "I'll go and settle up."

"No, that's not allowed," said Caz sharply. She proffered a ten-pound note. "I think this is about right. Can you get them to give you a receipt?"

"Okay, then." Thea performed the transaction, and they went back to the quiet village street. All Thea's thoughts were on Drew and her utter failure as his wife. She wanted to phone him the moment she got back to the house, but he was highly likely to be conducting a funeral. It would have to wait until later in the afternoon. Generally, there would be no pressing commitments after about 3p.m. "Thanks a lot for coming to tell me all that," she remembered to say. "Tell Gladwin I'm not panicking at the thought that I'm suspected of murder. I'm panicking a lot more about forgetting the anniversary, to be honest."

"She'll think it's her fault. Wasn't this whole thing her idea in the first place? I think she already feels bad about it."

They were standing in the driveway of the Corner House, right beside Barkley's car. "She's hopelessly busy with this pangolin thing," Caz went on, with a dark look. "Honestly, I thought I'd seen the worst of human nature, but this is a whole new level of barbarism. There really aren't any words for it. And I've only heard some odd bits — Gladwin's up to her elbows in it." The detective's face seemed to glow with black thoughts. "If you ask me, it's almost as vile to torture and kill animals as the things they do to children and other human beings. I know I'm not meant to say that, but I think I've got the right. After all, I was an abused child, and I've got over it. I can even almost understand what drove them to do it, and how having a kid tipped them over the edge. But when these total monsters do it for *money*, and it's all based on such utterly brainless superstition, I see red."

"I know," said Thea, still not properly attending. "That idiotic Chinese medicine."

"If you ask me, there's too much respect paid to primitive beliefs and practices. Look at FGM. And about a million other things."

It was a rant with which Thea had some sympathy, but she was in no mood to encourage it. Barkley was young and ideological and uncompromising, as well as a lot more experienced than Thea herself was, at least in some respects. She would no doubt make a fine police detective when she'd had time to absorb some of the nuances that governed human behaviour. She had sharp wits and more than adequate self-confidence. "Mm," she said. "I guess we'll have to leave all that for another day."

"What? Oh — right. I should go. Good luck with the Cirencester people. I'll try and call you to see how it went — maybe tomorrow."

"Thanks, Caz," said Thea.

"Sorry about the anniversary date," said Barkley as she got into her car. "You'd never have remembered if it hadn't been for my big mouth."

"I should be grateful, then. What if I *never* remembered it?"

110

"That might have been the best thing," said the detective, before starting the engine and driving away.

The older builder met her in the hallway, holding a steaming mug. It smelt like strong sweet coffee. "Bloke came looking for you," he said. "You just missed him."

"Oh?" Her first thought was that it must have been Drew. Then, that it had been somebody from the Cirencester police station, arrived early. "They could have phoned me, whoever it was."

Sid shook his head. "Didn't seem to want to do that. Said he'd rather see you in person."

"What did he look like? Did he have a bad leg?" It must have been the man from the churchyard, she assumed, come to offer her some company.

"Not that I noticed. Youngish. Tall. Bit of a beard. Nice smile."

Something chimed in the depths of her memory. "Was there a dog with him?" Although the man with the dog was unlikely to have a pleasant smile, on reflection.

"Didn't see one. Might've tied it up at the gate. He came round the back when nobody answered the knocker at the front."

She was still thinking about the sour-looking man with a large dog that she'd met on the path the day before. He'd been the first person she had seen after her arrival, before encountering Grace under the trees. Why in the world he should come calling on her now was beyond imagining. And anyway, she thought confusedly, it wasn't him, because she was fairly sure he

111

didn't have a beard. So who was it? The idea of a strange visitor, given recent events, was profoundly unnerving. "Didn't he leave his name?" she said.

"Oh, well — he did, actually. Said he was called Clovis, and you'd remember him."

CHAPTER
NINE

"Why didn't you say that at the start?" she burst out, loud with relief and surprise.

"You didn't give me a chance," he said reproachfully. "All those questions."

"Right. Sorry. Did he say if he was coming back?" Did she *want* him to come back? Could she cope with the disgracefully glowingly handsome importunate Clovis Biddulph? How on earth had he found her, anyway? Could he have simply gone to the Broad Campden house and asked Drew where she was? And would Drew have told him?

She had met him a few months earlier, during a very upsetting murder investigation and, completely against her will, had found him disconcertingly attractive. *Nice smile* was a massive understatement. When Clovis Biddulph smiled, the world was bathed in light. She had just about kept her feelings hidden from Drew, even after the case was over and she assumed she would never see any of the Biddulphs again.

"Said he had to be somewhere, but might manage a quick return visit later today."

"Okay. Thanks, Sid." She wouldn't be there then, either, she told herself. She'd be out showing police officers points in the Barnsley undergrowth, and then answering questions at the police station, and perhaps acquiring a car through Gladwin's kind offices. If Fate had any sense, she would make absolutely sure that Thea Slocombe and Clovis Biddulph would never find themselves alone together in a lovely old Cotswold house.

She should phone Drew. She needed the grounding that he would provide, and a reminder of her identity as his wife. She also needed to update him on the matter of the dead Grace. The woman had been murdered. Somebody had stolen into the house during the few minutes that Thea had been just down the road admiring a forgotten barn and inventing fairy tales. That was a lot more frightening than she had permitted herself to acknowledge. It could only mean that somebody had been watching her and Grace, waiting for an opportunity. But then, as she rehearsed her account for Drew, it struck her with a shock that there was another possible scenario. The killer could have come into the house and crept up to the attic while Thea was still asleep in the spare bedroom. He could have silently listened at her — Thea's — door. Luckily, the chair she'd used as a barrier would not have let him get in. Without Hepzibah to sound the alarm, it would have been easy for anyone to gain access to the attic. Thea had always slept deeply. As a child, her siblings had performed numerous practical jokes on her while she slept, and now Stephanie and Timmy were learning that they could get away with all sorts of mischief within inches of their dormant stepmother. But no —

the back and front had at least been securely locked overnight. There was no chance that a killer could have gained entry without noise and damage.

She could reassure Drew, then, that she personally had not been in danger. She would emphasise the walk she'd taken, exaggerating its duration, and the way she had so carelessly left the door open at the house. She would tell him about Sid and Dave and how sensible and hunky they were. It was much more permissible for her to flirt with the builders than to entertain seriously adulterous fantasies about Clovis Biddulph.

She spent the next ten minutes thinking about Drew, their life together, the business, and the various ways in which the future might unfold. She thought about where he was at that moment — almost certainly outside with Andrew. It had become their daily habit to meet at the burial ground, whether or not there was a funeral, and discuss plans for the coming days, monitor the existing graves and any saplings or markers for which they were responsible. "People pay us to make sure they're looked after," Drew had explained, when Thea had remarked that he seemed to be as much a gardener as an undertaker, at times.

But this week would be different because he was in charge of his children. He might take them with him to the field, or even leave them for half an hour — but he might equally well decide on a family outing at short notice. She wouldn't know until she phoned.

The knock on the door came five minutes late. A man and a woman stood there, both wearing plain clothes. They did not smile. The woman carried a large

115

camera. "Mrs Slocombe?" asked the man. "We're from Gloucestershire CID. I'm DS Goodbody, and this is DS Tompkins." He showed his identity card, for good measure. "We understand you have agreed to take us on an examination of a . . . position on a footpath?"

"Sort of," she agreed. Fancy sending two sergeants, she thought. Wouldn't a constable have been good enough?

"Lead the way, then," Goodbody invited.

"Right. Yes. Although . . . um . . ."

"Yes?"

"The thing is, the path I took starts behind the church. But there's really no need to do that again. We could take it from where it crosses the road, which is that way." She pointed to the left. "It's a bit dangerous, though. There's a bend, and no footpath. But it would be a lot quicker."

"I see," said the man, not quite convincingly.

"We'll be all right. We'll go in single file. There's not a lot of traffic, is there?" The female officer spoke decisively. "Let's get on with it."

So Thea led the way at a brisk march, along the road towards Bibury, only with difficulty recognising the stile she'd used to get onto the track that ran alongside Barnsley Park. She climbed over quickly, anticipating with some amusement the faces of the officers when they reached the monumental crossing place over the high wall, at the far end of the track.

Again, she followed the footpath up towards the big beautiful mansion behind the politely forbidding gates, and tried to construct a viable scenario for what might

116

have happened to Grace. Mostly she kept her thoughts to herself, simply escorting the police officers at a steady pace and saying very little.

But her companions were more voluble. "She ran away from someone over there, then, did she?" said Goodbody, indicating the business park. "Then over these fields to the woods up there?"

"I suppose so," said Thea. "But there's no way to be sure."

"Not much cover," observed Tompkins. "They'd be able to see where she went."

"They could have left her alone in the car," Thea suggested diffidently. "If there really was a car, that is. I can't be sure that anything she said was true."

"Why? Did she come across as a liar?"

"Not exactly . . ." Thea tailed off, uneasy at speaking ill of a murder victim who could no longer defend herself. "Some of what she said sounded a bit . . . rehearsed."

"Hm," said Tompkins. "According to the file, she told you she'd hurt her shoulder. Is that right?"

"She said it was dislocated. That was more or less the very first thing she did say, actually. But after a few minutes I came to the conclusion it wasn't as bad as that. Just wrenched, I think."

They got to the immense stile in a few more minutes, and stood staring up at it. "Wow!" said Goodbody.

They slowly climbed over it, Thea first, then Tompkins. Goodbody stood back to watch, observing that anybody in a frantic hurry could trip and fall from the top. For a small person like Grace it would be quite a tumble. "If she landed on her shoulder, she might well hurt it enough to think it dislocated," he mused.

With elaborate care, Thea demonstrated how exactly she had found the fugitive, and what happened next. "It was just here," she told the officers. "She said she'd been hiding under all that bracken and stuff, for a long time. Hours. You can see it would be quite easy to stay out of sight — and it doesn't look as if people ever come along here, anyway."

"Better have a proper look," said Goodbody, and started to push his way into the point indicated. Almost immediately, he was forced onto hands and knees. "Did you do this?" he asked Thea, over his shoulder.

"Definitely not. She came out almost before I was down from the stile. Can you see anything?"

"It's a bit flattened. Er . . . a couple of threads caught on a thorn. Hey, T. Come and take some pics, will you?"

DS Tompkins activated her camera and approached in a crouching posture. Thea stepped back, content to leave them to their forensic investigating. It was both like and unlike scenes from TV dramas. No white paper suits, but an impressively thorough search for all that. Small plastic bags were filled with minute threads and hairs. Pictures were taken of indentations on the ground. It took at least ten minutes.

"Well, that seems to confirm what you've told us," said Goodbody, finally crawling out and standing up again. "Where to now?"

Thea explained the route she and Grace had taken back to the house, and awaited a decision as to whether it was necessary to follow in their footsteps. "She was obviously terrified of being seen," she told them. "The walk must have seemed endless to her."

"And did anybody see her?" asked Tompkins.

"Possibly. Two cars passed us on the way."

"But neither of them stopped? Did they slow down?"

"No, I don't think so. But I suppose they could have recognised her, but just kept going, so as not to attract attention. Or something." She began to consider the possibilities more closely. Had someone in one of the cars phoned a co-conspirator watching from some point in the village? The driveway of the house could be seen from a variety of viewpoints, after all. If it was a matter of great importance for Grace to be recaptured without causing a commotion, the sensible strategy would be for a car — or two or three cars — to circle the area, on the assumption that eventually the fugitive would have to emerge onto a proper road, in order to get away from the area. Then the watchers might have quickly established where their quarry was spending the night, and who it was who had rescued her. But again, she kept these thoughts to herself. If she did choose to share them with the police, it would be better done during a formal interview at the police station.

She did, however, find it oddly satisfying to have a credible explanation worked out, albeit hypothetically. It rendered the murder somehow less frightening, once it became clear that ordinary levels of common sense and persistence had been all that was needed to find and kill the woman they were chasing. Even if the whole thesis turned out to be completely wrong, it was still theoretically practicable, and therefore possible to confront without panic.

"We'll go back the way we came," decided Goodbody. "We've got all we need for now. They'll be wanting to question you back at the station. We're to take you there. Then we'll come back to the house and give the attic room a proper going-over. We'll probably be gone by the time you get back."

"What about the builders?"

"They won't be a problem. We might ask for their fingerprints, for purposes of elimination."

The return walk was soon accomplished, and Thea was being urged to waste no time in accompanying the officers to Cirencester. Quickly gathering bag, door key, phone and coat, she went round to the builders to explain that she would be out for a bit, and there would be a team of forensic people all over the house.

"Whoa!" said Sid.

"They might want your fingerprints, if that's okay." Both men shrugged, not quite able to hide their excitement. Neither one seemed worried about being fingerprinted. Thea added that they should put up the barricade into the kitchen and leave through the front, pulling it firmly behind them, if she wasn't back by knocking-off time and the police people had gone by then.

"Leave it to us," said Sid jauntily.

"Thank you," said Thea, with a sigh.

CHAPTER
TEN

The interview took place in a small room with a bank of machines against one wall. "Are you going to film me?" Thea asked facetiously, eyeing something that looked like a camera.

"Not today," said the man, without a smile. "What we'd like from you is as much information as possible about the deceased. Ideally, we'd like you to recall every word she said to you."

For a few seconds, Thea was transported to another police interview, some years earlier, in a very similar room. She had been on her very first house-sitting job and had heard a man being killed in the garden outside. The detective superintendent who interviewed her had become rather more than a friend in the following months. He had been kind and understanding — a very nice man, as all her friends and relations observed. Just as Drew Slocombe was a very nice man, of course. She sighed and did her best to concentrate on the matter in hand. "I'll try," she said.

It turned out to be easier than she'd expected. The interviewer prompted her with just the right questions, and she found herself repeating many of Grace's actual words. "She didn't say very much, actually," she realised. "A lot of it was just sort of *implied*. But I do remember her saying, 'My father's British and my mother's Chinese.' She spoke perfect English, so I guess she's lived here for most of her adult life."

"Okay. The pathologist thinks she's about fifty — would you agree with that?"

"She looked younger, but I wouldn't argue about it."

"Did she say any more about her family? Children?"

"Nope. Just parents. I think they're dead." She paused. "Actually, I'm not sure about that. Perhaps just her father's dead. I don't remember anything about her mother."

"But she never gave a surname? Presumably it's something British — that's if her parents were married, I suppose."

"Definitely no surname," said Thea. "And I'm not totally sure I believe the 'Grace'. The trouble is, even at the time, I wasn't sure I could believe much of her story."

"Interesting," said the interviewer dubiously. "Now — you told our officers yesterday that she'd come here from Manchester."

"So I did. That's what she said. As far as I can recall, she'd been met in Manchester — I guess the airport, but she didn't say that, so it's probably just me jumping to a conclusion — and driven down here. Something happened in the car to frighten her, and she made a desperate escape, leaving all her things behind. She didn't have money or phone or passport or *anything*. She seemed to think she could be traced if she used a cash card or a phone. I told her that was ridiculous."

"Hm," said the interviewer. "So it didn't seem very credible to you?"

"Right. Although she was genuinely frightened. I am sure about that. I mean — something bad must have happened to send her off into the woods with absolutely no possessions."

"You've seen the TV reports of refugees and migrants arriving empty-handed, haven't you? They deliberately destroy their passports. It makes it more difficult for the immigration people to decide what to do with them. They don't know where to send them back to, if they think that's what ought to happen."

"So?"

"So it makes it extremely hard to separate the sheep from the goats, the legal from the illegal. And it creates a whole subculture of migration tricks, designed to get a foot in the door of a nice peaceful country where work's easy to find."

Thea shook her head. "That doesn't fit. She was too self-confident, too well educated, to be one of those people."

"You'd be surprised. We've had people at the top of their profession turning up pleading for asylum, looking as if they've spent a month in a ditch. Which some of them have, probably."

"I still don't think it applies to Grace."

"But she was frightened? She behaved like a fugitive?"

"Yes. She cowered behind me with her face turned away when the cars went past. And I'm sure she had a damaged shoulder. It can't all have been an act."

"But she didn't say how that had happened?"

"Well, yes — she said she fell off that stupidly high stile. But she also told me it was dislocated, when I first met her, and I could see it wasn't as bad as that."

"But she refused to go to a doctor?"

"Well, not exactly. I wouldn't have been able to take her to one, even if I knew where to go on a Saturday afternoon. It didn't occur to me to call an ambulance — it wasn't bad enough for that. And it seemed to get a bit better on its own once she was in the house. We decided it didn't need a sling or anything like that."

The man gave her a steady, considering look. "The pathologist couldn't find anything wrong with her shoulder," he said.

"Oh! Well, pulled muscles must be hard to spot. Would there be any signs, once she was dead?"

He actually winced at the starkness of her words. "It would have to be a very minor injury."

"Sorry," she said. "I'm married to an undertaker, remember. I'm used to dead bodies."

"Ah." He glanced down at the page of notes in front of him, turning back to look at earlier sheets. "Nobody thought to mention that."

"It's not important. Just means you don't have to worry about being unduly delicate in what you say to me."

Again he looked long and hard at her. "You are aware, aren't you, that on paper you look like the best — and only — proposition for having perpetrated this unlawful killing?"

124

"Prime suspect," she said, with a rueful smile. "But only on paper, surely? I mean — nobody can possibly think I really did it. Why would I?"

"'Why' questions are not always helpful," he told her ponderously. "Why would you take a total stranger into the house, to start with? Not even your own house. And then leave her there completely unattended and vulnerable, when you knew she was afraid of being found?"

Thea experienced a moment of self-knowledge. "You know what? I think I was hoping she'd just quietly creep away, if I left the door unlocked. When she didn't answer my call before I went out, I was half-thinking she might already have gone. I went off like that to give her a chance to get right away. But at the time, I wasn't consciously thinking that. It was all instinct and gut feelings, until now."

The man nodded and made a note on his pad. There was a recorder running, which he had pointed out to her at the start. Then he went through the exact state of the house doors, which felt superfluous to Thea. She had explained all that the day before to the officers who came to the house. When she suggested this was repetition, her interviewer put his pencil down and adopted a severe expression. "It was not an official murder investigation at that point," he reminded her.

"Point taken," she conceded. "And I admit it was very sloppy of me when I knew Grace was so frightened. I should have been more careful for her sake, but she was up in the attic and I wasn't scared at all. I suppose I thought all danger was gone, with a new day and everything seeming perfectly normal."

"It's still not easy to understand," he insisted.

"But isn't that always how it goes? Real people doing unpredictable things for no apparent reason. Not just telling lies and keeping secrets, but being thoughtless, acting on impulse, contradicting themselves. Real life is terribly messy, don't you find?"

"No, not really," he disagreed. "Most people are very predictable, and their lies are usually easy to spot. Even the secrets generally boil down to love affairs or stealing money."

"Not in my experience," she insisted.

The man gave himself a little shake. "We're not here to discuss human behaviour. Let's stick to this specific case, all right? Can we go back to when you first met her? She told you her shoulder was dislocated, but what did she want from you? What did she ask you to do for her?"

"Um . . . nothing, really. She left it all to me. I told her I hadn't got a car, but I could offer shelter and a bit of food. I hardly had anything. I didn't bring nearly enough with me on Saturday. I'm always hopeless with food. The whole business is so *boring*."

"Was she hungry?"

"Very. Even though she was tired and overwrought, she managed to eat and drink everything I gave her. She said she'd been out in those woods all afternoon, and was thirsty."

"All afternoon?"

"That's what she said."

"So, according to her, she was up in Manchester for some reason — you think she must have just landed at the airport, do you?"

"She must have said something that implied that, but I can't remember what. It could be that I assumed it and she agreed. I might have put the idea in her head."

"Well, we have to check it as far as we can. So, she could have been met there and driven to the small village of Barnsley by people she decided were posing a threat to her, so she ran away from them — all during Saturday morning — right? That's entirely feasible. She could have been telling the truth."

"Can't you check the passenger lists? They probably have photos of everybody, don't they? You can easily find out if she was on a plane."

Another severe look came her way.

"Sorry," she said. "I shouldn't be telling you your job." She paused. "But it might all be resolved, if you find her on a list. You'd have identity, home address, next of kin, passport details." She grew more animated. "It would give you a whole lot to go on."

"Indeed," he said repressively, before opening a familiar map of the local area and spreading it out on his table. "So, is there any more you can tell me? You walked back to the Corner House via the roads, instead of using the footpath? Have I got that right?"

"Yes. Grace didn't want to go past the business park. She seemed to be saying that that was where she'd escaped from."

The officer traced the paths and roads with the end of his pen. Thea watched, thinking again how very different the printed marks were from the reality on the ground. "Your detective sergeants have got all sorts of bits of fluff and photos from there that will confirm what I've told you. You'll see how terribly overgrown it all is. She could easily have kept out of sight under all that vegetation."

"That's a distance of less than half a mile, then, from the business park."

"That's right. I'd say hardly more than a quarter of a mile, actually."

"Don't you think a determined search would soon have found her?"

"No, not really. They wouldn't know which way she'd gone, once she was over that enormous stile. The wall's much too high for anybody to see over it."

He sighed and shook his head.

She pointed again at the map. "It must be a local landmark. You have to understand what it's like there. You can't see what's happening on the other side of it. Grace could have gone in any of three directions. Given that there would have been at least a few people and dogs around on a Saturday, it would be risky for anybody with malicious motives to start crashing about searching the undergrowth for her. Any walkers would think it peculiar if they saw men charging through the woods beating the bushes and so forth. If they wanted to be discreet about it, she'd easily have managed to stay hidden. And she didn't say how many there were. There might only have been one."

"Did she say 'they' or 'he'?"

"Good question. Let me think. 'They'. She definitely said 'they'."

"So what else did she say?"

"Well, she definitely didn't want me to go to the police. She said she'd been deceived somehow. She said she'd made a stupid mistake, something to do with greed." More was coming back to her, even after she'd assumed she'd reported the whole conversation. "Yes, that's what she said, more or less. She obviously didn't want to tell me any details. Perhaps because she thought I'd disapprove. Or worse. If she was involved in trafficking rare animals, and let that slip, I'd have certainly called the police. Obviously."

He leant forward. "Is that what you thought she was doing?"

"No, no. Not at the time. Gladwin told me about finding the pangolins in Cheltenham later on." She stopped to reflect. "No, I didn't really think Grace was doing anything criminal. I thought she was more of a victim than a wrongdoer. Although she seemed to be feeling guilty about something, all the same. She said, 'We fear those we hurt,' which I took to mean that somebody was out for revenge. And when you think about it, she did seem more the sort of person who'd victimise other people, rather than having it done to her. If you see what I mean."

"But you did eventually make a connection between her and the rare species investigation. Can you tell me why?"

"Because she was Chinese," said Thea unhappily. "Does that make me a racist?"

"Not for me to say," he replied with the faintest of smiles. "From what we can gather, there is some Chinese involvement, among a lot of other people from a lot of other countries."

"It *could* fit," said Thea thoughtfully. "I mean, she might not have realised what was going on until she got to Barnsley, and then decided to run away, rather than take part in something so horrible."

The man nodded, saying nothing.

"It feels more likely than her being trafficked as a prostitute, anyway," Thea went on. "I mean — that was my very first thought. But she seemed too . . . confident. And she's much too old, if she's fifty — isn't she?"

"You'd be surprised. But we would need a lot more evidence before we pursued that line of enquiry."

"Isn't there any CCTV at the business park? Surely there must be. Some of those businesses must worry about security. And people *live* there as well."

"There are a couple of cameras. On first glance, they don't seem very helpful."

It struck Thea that she was being given much more inside information than was usual. That had to be because of her friendship with Gladwin, conferring a semi-official role on her. There had been talk, a little while before, of Thea becoming a paid employee of the police, in a civilian role, helping with local knowledge and insights. But it had come to nothing, when the precise job description proved impossible to establish. All that had happened was that Gladwin continued to treat her as a special case, sharing facts about her

130

investigations and trusting Thea to provide whatever assistance she could.

The interviewer looked up from his notes, meeting Thea's eyes. "Did you *like* her?" he asked.

"What? Oh, gosh, there's a question. I can't give you a straight answer. I *wanted* to like her, but it was all so peculiar, and I was fairly sure that she didn't much like *me*. There was something calculating about her, right from the start."

"You felt used? Manipulated?"

"I did rather. But I admit I liked the adventure of it. It gave me something to do, something to think about. If she'd still been there when I got back from the walk, I was going to ask her a hundred questions and try to get to the bottom of the story. That's what I mean about people being irrational, inconsistent. I sort of wanted to be rid of her, but I was also very keen to have more talk with her. It's been extremely frustrating not understanding what was so secret."

"Secret? Did she use that word herself?"

"I think she did. I think she made it obvious that behind everything there was a nasty great secret."

"One last thing," said the officer. "Where did you go? When you went out leaving the house open, on Sunday morning?"

"Oh . . . just round the village. As far as the big hotel and back, more or less." She found herself oddly resistant to mentioning the romantic abandoned barn. It could not be the least bit relevant, and it would ruin the fairy-tale notions she had about it if the police were to start noticing it.

"You just walked down the main street and back?"

"Not quite. I took a little road that goes off just past the church, and then came back to the main street through the garden of that big hotel. It was just an aimless stroll to stretch my legs a bit."

"Did anybody see you?"

"Quite a few in passing cars, I suppose, but I don't imagine they'd remember. I didn't speak to anybody. Not like this morning. I had quite a good chat in the churchyard then."

He shook his head impatiently. "So, no evidence that you actually did go for a walk on Sunday?" he said with brutal directness.

"What? Oh, gosh, I see now." She had managed to forget that she was still theoretically suspected of having committed murder. "You mean I should find myself an alibi. Well — a woman came out of her house and got into her car. She might remember seeing me. She'd probably know the time, as well. People usually look at the clock before they go out, don't they?"

"Do they?" He sighed. "Can you remember which house it was?"

"I think so. I could point it out, anyway."

He made a note, and then lapsed into silence.

"So . . .?" she prompted him.

"So I think that might be enough for now. We'll collate the findings from the house, and take it from there."

"Right." She hesitated. "Gladwin said there might be a chance of you lending me a car. Did she tell you that?"

He blinked at her. "Not me, no. We'll ask at the front desk. There's usually a spare vehicle knocking about, but there'll have to be a fair bit of paperwork before we can let you have anything."

CHAPTER
ELEVEN

There was plentiful paperwork to deal with before Thea was allowed to take the five-year-old automatic Fiat away. There had also been a crash course in how to drive an automatic, and dire warnings as to the avalanche of trouble there would be if she damaged it. "We'd only do this for a friend of the superintendent," said the sergeant who was handing the car over.

"I'll only use it when I have to," she promised. "Just for shopping, really. When do you want it back?"

"End of the week?" he offered. "There's no great rush."

She managed the short drive back to Barnsley at a careful crawl, getting the feel of the car and terrified of stalling it at junctions. She got back to the house on the corner just after four, tucking it in beside the truck that Sid and Dave used. There were no police vehicles, which suggested a rather rapid forensic exercise. Had they scanned every surface for fingerprints and collected invisible flakes of skin to be tested for DNA? Or had they just had a good look round, concentrating on the attic and noting the way Thea was effectively camping in the living room? They weren't specialist SOCOs, anyway — which was odd, when she thought about it. Had the hunt for pangolin smugglers taken every trained officer away from other work? More than likely, she decided, given the strictures the police were currently working under.

The act of walking up the driveway triggered a rerun of the conversation she'd had with Sid when she'd returned from the lunch with Barkley. Clovis! There he was, tucked into a small corner of her mind, patiently awaiting his turn for her attention. What was she going to do if he came back again? Would she slam the door in his face, or at least let him explain what he wanted? She had assumed the danger was past, her turbulent hormonal responses kept hidden from her trustful husband. And now, if she readmitted him, saying nothing about it to Drew, that would compound the secret. Thinking this through made her feel trapped and cheated. Hadn't she behaved impeccably so far, telling herself that the man had no feelings for her, and that her own reactions were therefore stupid and shameful? Clovis Biddulph was just an automatic philanderer, who gave the same Gallic treatment to every woman he met. Barkley had pointed out, on her first sight of him in Broad Camp den, that he made no attempt to ameliorate his charms, wearing an expensive male fragrance and paying close attention to his clothes. His grandmother had been French, which apparently was enough to confer that special streak of sex appeal that rarely manifested in an Englishman.

It was ten past four and the builders were obviously finishing up for the day. "You're back, then," said Dave. "No need for us to set up the barricades, after all."

"Did you have your fingerprints taken?"

He shook his head, almost regretfully. "They were no bother — hardly noticed us at all. Said they just needed to get an idea of the layout and so forth. Took some pictures and were up in the roof for thirty minutes or so. Sounds as if they've got a lot on at the moment, and this was just what they didn't need. Not like on the telly," he concluded.

"No," said Thea doubtfully.

"We'll be back tomorrow, then, bright and early. Have a look, why don't you? See where we've got to today."

She obediently stepped through the doorway that was eventually to become an archway and duly admired the installed kitchen equipment, and the completed hole where the window would go. "Amazing!" she enthused. "It's a transformation."

"Surprising what you can do in a day," said Sid, with a smirk. "Mind you, we had everything ready and waiting, last week. Just a matter of slotting it all in."

"When will there be a back door?"

"Wednesday," said Dave. "It's being delivered tomorrow. Won't take long, then. Thursday's tiling and painting and making a start on the bathroom. Same thing up there — it's all ready and waiting. We're still hoping to get finished by the end of Friday."

It was all blessedly practical. A job to be done and men with the right skills to do it. No secrets or mysteries — unless they were cunningly concealing terrible mistakes in the plumbing. She gave them her most dazzling smile and went through into the rest of the house. "Bar the door now," Dave called after her. "And don't touch it till we come back tomorrow."

She did as instructed, despite feeling no apprehension about intruders. Even if someone out there had malevolent intentions towards her, they had probably done their worst by framing her for the murder of Grace. There could be no possible reason to physically harm her; no sense in taking such a risk. *Except*, said a little voice, *that you have a reputation for pinning down killers and helping the police. That might be enough for somebody to want you dead.* She confronted this idea full on, doing her best to take it seriously. Murder *was* serious. That sometimes had to be repeated and emphasised, when she was immersed in a puzzle involving people she didn't know personally. She could all too easily detach her emotions when trying to figure out a matter of logic and logistics.

She had not warmed to Grace and was shamefully unmoved by her death. Whether the woman had been a victim or a member of some revolting gang, she did not seem a very great loss to the world. That alone was a disgraceful way to think. "No man is an island," she reminded herself. "Every death diminishes me." She had frequently struggled to accept this assertion as literally true. So many deaths occurred every day. Little deaths, of birds and fish and aborted human foetuses. She wished she hadn't added this last, because she found the subject of abortion too big and too sad to contemplate without severe discomfort. She carried with her somewhere the conviction that the death of these countless thousands of little half-formed human beings cheapened life in its widest sense. So did the slaughter of animals for food and the wanton hunting and shooting of them for sport. Sometimes she would reach the conclusion that the murder of one more person did not weigh so very heavily in the balance, after all.

Nonetheless, she did want to find an answer to what had taken place here in this house on Sunday morning. A person had gripped Grace by the neck, pressing hard enough to block the blood flow to her brain, and thereby killed her. Thea herself was small and not especially strong. She did not know the exact place to squeeze in order to kill someone. If she had done it, Grace would have had plenty of time to kick and scream and scratch and bite in resistance to the assault. She, Thea, would have fumbled and faltered and thoroughly failed to inflict anything in the way of damage. And why would she want to, anyway? This unanswerable question was enough in itself to reassure her that nobody would ever seriously consider her as a viable suspect.

She made herself a mug of tea and constructed a sandwich from her purchases made at Waitrose. The house wrapped itself contentedly around her, enduring the battering its back wall had taken, and oblivious to the sudden death that had happened upstairs. There was no suggestion of a ghostly reappearance of the murdered woman. She had already seemed oddly insubstantial when Thea had met her; entirely self-contained and unwilling to share anything but the most basic facts about herself. And even they might not have been true. And if they were, then the police might already have located her on an airline passenger list, and be matching her up to some definite identity that explained who she was and why she had come to Britain.

There might even be a CCTV recording of her getting into a car, its licence plate clearly visible and its owner quickly apprehended. The car's journey down to the Cotswolds would be captured on a succession of motorway cameras. There would be no escape in these days of total surveillance. While Thea abhorred this development in principle, she could relish the idea that only the most cunning criminals could evade detection. Except, she remembered, they very often did, regardless of the cameras. The monsters who slaughtered and then sold rare wild animals, for a start. Would Gladwin and her colleagues really manage to catch them and bring them to justice? And what would that justice be, anyway? What difference would it make to the worldwide trade that was going on?

Her thoughts see-sawed through optimism and dark despair at the wickedness of the human race. In the quiet of Tabitha Ibbotson's living room, she pursued her stream of consciousness wherever it might lead her, with nothing to distract or interrupt her. She had experienced such interludes before, meditating on situations and dilemmas without flinching at the implications. It was something she shared with Drew, who was given to a very similar kind of musing. It had to do with his work, and with the fact that both he and Thea had lost partners they had expected to enjoy for many more decades. They shared an impatience with trivia and evasion. It had, she supposed, been quickly apparent to them both, from their first meeting, that they had this in common.

All of which prompted her to phone her husband some hours earlier than usual. She had a lot to say to him, starting with the abject apology due for forgetting their anniversary.

She tried the landline first, and was answered on the third ring by a young female voice saying, "Hello? How can I help you?"

"Stephanie! Does Dad know you're answering the phone? What if it's a funeral?"

"I can manage," said the child stiffly. "I know what to say."

"But where is he? Why can't he answer it for himself?"

There was a pause, in which Thea could hear some whispering, and then, "Oh, he's upstairs. Do you want me to call him?"

"Yes please," said Thea firmly. "And who are you whispering to?"

"Only Timmy. I'll ask him to go and call Dad, shall I?"

"Yes," said Thea impatiently. "Why's he upstairs? What's he doing?"

"Oh — making beds or something. I don't know exactly."

The tone was artificially airy and Thea began to feel suspicious. The forgotten anniversary came back to bite her, and the need to speak to her undervalued husband

140

became more pressing. "Hurry him up, then," she said. "Shout for him if you have to."

"Wait a minute, then." The receiver was put down and an echoey silence ensued for at least a full minute. At last Drew was there. "Hey — sorry," he said breathlessly. "What's the matter?"

"Nothing, really. At least — a few things, but you don't have to worry. The first is to offer my grovelling apologies for forgetting our anniversary. It was yesterday, wasn't it? I just never registered the date properly. I feel so awful about it, I had to phone you as soon as I had the house to myself."

"Oh, Thea. Did you think I'd care about that? I just assumed we weren't going to go in for any of that mush. Karen and I never bothered about it."

"Oh." Outrageously, she felt distinctly slighted, until she gave herself a shake. "But *you* didn't just forget about it, did you? You knew which day it was and just never said anything. That's much less awful than me not giving it a thought." Was it, though, she silently wondered. Wasn't there something wrong, either way?

"Stop it," he said, sounding tired. "Make it up to me when you get home."

"I will. So — how's things? Why was Stephanie answering the phone? How's Hepzie?"

"She's fine. Being lazy. Feeling her age, I guess. Steph's very good on the phone now. She's heard me do it often enough. She knows what to say."

"Yes, I know she has — but a *child* answering a funeral call isn't right, is it? What will people think?"

141

"They know we don't go in for undue formality. They'll think it's nice."

"Oh, well — it's your business. So, everything's all right, then, is it?"

"Everything's fine," he said emphatically. "Just leave us to get on with it, okay? I'm assuming you're all right? Are you involved in any police investigation over the woman that died?"

He sounded strangely detached, as if he only wanted to hear platitudes and blithe assurances. It felt impossible to burden him with her own alarming news that Grace's death had been deliberately inflicted by a mysterious stranger, and that Thea herself was possibly under suspicion. The reappearance of Clovis. The powerful sense of loss at the absence of her spaniel. The cost of a modest meal at the local pub — even that seemed too much of an imposition, the way Drew sounded. "Yes, I'm alive and well," she chirped. "The police have questioned me a bit more today, which was all very interesting. Now I've got a whole evening of nothing. I'm missing you all, and still immensely remorseful about the anniversary, whatever you say."

"Then let's just get on with it," he said softly. "You don't have to worry. And you really don't have to phone every day, you know. Not unless there's something important. It's only a few more days. Nothing to get in a stew about. Just relax and have fun — leave it till Thursday now, why don't you? Bye, love."

And he was gone. She stood holding her phone, staring at the blank screen. Had that really been her husband, or had an interloper taken his place? He had

142

sounded so . . . impenetrable. As if he'd put up barriers against her. Was he secretly furious with her for abandoning them, to the point where he could barely speak to her? Drew, who did not do secrets; who had always insisted they share all their thoughts and feelings, however unpalatable? Although Thea had known that such an ambition was unachievable, she liked the basic intention. The two of them had shared their doubts and anxieties concerning the business, and where they should live when faced with a sudden need to choose between Drew's former home and Broad Campden. But Thea had concealed her reaction to Clovis, seeing no possible benefit to letting Drew become aware that his wife was in thrall to another man. She had believed it to be all over and done with, anyway. She had been entirely convinced that there need never be another encounter between her and the darkly handsome Mr Biddulph.

Drew had tried to discourage her from phoning so often, which had felt a bit odd at the time, and now escalated into a much bigger deal. It suggested annoyance with her, at the very least. The message seemed to be, *You've made your bed, now lie in it.* He hadn't wanted her to go off and leave him to cope with his children, and he wasn't going to pretend to be happy about it. And she had forgotten their anniversary, only a year after marrying him. But then she recalled the whispering between Stephanie and either Timmy or her father. Did they perhaps — incredibly — have something secret going on? Had something happened to Hepzie, and they couldn't

143

bring themselves to tell her? Or was it something *nice?* A welcome-home present they were making, or a new interest that the children were working on, to surprise her.

None of that entirely explained why they couldn't take a phone call from her. Drew knew that she was at the centre of another murder investigation — but no, he didn't. He had not let her talk for long enough to convey the full story. The only thing she'd really been able to say was how sorry she was about the anniversary, and he had brushed that aside as unimportant. The distance between them suddenly felt like a great gulf that he was making no attempt to bridge. A reciprocal annoyance seized her. There was no need for him to be quite so cold, after all. It was bordering on punitive, which was something she would never have expected from him.

It was time to stop all this thinking. There was a whole evening still to get through, with the TV not working and no prospect of any congenial company.

Except — the name she had been resolutely pushing out of her mind forced itself past the barriers she had erected and flashed up in neon lights. Clovis Biddulph had been to this house, looking for her. This was impossible to explain or account for, given the absence of any proper message via the builders.

There was nothing she could do but wait to see if he came back. She had no phone number for him, and would have resisted any temptation to call it, even if she had. The very helplessness was anathema to her. She regarded herself as a person who made things happen.

She did not sit waiting like a Victorian damsel for a man to confer his attention on her. And yet, that was exactly the situation in this instance. It made her fidgety, after the hour spent in quiet meditation. All that thinking had led nowhere, anyway. Without action, it was meaningless. And without any idea of what that action could or should be, there was a growing feeling of frustration.

Everybody had deserted her. Gladwin, Drew, her dog, even Grace. Well, to be fair, it had been entirely involuntary in the case of the last two. But the result was that she was here on her own, entertaining increasingly dark thoughts, with several hours still to pass before bedtime.

But she did have a car. And there was still some daylight to enjoy. She could go out, if she decided that that was what she wanted to do, and drive anywhere she liked. At that point, her imagination failed her. She disliked eating alone in a public place. There would be no shops open, other than supermarkets. She didn't have anybody she could visit.

"Arrghh!" she moaned aloud. Everything had turned sour, and it was all her own stupid fault.

Then her phone jingled, and she answered it on the assumption that it would be Drew, relenting from his uncharacteristic chilliness. The fact that the screen announced "Caller Unknown" did not register, in her haste to respond.

"Thea? I'm really sorry if I'm intruding, and I hope I didn't startle you by trying to find you today. I expect your builders told you I'd been? I was hoping to talk to you in person, but you're rather elusive."

"Clovis Biddulph," she said faintly. "How on earth did you manage to find me?"

CHAPTER
TWELVE

"I had to turn detective. There was an item on the news about a suspicious death in Barnsley, and a brief mention of a house-sitter. I guessed that might possibly be you, so I tracked down the house and asked the builders if a Mrs Slocombe was staying there. Simple, really."

"But my phone number?"

"That was a bit more tricky. But everything's out there somewhere, and you might remember you placed an ad for your services as a house-sitter on a Cotswolds website, about three years ago, with mobile number? Well, it's still there."

"Good God! That must have taken you *ages*."

"No, not really. I've got quite good at that sort of thing lately. And, of course, I could simply have phoned your husband and asked where you were, but I figured that might be a bit undiplomatic."

"Seems to me the whole Internet is a stalker's charter," she said daftly, not really meaning to accuse him of any such thing.

He seemed unwounded by the implication. "You needn't worry. I just wanted to pick your brains about something. It's all quite innocent, I promise you. But I thought I should phone before coming to the house again. I honestly don't want to alarm you."

His voice was soothing and yet arousing. His words were reassuring and yet her heart was pounding with panic. "Can't you ask me whatever it is over the phone?" she said.

"Well, no, not really."

"Is it something to do with your father's grave? Or what?"

"No, no. It's nothing much, really. I just want to make use of your obvious talents."

She had a strong sense of drowning; of being swept out to sea by forces too powerful to resist. "I don't know," she said weakly. "It sounds as if you might need a counsellor or something. It must have been traumatic for all of you with your father dying as he did, but it's way beyond my job description to try to help. I don't even *have* a job description, really. You'd be better off talking to Drew, and even he'd probably be out of his depth." *Because,* she wanted to tell him, *whatever happens between me and you, happens between me and my husband as well.*

"You don't understand. I don't blame you — I haven't explained anything yet. So you won't even meet me somewhere for lunch, then?" He sounded profoundly reproachful. The way men so often sounded when they wanted something from you that you knew was dangerous, and they pretended was entirely harmless. The little-boy wheedling that was far more successful than it ever ought to be, because it left you feeling stiff and mean-spirited and needlessly cautious.

148

"I would if I thought I could be of any help to you," she said. "But there must be countless people who'd do a better job than me."

"I think I might be the best judge of that. Look, I just want to talk something over with you, that's all. I want to see if you can help me to understand myself a bit better, if that doesn't sound pretentious. No strings. Nothing sinister."

She knew, then, that everything he was asking her was a smokescreen, a pretence in order to get beneath her defences. He knew that she knew, as well. They both knew that there had been a violent physical spark between them the moment they set eyes on each other. Two highly attractive people in their forties, she in a new and loving marriage, he a single man of indeterminate background — by some malign hormonal chemistry they could scarcely keep their hands off each other. But nothing had happened and Thea clung to a desperate hope that nothing ever would or could.

All this knowledge was providing only the flimsiest of barriers against him. Just the mental repetition of his name had been enough to make her warm. Now she was actually speaking to him, hearing his voice inviting her to meet him again, she was unequal to the test before her. There was almost no rational thought involved. She was nowhere close to having to justify herself. She was a rabbit staring into the hypnotic eyes of the fox, somehow accepting that her eventual fate was going to be worth the extreme gratification that was being promised.

"Tomorrow, then," she said. "I hear there's a good pub in Quenington. Can we meet there, say half past twelve?"

"If that's the best I can hope for, then fine. What's the name of the pub?"

"I can't remember. It's the only one in the village, I think. Should be easy to find."

"Please don't worry, Thea. I'm not going to harm you. You sound so scared, and that's hurtful. I'm not a monster. I just want to talk to you. Okay?"

"Okay," she murmured, wondering whether all the shameful expectations lay entirely within her, while knowing that absolutely was not the case. Perhaps, an insistent voice repeated, after all, he was much less concupiscent than she thought. *Concupiscent*, she mentally repeated, enjoying a word she had used a lot in her teens. It had been a favourite amongst the sixth-form girls for a while.

At least he hadn't threatened to invade the house that evening. He knew she was alone; he knew how to find her. Didn't it prove his decency that he had agreed to hold off until the arrival of the purifying light of day in a public place? Bit by bit she relaxed and savoured the glow of anticipation. It would be pleasurable just to see him again. He could harmlessly feed her fantasies, while leaving her conscience clear. And on top of that, he might actually have some intriguing puzzle to run past her, which would give her something new to think about.

Thanks to close questioning of Sid and Dave on the subject, she achieved a long hot bath at ten, with a book. The habit had been broken once she was living with Drew and his children. There was never quite enough hot water, and the Slocombes all thought there was something a bit mad about lying in a six-inch puddle reading for half an hour or more. The water went cold, they said. How could it be enjoyable? Somebody would bang on the door after ten minutes to ask if she was dead. Now she could relish Tabitha Ibbotson's facilities, having wantonly used the immersion heater to get the water good and hot. Sid and Dave would have to wait for their plumber to activate the nice new boiler they had installed just that day along with the cooker, dishwasher and fan extractor. It had been eight hours of impressive work, by any standards.

The book was diverting, and the hot bath soothed away at least some of the current anxieties. The most persistent was the question of Drew, and what was really going on with him.

Tuesday dawned gradually, the sun blocked by dense cloud. It was almost eight when Thea woke, and she rolled out of bed with a sense of urgency. Only when she was washing her face did she pause to ask herself why she was rushing. All she could come up with was that the builders could arrive any time, and some old-fashioned sense of propriety suggested she should not greet them in her dressing gown. And there was Clovis to think about.

The main thought was that Drew must never know that she had met the man she so shamefully fancied. She obviously wouldn't lie if it occurred to him to question her about the people she'd met while in Barnsley. She just wouldn't voluntarily mention it if she didn't have to. It wouldn't even feel like a secret. Just something he was better off not knowing. Any woman in the world would thoroughly agree with that.

She made coffee and ate a piece of cold bread spread with butter and Marmite. Outside it was dry but grey. The trees looked dusty and tired, preparing to shed their leaves and call it a day. There was a patch of honeysuckle in one corner of the front garden, its flowers a distant memory and most of its leaves brown and crisp. July had been very dry, and the plant had evidently not recovered from the weeks of thirst. Tabitha couldn't have watered it during her stay at the house.

Forcing her thoughts away from Clovis, she concentrated on the group of women who deserved her attention. Gladwin, Grace, Barkley, Tabitha. They all swirled around, offering trouble and friendship in equal measure. They had all depended on her, Thea Slocombe, in one way or another, and she was determined not to let them down. Even Grace, already the recipient of genuine benevolence, deserved to have her story revealed and her death avenged. Tabitha was relying on her to keep her house intact, her piano undamaged.

She was going to need all her resolve if the day was not going to lead to disaster. She needed to hold on to an idea of herself as a good dependable person. Her husband should be able to rely on her fidelity, and Gladwin needed her to contribute positively to the

152

murder investigation. She must face facts and stay firmly in the real world. Such internal admonitions were tiring, she discovered. Combined with far too much thinking the day before, the unwonted earnestness was all a bit too much. She found herself craving some frivolity to counteract it all.

The problem, of course, was that frivolity would come in the form of Clovis, if she let it, and was therefore not to be entertained. Instead she must do her civic duty, protecting the house and helping the police. With this in mind, she waited for the builders and planned her morning.

Sid and Dave arrived at half past eight, their expressions slightly wary. She could hardly blame them for that after the shocks of the previous day. They were probably anxious to finish the work and go as quickly as possible. "Had a good night?" asked Dave.

"No problems," she reported. "Everything was nice and quiet."

"That's good." He looked as if he did not entirely believe her. "Going out for a drive today, are you?" He eyed the car in the driveway speculatively. Thea realised she had not explained how she'd acquired it.

"The police have let me borrow it," she said. "Just so I can get some shopping when I need it."

"Nice," he said doubtfully.

"I think I'll go for another walk this morning. I'll be out for lunch with a friend. The man who showed up yesterday — Clovis."

"No more forensic bods coming here, then?"

"Not that I know of. The trouble is, they've got a big investigation going on, and there's nobody available to do a proper job on this one. It's all wrong, you know. They can't be everywhere at once, with all the cuts and restrictions."

"You'd think murder would trump all the other things, wouldn't you?"

"You would," said Thea. "But it's not always very logical." She had had the idea of revisiting the business park, perhaps from a different approach, trying to understand how it operated. It had seemed obvious that Grace was afraid of going near it, because that was the point from which she had escaped. The policeman at Cirencester had said there were at least a couple of cameras with recordings they were looking at. The fact that they had requisitioned the recordings must have alerted the people at the park to their supposed involvement with the murder. Would that have made any guilty individuals nervous? The website had talked of offices and workshops and businesses of varying sizes, all sharing the cluster of attractive stone buildings. It was impossible to know how much of a community it was, and who exactly made use of it. If Thea simply walked up the front driveway and started to look around, from one unit to another, would anybody stop her? She had done similar things before, usually with impunity. But what could she hope to gain by it, a sensible voice enquired. Who would she speak to, if anyone? In what way could such intrusion constitute responsible behaviour?

154

Better, then, to retrace her original steps from Saturday without two police officers watching every move, looking for hidden clues, trying to make sense of what had happened. That would be a lot more focused and therefore easier to justify. Small details might come back to her. And if there was nobody from the police with her, making notes and asking questions, the very solitude might help to nudge her memory. And yet — did she *really* want to do it all again, for a third time? Wouldn't it be nothing more than wasted time? She sat in the living room with a cooling mug of coffee and considered her options.

Perhaps she could just regard it as going for another walk. Perhaps she would follow a different route from before, responding to whim and letting her thoughts roam freely. That was, after all, how she had envisaged this week before coming here. It would be a restful interlude, where she could indulge in drawing, reading, thinking, away from insistent children and the nagging demands of domestic routine. Couldn't some of this yet be salvaged? There were four or five days still to go, in which she might yet make some sketches and read a book. She could go to Bibury and beyond, get to know the Ampneys and the outskirts of Cirencester. The fact of a murder, right under her nose, closer than any she'd been involved in previously, ought not to be allowed to consume every waking moment. It could be pushed to the edges of her attention, leaving space for some of the indulgence she had originally anticipated.

So she took herself out into the village, with its smattering of houses, pub and hotel, church and village hall. And a mysterious old barn. A place that had offered refreshment and rest to passing drovers and their flocks or herds. There would have been a field close to the inn where the animals could also gather their strength for more miles of walking. There'd be water for them, but perhaps little or no grass, if times were busy and numerous previous travellers had already bitten it down to nothing and then trodden the ground to bare earth or mud. Thea ambled slowly past the various buildings, dreaming of bygone times, listening for echoes of hooves and whistles, barking dogs and even the occasional drover's song.

She went into the churchyard, as a place where she had enjoyed a brief friendly chat with interesting people, though deserted now, and climbed over into the field with the cowpats and the walnut tree. There was a bird singing sporadically in the tree, and three or four nuts in their green outer cases lying in the grass. She picked them up, thinking Stephanie and Timmy might find them interesting. A plane passed overhead and cars went by on the road fifty yards away, but Thea felt she was alone in the world. It was a feeling she'd had before in the Cotswolds, as if the entire region was nothing more than a film set. The beautiful facades in their edible cream-and-piecrust hues, held nothing but empty space at their rear. Nearly every village she had spent time in had an air of secrecy about it. And here in Barnsley, in something as prosaic as a business park, there were apparently even darker secrets than most.

She decided to go no further, but retraced her steps, back over the stile into the churchyard, still musing on

156

the absence of any human life. Never mind that it was August, and that thousands of visitors came to the Cotswolds every week, not one of them would venture onto a barely visible footpath to explore empty fields and handsome old trees. Coachloads of them would be swarming around Bibury, Chipping Campden, Snowshill and other famous spots, ignoring the spaces in between.

But then, all of a sudden, as she was loitering in the churchyard, two men appeared in the wide opening onto the road and turned up the approach to the church, towards her. She quickly recognised one of them, from his limping gait — it was the man from the churchyard the previous day. But his companion was not the same one as before. As she waited for them to come closer, she could see that this one was also fairly elderly, with a face very similar to the man with a limp. She wondered if they might be brothers.

She made no conscious decision to speak to them, but simply stood there, watching them and waiting for them to reduce the space between her and themselves. Eventually, she said, "Hello! Looks as if the sun's trying to come out."

"Ah! Good morning to you," said Dick, the man she'd met before, after a brief hesitation. Had he not wanted to speak to her, she wondered. Was she nothing more than a nuisance to him? "Been for a walk, have you?" His eyes were small and blue, his chin slightly pink, as if very recently shaved. He wore a short-sleeved checked shirt and light summer trousers with a careful crease down the front. He did not meet Thea's gaze for more than half a second at a time, but kept his focus on a point somewhere over her shoulder.

"That's right." She adopted a falsely buoyant tone, which she quickly realised must appear very foolish, given events of the past few days. "Not much else to do, really. And it's all so lovely, isn't it. That house further along the road, with the business park all round it —" She nodded towards the mansion she had so admired. "Must be Georgian, I suppose."

"Quite right. Still privately owned and well maintained." A hint of local pride was readily detected.

"I noticed the ha-ha as well," she went on. "Even though it's rather overgrown. You could fall over it at night. I do like a ha-ha," she added. "Such a simple idea."

"Nobody goes that way at night," said the second man. "There's a perfectly good driveway the other side of the yard." In contrast to his companion, he gave her a steady look, with eyes of a darker blue.

"The stiles are rather a challenge, though." She found herself wanting to keep them there for a few minutes. It was good to have someone to talk to, even if it was only trivial chit-chat.

"You mean because of my bad leg, I suppose," said Dick. "Actually, it's really no problem. I twisted my knee falling down some stairs, which slightly damaged my cruciate tendon, but it's not serious. I'm not letting it prevent me from following my usual routines."

"Oh good," said Thea weakly. She had never heard of a cruciate tendon.

158

"But he doesn't climb over stiles if he can help it," said the second man, with a quick smile. "Permit me to introduce us. This is Richard and I'm Edward. Jackson, in both cases."

"Pleased to meet you," said Thea, wondering whether to extend a hand. "I'm Thea Slocombe."

Richard appeared to be gradually relaxing his decidedly stiff manner. "You're all right, are you?" he asked her. "After what happened? I must say I'm surprised to see you still here."

"Must have nerves of steel," said Edward, with a laugh that sounded as if his own nerves were made of something more flimsy.

"I'm quite all right," said Thea. "You're brothers, then, are you?"

"That's right," said Richard.

But the other man was still focusing on the image of a lone woman spending nights in a house of death. "But surely . . ." he stammered. "That is — aren't you at all anxious? I mean . . . isn't it a bit . . .?"

She gave him a moment to recover the use of his tongue, and then smilingly corrected his assumptions. "Not really. It's not the first time, you see. And I've got the builders there during the day, and the police are keeping an eye on me. If anything, it's rather boring. I've got all of this week still to go, if we stick to the plan."

"And you will, will you? Stick to the plan, I mean?" It was Richard again, rapping out brisk questions as if he had every right to interrogate her. "Who made the plan, anyway? Are you a friend of Tabitha's? She's a

159

very elusive person, in our experience. Half the local people still haven't met her."

"But you have?"

"Once," he nodded. "So — what's the plan, then?" he persisted.

"It depends," she shrugged, being instinctively vague. "Who knows what'll happen?" Both men gazed at her, as if at a rare specimen at a zoo. The likeness between them became more apparent. "You both live here in the village, do you?" she asked, determined to match question for question.

"Born and bred," said Richard. "Our grandfather had a farm here originally, but our father sold off most of the land, very unwisely and totally against Mother's wishes. We've only got a small fraction of it left now. But we've managed to keep going one way and another."

"And they're buried here in the churchyard, I suppose," said Thea, remembering when she had first met him. "Your forebears, I mean. Although I don't remember seeing Jackson on any of the headstones."

Edward took over, so smoothly that it felt as if the brothers habitually finished each other's thoughts and spoke for each other. "They're here, right enough. The whole clan, pretty nearly. The occasional youngest son got away, as in most families, but you'll find us easily enough if you go looking. My grandmother's people are there, too. In fact, if you delve back far enough, you'll find we're related to at least half the people buried here."

160

"You said something yesterday about the parish records being damaged," frowned Thea. "Is that right?"

Richard nodded, but again hesitated before elaborating. "All a bit of a mystery, that is. No obvious reason for it — quite a lot of the paper's just fallen to pieces, so it's just a scatter of illegible scraps. The vicar says it must have been beetles or weevils. Some sort of insect."

"That's terrible," said Thea, who had a feeling for old archives and primary historical sources. "There's no substitute for the original records."

"Well, we're hoping we can reconstruct most of them," said Richard. "It's become quite a major project amongst several of the local people. We've got them coming up from the Ampneys as well — there are several connections, of course. We had a great-uncle who was churchwarden of Ampney Crucis at one point."

His brother showed little sign of concern for the lost documents. He was scanning the fields that lay behind them, as if searching for a missing dog or child. "Sun's coming out, look," he said, apparently forgetting that Thea had said the same thing ten minutes earlier.

It was an effective interruption. "Yes, yes. Must get on," said Richard Jackson.

They were both retired, Thea presumed. One spent his time delving into family history and the other apparently did not. "I'm sorry to ask, but it's going to nag at me all day otherwise," she burst out. "The thing is, I wondered if you might be twins?" It had come to her attention long ago that making a direct enquiry such as this was considered impolite by society in general, for reasons that were obscure to her. It was the obvious way to acquire information, after all.

"Oh no," said Richard. "He's three years older than I am. Are you suggesting that I look as ancient as he does? If so, I think I should feel insulted."

She was unsure as to whether this was meant as a joke, but a glance at his face suggested something heartfelt just below the surface. "Sorry," she smiled. "I'm hopeless at guessing people's ages." This was not strictly true, but she hoped it would appease him.

He returned the smile, as if it was of no importance at all. They had been conversing close to the wall between the churchyard and the field, but now Richard made a move towards the road, forcing Thea to move aside. Within a few seconds, both men were walking away, leaving Thea to go when and where she pleased. "I expect I'll see you again," she said.

"I don't suppose you will," said Richard. "We're going to be fully occupied until the end of the month with visitors."

Edward gave her a softer response. "Nephew and nieces, mostly. There's been a tradition for decades now that they all descend on their old uncles for their summer holidays."

"Actually not uncles but cousins, to be strictly accurate," said Dick.

"How nice," said Thea fatuously.

She was back at the house before eleven, finding the builders sitting in their van with mugs of coffee. "Waiting for the plumber," explained Dave. "He's late."

162

Thea merely nodded and flapped a hand as if to say it wasn't up to her to keep them at it. Now the time was growing so close, all she could think about was her lunch date with Clovis Biddulph.

CHAPTER
THIRTEEN

She had suggested the pub in Quenington from some obscure sense of keeping Clovis well out of sight of anyone in Barnsley. Word was less likely to get back to Drew, or even Gladwin, that way. Whatever happened next, the whole encounter would be far best kept secret, if she could manage it without telling any direct lies. A quick check on the Internet reminded her that the pub was called The Keeper's Arms. Ruefully she noted that it welcomed dogs. She felt sorely tempted to rush back to Broad Campden to collect the abandoned Hepzie, regardless of what Tabitha Ibbotson might think. It was not getting any easier without her. The morning's walk had been just as flat and empty as those of previous days. Watching the spaniel nosing around, with bursts of exuberant flight, ears flapping, had always been more than half the point of a country walk.

She did her best not to be early, but somehow found herself setting out just after noon. The unfamiliar car might cause trouble; there could be roadworks or a great logjam of coaches at Bibury, which was on the way. While not wanting to appear eager to meet Clovis again, neither did she want to keep him waiting, in a show of female hard-to-gettery. *Just be normal,* she kept telling herself.

Quenington was itself full of historical and geographical interest. The buildings were ancient and unusual; there was the River Coin, which gave its name to a number of local settlements. Thea had been there once, two or three years earlier, on a day out that had included so many points of interest that she could now remember none of them in any detail. She drove a short way past the pub, with ten minutes to spare, and decided to take a quick walk up to the Knights' Gate, that had taken her fancy on the previous visit, mainly because it claimed some connection with the Knights Templar, which were always fascinating.

She located it without difficulty and stood admiring its age-old charms for a minute or two. Then, as she walked back, the driver of a dark-blue car tooted at her and she realised her assignation was about to begin.

Clovis parked in the road outside the pub and sat waiting for her. With a brief greeting, he stood back and let her lead the way into the building. Tables were arranged like an ordinary pub, rather than a blurry combination of pub and restaurant that was more or less the norm in the Cotswolds. Without discussion, they settled at a corner seat by a window, with pints of beer in front of them. "We'll order lunch in a minute," Clovis told the man behind the bar. He had not given Thea time to properly look at him, barely meeting her eye and moving briskly. Now, sitting across a pine table from him, she stared bravely into his face.

It had been the eye contact that had sent her melting and throbbing when she'd first met him. That, and his outrageous good looks. He was dark and chiselled, tall and muscular — everything a good romance demanded. And now he had added a neat beard, trimmed to a quarter of an inch all over, which looked soft enough to stroke. He also had a rich voice and impeccable manners. Except, she reminded herself, that her first conversation with him, on the phone, had consisted of him making loud and intemperate accusations and threats. Clovis Biddulph could be dangerous in more ways than one.

But as she kept his gaze, she found that almost nothing was responding inside her. She could not help thinking about Drew, as well as Barnsley and the builders, with Clovis dropping rapidly down the list. He was so sleek, so flawlessly handsome, that he scarcely seemed real. She thought of the effort he must go to every morning to ensure that his image remained immaculate. The danger was receding, the longer she looked at him. After several seconds, she realised that the change was in him, not her. He wasn't activating charm mode at all. Instead he seemed to be waiting for her to get past the initial inspection and move on to the important stuff.

"You said you wanted to pick my brains," she said. "I can't imagine what I can possibly have to offer, on any conceivable subject."

"Marriage," he said succinctly. "I'm thinking of getting married, and I thought you might have some words of advice for me."

She sat back in utter astonishment. Wasn't this rather a cliché? Didn't it happen in old movies and popular romances? How could he sit here and say those words to a woman he had so shamelessly treated to all his charismatic wiles, only a few months before? "Oh!" she said. "I didn't see that coming."

"Listen," he said urgently. "I know how I came across last time, and I admit I did it deliberately. There you were, so pretty and confident and intriguing. I just couldn't resist. But you have to admit I didn't keep it up. When it all got so serious with the murder and everything, we simmered down, didn't we? Your husband's such a decent bloke, for a start. And you're so well matched and happy together. Anyone can see that. I don't want you to think . . . well, you know. I can't help how I look, but I can't pretend I haven't exploited it. After a bit, it gets to be a curse. You must know what I mean — you're quite an oil painting yourself, after all."

She felt her shoulders loosen, and gave a relaxed little laugh. "That's an original way of putting it."

He drank half his beer and turned towards the bar. "We should order the food before it gets busy. If it ever does get busy, of course."

"I'll have the steak and mushroom pie," she said. "I need something substantial. There's no proper cooking facilities at the house." She had a thought. "Although, now they've got the new cooker in, maybe I can start using it."

"I met your builders. Seemed like nice chaps."

"They're not *mine*. I'm just keeping an eye on things."

"Yes, I know," he said. "I've read about you in the papers, once or twice. You're the famous Cotswolds house-sitter who solves complicated rural murders. Everybody knows about you."

She grimaced. "None of it by choice, I promise you. It's a tawdry sort of fame, always associated with somebody getting murdered."

He got up. "I'll go and order, then. Are you ready for another drink?"

"Nowhere near. Besides, I'm driving. This one'll have to last."

While he was gone, she explored the notion of Clovis being married. It would have to be a tough woman, well supplied with self-confidence. Or would he be crass enough to go for some young thing who had no idea what she was getting into? Having met his mother, who seemed entirely well balanced and a good sensible influence on her son, she tried to give him the benefit of the doubt. The very fact that he was seeking advice seemed to be a good sign. She laughed gently at herself for her earlier panic. There would be no need to keep this encounter a secret from Drew, after all. That in itself was a great relief.

He came back and sat down and looked at her. He was still impossibly handsome. To have such a man as your lawful wedded husband would bring great kudos, even in this era of near equality. Heads would turn, and women would narrow their eyes at the wife and wonder what her secret was. "So what do you think?" he asked her, seeming to be reading her thoughts without asking.

"I need more information. Who is she? How old is she? What sort of baggage is she bringing with her? I mean — children, mainly."

"She's called Jennifer and she's thirty-two. No children, but two dogs. A job that pays silly money and a severe allergy to sesame seeds. You'd be surprised how tricky that can be, let me tell you."

Thea was not one to prevaricate with euphemisms and implied meanings that might easily be missed. "You're over forty and never married, right? Doesn't that frighten her?"

"It frightens *me*," he said. "I'll have to learn all those rules from scratch. I'm handicapped, remember, by not having a normal family background to rely on. I never saw a functioning marriage at close quarters in my formative years."

"I wonder how much that matters." She thought of her own settled family, with two parents, three siblings, and all the associated trimmings. Nice house, pets, adequate finances, no traumatic deaths and hardly any accidents. All that sort of thing had not started happening until she was past forty. And still she was doubtful about her performance as a wife — not just to Drew, but retrospectively to Carl as well. In the past few months she had begun to wonder just how good a job she'd made of it the first time around.

"She's very good-looking," he said, managing to convey a wealth of meaning in these words. Thea thought she had caught most of it. He meant there would be no imbalance in the eyes of the world, no sense that Jennifer had somehow used underhand methods to capture him. They would be Posh and Becks or whoever the more recent golden superstar couple might be.

"That'll help," she said.

He flinched. "We're both very ordinary, you know. The main worry is probably going to be that she's got far more money than me. If we have children, I'm going to be the one staying at home to mind them while she forges ahead with her career."

"Which is?"

"Oh — she's a consultant to the big charities. All very worthy and politically correct. She advises them on how to get the best value for money, and which projects are likely to have the most effect. She favours the conservation side of things."

"Sounds great," said Thea, wondering how ethical it was for someone in such a line of work to earn big money. "Which charities in particular?"

"Most of the big names. World Wildlife Fund. RSPCA. RSPB. A few of the smaller ones. She's independent, you see. Goes wherever the need is. They put her on short-term contracts, and she spends a few months going through their procedures and setting them straight. She's very clever."

"But she doesn't go into their basic ideologies? I mean — she doesn't tell them whether to save rhinos over elephants, or African children over South American ones?"

He frowned. "Indirectly, she probably does. It's not just her, obviously. There are legions of people doing similar work. It's a whole industry."

"Does she have to travel much?"

"Not really. Mostly she can do it in London, or wherever their head offices are. I travel quite a lot myself, remember."

Thea never had fully grasped the nature of Clovis's work. Something about music, and going to Prague. "Remind me," she said.

"I scour the world for original music. New young composers in need of a publisher. All very high risk and low reward, except when I hit the jackpot. That happens about once every three or four years. There's some good stuff coming out of Eastern Europe, funnily enough."

"Why is that funny? What about Chopin? Wasn't he Polish?"

Clovis looked down his shapely nose at her, and gave no reply.

"Sorry. Tell me more."

He relented and treated her to a short lecture on the many vibrant new forms of jazz and rock and metal emerging from the region. Then, for good measure, he added a few remarks about Bulgaria and Croatia. Their food arrived while he was in full spate, and he began to eat at the same time as talking. He had selected a curry, with popadums, which he crunched cheerfully.

Thea listened while tackling her own good-sized pie. When he finally stopped, she gave him an approving smile. "Sounds thrilling," she said. "The woman whose house I'm looking after is a musician, as well. She plays the piano."

"Tabitha Ibbotson," he nodded. "Of course."

"You know her?"

"*Of* her," he corrected. "I don't think we've ever met. She's a bit too traditional for my taste. But she's a fine performer, for all that."

"You do know a woman was murdered in the house on Sunday, don't you?" The words burst out of her, with scarcely any conscious thought. It was as if she couldn't hold them back any longer; that everything they'd said thus far was beside this main point. Clovis and his upcoming marriage no longer seemed to be the real motivating force behind this encounter.

"Yes," he nodded, with unmistakeable eagerness. "I mentioned it yesterday on the phone, if you remember."

"So you did. Well it's looming rather large in my mind, as you'd probably expect. I'm not sure I can think about much else, just at the moment."

He gave her a long look that implied complete understanding. "That's not surprising. So tell me."

"How come you don't know? It must be the talk of the whole area."

"I know a couple of basic facts. I'd be very interested to hear the story from the inside, so to speak."

She told him the whole story over the next five minutes, including the police interview and her frustration at not being able to talk to Gladwin. "But Barkley's doing her best to keep in touch," she conceded. "You remember Barkley?"

172

"Vividly."

She laughed at that. "Well, that's more or less it. I suppose I should be feeling a lot more scared than I am. Somehow, I can't believe anybody's after *me*. And after today, I think there'll be a proper door at the back, which will help."

"So who are the main suspects, then?"

"Well — on paper you could probably say I am. But luckily nobody takes that seriously. I ought to be thankful the media haven't made more of the story — they'd be tearing me apart by now. Think how ghastly that would be! I suppose it's because it's August and they only want silly soft news. Plus, all this about the pangolins, of course. Nobody's very interested in an unidentified woman getting killed in a sleepy Cotswold village."

"I heard about the pangolins," he said, with a serious expression. "Vile business!"

"I know," she nodded. "Horrible for the poor things."

"And that's just the tip of a loathsome iceberg." He took a last draught of his beer. "So I'm not lunching with a murderer, then?"

"Wasn't me, guv. I wouldn't know where to squeeze to strangle somebody so quickly and quietly."

"Who says it was quick and quiet?"

"It must have been. I was only out for twenty minutes at most. And if she'd screamed, even in Barnsley somebody would probably have come to investigate."

"Hm. Not too sure about that. People mind their own business around here, in my experience."

"That's true. But the only possible explanation appears to be that somebody knew she was there, and just walked in and killed her when I was out. They must have been watching the house pretty closely to seize the moment like that."

"Not so difficult, actually. They could have put a camera in a parked car, with a feed into a house or van just down the road. Technology's amazing nowadays, you know. There could have been some sort of tracker on the woman who was killed, so they knew which room she was in. Almost anything's possible."

She stared at him. "How do you know all that?"

"It's common knowledge. And I know people who use cameras like that. Neighbourhood disputes are fertile ground for all that sort of thing. And then there are the drones. You can put a camera on them, as well."

"Surely not in the Cotswolds?" She hated to think of it.

"Why not? There's a man round the corner from me who's got three separate cameras on his house, with a bank of monitors in his spare room. He sees everything that goes on within at least a quarter of a mile. The cameras can be swivelled by remote control. And he's just an ordinary Joe Bloggs with an obsession about his marrows."

"You're joking," she accused.

"Marrows, pumpkins and prize tomatoes. It sounds like a joke, I know, but it's deadly serious — and not even very original."

174

"Blimey," said Thea faintly.

"So, you see, it would be easy enough for your killer to grab his chance the minute you went out. He probably knew already that the back door was missing."

Thea waved her fork at him. "Actually, the back was quite well barricaded. It was the front that I didn't bother to lock."

He laughed. "Why doesn't that surprise me?"

She found herself smarting at this. "What do you mean? You can't possibly think you know me well enough to say a thing like that."

"I'm sorry. Was that rude of me? I meant it to sound approving, as a matter of fact. The thing is, my mother really took to you, and said you were a kindred spirit. She never locks anything, either. She just ... recognised you, I suppose."

"Hmm," said Thea, wondering whether everyone found her as transparent as Clovis and his family seemed to.

"Anyway, let's stick to the point. I presume it wouldn't take long to search the house for the woman, even if there wasn't a tracker on her somewhere. As for knowing where the pressure points are, that does imply some kind of medical training. It's not as easy as people think."

"I don't think it's easy," muttered Thea. She found herself thinking of a strangled child in the village of Snowshill, where there had been nothing very subtle about the attack. "And how do you know whether it's easy or not?"

175

He grimaced. "I don't really. I'm not claiming to have any direct experience, if that's worrying you."

She merely shook her head at that, and they finished the final morsels of their lunch. "I'm having another beer," said Clovis defiantly.

"Go ahead," she shrugged. "With your body weight, you'll be fine. With me, a pint's probably enough to put me over the limit."

"Are you saying I'm fat?" He looked down at himself in wonder.

He was back to the old philandering manner, putting on a playful act and forcing her into a defensive response. Except she dodged it all and told him to shut up. "Don't start," she added warningly.

He collected his drink and they continued to analyse every detail of Thea's weekend. In summary, Clovis suggested that there might be two possible lines of enquiry. "Either she was involved in the trafficking of rare animals, working with a criminal Chinese gang or else she was being trafficked herself. They could have told her she was coming to work in a hotel or other respectable business, and then broke the news that she was their prisoner in some way."

"I can't see it," Thea objected. "Neither one seems to fit with what I saw of her."

"But she was escaping? So she must have been a captive, surely?"

"I suppose so. But there are just too many possible explanations. I really hope the police can find out who she was, and with any luck they might track down some film of her running away from the business park."

Before they knew it, it was half past two and every scrap of food and drink had long ago disappeared. "You've missed your vocation," she told him. "You're a born detective."

"I enjoy a good puzzle," he admitted. "So many people's lives are riddled with secrets, and I like to ferret them out."

"Not much chance of secrets, with all these cameras everywhere."

"You'd be surprised," he said. "They still haven't invented a camera that can see inside people's heads."

They'd drifted a long way from his stated intention to seek her guidance concerning his forthcoming marriage. She began to wonder whether that had all been a ploy, in any case. Had he just used it to gain her confidence? To convey the message that he was not looking for a passionate affair? Neither idea explained why he should seek her out as he had. If it wasn't sex, then what exactly *did* he want from her?

"Did you ask me out so we could talk about the murder?" she asked him on an impulse. "You seem awfully interested."

He hung his head, and looked at her from under his immaculate eyebrows. "You weren't supposed to suss that out," he said. "But yes — the fact is, I did want to hear more about it. It's all totally hypothetical at the moment, but we did just wonder whether there could be a link to the pangolin smuggling. It seemed too good a chance to miss, with me knowing you and you being on the spot — do you see?"

"We?" she echoed. "Who's 'we'?"

"Me and Jennifer," he said simply. "Who do you think?"

CHAPTER
FOURTEEN

"We can't just leave it like this," he said, as they went back to their cars. "I'm free for a couple of days, and you're here all on your own. Can't we team up and solve this murder together?"

"You sound like Just William or some boy detective, talking like that. You don't just solve a murder like a Rubik's Cube." She knew she sounded tetchy, but his confession of a deliberate plan to extract information from her in collusion with his girlfriend had annoyed her.

"Don't you? I thought that was what you did."

"You thought wrong. I'm a house-sitter, that's all. Or I was. Now I'm an undertaker's wife. This job is a one-off. It was all Gladwin's idea. She seemed to think I needed a break from looking after Drew's kids." It sounded worse, every time she said it — or even thought it. It was so irresponsible . . . selfish . . . unkind . . . to go off as she'd done, leaving poor Drew to cope.

"Be that as it may, I think we might want to take this a bit further. I didn't mean to deceive you. It's all terribly tentative, but there's a niggling little idea that Jen wants sorted out. It's horrible to talk like this, I know. Something and nothing. But I can't tell you any more until we've got something concrete to go on."

"Is it something that might identify Grace?"

"We thought it might be. But that isn't the name of the person we're following up. So it's almost certainly a complete mistake. And that's why I can't say any more." He looked genuinely wretched at having to be so evasive.

"Well I can't force you," she said tightly. "But thanks for the lunch." Clovis had insisted on paying for her pie. "It was delicious."

"Good. Well don't take any silly risks, at least. Lock all the doors when the builders have gone and keep your phone by your side. Make sure it's charged, as well. The damn things can let you down at the crucial moment if you don't watch out."

She took her mobile out of her bag and gave it to him. "Put your number in, then."

He thumbed the screen, and reported that she only had sixteen per cent battery life left. "Plug it in the minute you get back," he ordered her.

"Yes, sir." It was nice, of course, to have a big handsome man looking after her welfare. It reminded her of former times, with attentive boyfriends all competing for her favours. But then she had married two men who each insisted that she could quite well stand up for herself. Somewhere inside, she presumed, there was an assertive female who actually wanted to go her own way, without a champion hovering behind her to catch her when she fell. But even the most ardent feminist must be permitted the occasional lapse, she supposed.

"Is it all right with you if I tell Jennifer everything you've told me?"

"That's not for me to say, is it? The fact that the woman was killed at the Corner House is common knowledge, anyway. And you don't want Jennifer thinking you're keeping any secrets from her, do you?"

Her words were almost instantly drowned by a cheerful voice calling, "Hi, Thea! Fancy meeting you here."

Thea was stunned to the point of immobility. The person calling to her was both intensely familiar and wholly alien. "Jocelyn! What . . .? How . . .?"

Her sister laughed. "Well, I was actually coming to find you, so it's not really such a coincidence." She stared hard at Clovis. "But I never expected to find you with a gentleman friend." Her expression added, *And such a beautiful one, too.*

This development was becoming more disastrous with every passing second. Jocelyn was the youngest in the Johnstone family, the mischief-maker and their mother's favourite. She was also the mother of five children, several stone heavier than Thea, and four inches taller. Nobody would ever take them for sisters. But they had grown up as "the little ones", both of them in possession of a strand of fecklessness and defiance in the face of two critical and impatient older siblings.

"Jocelyn," she said again. "This is Clovis. My sister," she explained to him. "Why were you looking for me?"

181

"A few reasons. I gather there's been a murder. I wondered how you were coping. And I wanted to talk to you about Jessica. Toni's just been to see her, and she thinks there might be something going on that you ought to know about."

Jessica and Toni were their respective daughters; cousins who had always liked each other, despite six years' difference in age.

"Oh," said Thea, thinking that it must have been at least a week since she had given her daughter a single thought. "She hasn't said anything to me."

"No . . . Well . . ." said Jocelyn with a small sigh. "Did you say 'Clovis'? That's a very unusual name."

"French," he told her, having followed their fractured exchanges with undisguised interest. "Thanks to my grandmother."

"You do know she's married, don't you?"

"Joss!" Thea was mortified.

Clovis just laughed. "Yes indeed. And I know and respect her husband. You don't have to worry."

Jocelyn's expression was complicated. Dubious, concerned, curious — and more. "Okay," she said.

"Where's your car?" Thea asked her sister. "Why have you come to Quenington? Are you on your own?"

"I'm going," said Clovis. "Nice to meet you, Jocelyn." He got into his car and flashed an all-embracing smile at them both. "Be seeing you." And he drove off.

They watched him go before Jocelyn said, "My car's up by that gorgeous archway. I thought I should go and have a look at it while I was in the area. Noel told me

182

about it — all that guff about Knights Templar is an obsession with him at the moment." Noel was her youngest, eleven years old and something of a geek. Thea was extremely fond of Noel.

"So is he with you?" Thea looked around hopefully.

"No — he came here with his father a few weekends ago. They've taken to Sunday outings, just the two of them. It's rather nice."

"I should get back to Barnsley," said Thea. "I'm supposed to be keeping an eye on everything at the house."

"I'm coming with you. I couldn't see your car."

"It's this one," said Thea, indicating the borrowed vehicle. "It belongs to the police. They're just letting me use it while I'm here. Drew needs ours at home."

"Lead the way, then," said Jocelyn.

Back at the Corner House, Thea was informed by the builders that she could move the kettle and microwave back into the kitchen, where one wall was finished. There were functioning power points, a spotless new work surface and running water. "Best not use the oven," said Dave, with a little frown of embarrassment. "But I guess the hob would be okay."

"Oh? Why?"

"Well, if I know Mrs Ibbotson, she's going to want to christen it herself, if you follow me. Even if it's only used once, it's going to be just a bit spoilt — do you see? You can never really get an oven looking new again, can you?"

It was a very delicate point and Thea was impressed at his sensitive handling of it. "I get it," she assured him. "I'll be fine with the microwave."

It was approaching four o'clock when she and Jocelyn settled down in the big living room with mugs of tea. "Nice house," said the visitor. "But I'm not sure I understand what you're doing here. Have you fallen out with Drew? He sounded pretty weird on the phone this morning."

"Did he? In what way?"

"Well, for a start it was his little girl who answered. How old is she now? Don't the funeral calls come through on that line?"

"She's eleven. She's been answering it since Saturday, apparently. People keep telling me about it." She frowned. "I suppose he must be training her up, because he's got too much else to do. She's heard us both doing it often enough."

"She didn't want to fetch him until I insisted."

"I'll ask him about it when — if — I phone this evening. He did say I shouldn't call again until Thursday, actually." She paused. "And you won't tell him about Clovis, will you?"

Jocelyn's eyes sparkled. "Why not? I thought they were best chums."

"They're not. And even if they were, that wouldn't make much difference. Drew's only human: he's bound to worry, however much I assure him there's nothing going on."

"Secrets, sis? Slippery slope and all that."

184

"Just saving him from needless bother. I could tell him — probably will, actually. It just needs to be the right moment. Besides, I thought everyone agreed there were times when it's best to keep quiet about things. Clovis is getting married. He's not interested in me."

"But he's so appallingly gorgeous! How can you resist?"

"It got easier," sighed Thea. "Three months ago, I'd have turned to jelly if he'd touched me. Now the spell seems to have been broken, thank goodness."

"I'll take your word for that. Now tell me all about this murder. Was it *right here*, in this house? That's what I'm hearing." She looked at the slightly ragged old carpet, as if for bloodstains.

"Upstairs. While I was out for a walk."

"Tell me."

But Thea didn't want to recount the whole story again. She'd had enough for one day, with Clovis turning out so unexpectedly different, and then her sister arriving out of the blue. "How long are you staying?" she asked instead. "I still don't understand why you came looking for me."

"School holidays, same as you," said Jocelyn astutely. "Every woman needs to escape for a bit. The whole thing is relentless otherwise. Thinking up amusements, wondering whether you're doing enough to stimulate them, inventing treats that won't break the bank. I don't blame you for bunking off, even if poor Drew seems to have taken to his bed."

"What? You don't mean that literally, I hope."

Jocelyn had gone pink, and put a hand to her mouth. "No, no. It's just the way he seemed so *absent*. Even when I finally got to talk to him, he wasn't paying much attention."

"But he told you where I was, didn't he? And what I was doing."

"Yes. Forget I said anything. I came about Jessica, remember?"

Thea chewed her lip for a moment. Something wasn't adding up — there was definitely a sense of being excluded from a secret known to everyone else in the family. And yet it was only what she deserved. If exclusion was going on, then she had wantonly done it to herself and could hardly complain if life carried on without her back home. And Jessica — was *she* keeping secrets from her mother as well? "So, what do you think I should know?" she asked wearily.

"Toni thinks Jess is drinking too much."

The starkness with which this was said left no room for evasion or dismissal. Jessica had brought work troubles and boyfriend crises to Thea over the years, and shared in one or two of her encounters with violent crime — but not recently. Well into her twenties, the girl seemed focused and ambitious, with a promotion to the rank of sergeant imminently expected. "Oh," said Thea. "That's the last thing I would have imagined."

Alcohol had never been much of a factor in the Johnstone household, and since becoming adults and leaving home, none of them had taken to drink. The eldest sister, Emily, had got into trouble in a particularly dramatic fashion, but even she was now back to almost-normal life, enjoying her first grandchild and taking things quietly. One or two of Jocelyn's offspring had been dragged home from wild teenage parties a time or two, but nobody worried too much about it. The suggestion that the sensible grown-up Jessica might take to drink was too surprising to process. "Would Toni recognise a drink problem when she saw it?" she wondered.

"I'm not sure. She is quite sensible these days — and she saw drunks when she was doing that hotel job. It was finding a cupboard full of bottles in the flat that really alarmed her. Whisky, gin, loads of wine. All tucked away behind other things."

"Lord help us," groaned Thea. "I suppose I'll have to go and see for myself, once I've finished here. Drew's going to love that, isn't he."

"There could be other explanations," said Jocelyn hesitantly. "Maybe she's preparing for a party, or keeping it for somebody else."

"Didn't Toni ask her?"

"She didn't like to. Couldn't think how to phrase it, I suppose. They went out both evenings with some of Jess's workmates and there was a lot of booze flowing both times. She came home pretty convinced there was an issue."

Issues, thought Thea. Everywhere she looked, there seemed to be stacks of them. Even murder was probably some sort of issue, as well. "I'll phone her tonight," she said. "And fix up a visit in a week or two. Stephanie could come as well, maybe."

"You can't take one without the other," Jocelyn warned. "Who's going to mind Timmy if you do that?"

"Oh, shut up," said Thea. "It's just one darned thing after another."

It was a family saying, gleaned from old Laurel and Hardy films, and Jocelyn obediently laughed.

At six, they ate scrambled eggs, prepared on the new hob, with Thea taking extreme care not to spill anything. "I'm going at eight," said Jocelyn. "Can we have a little walk before then? I want to see this village."

"No problem," said Thea, thinking there really wasn't very much to see. "There's just a pub, a church and a village hall and a big hotel, basically."

"Show me where you went on Sunday, while that poor woman was getting herself murdered. Maybe we'll find a clue or something."

"I don't see how, but we could do that, yes."

Thea led the way out of the front gate and headed towards the centre of Barnsley. The houses were reliably gorgeous in the setting sun, the shadows deep and dark. The road at that point ran north-south, thanks to the sharp kink on the Bibury side of the village. The church tower was one of the few buildings on the eastern side to catch some of the light. Jocelyn glanced at it as they passed. "Have you been in?" she asked.

"Only the graveyard. I went there yesterday and met some people. And I had a chat there this morning, as well."

"What else is there to see?"

188

"There's a rather wonderful barn. A little way along here, look." She pointed to the next junction and they walked on.

"Wow!" breathed Jocelyn, as they turned the corner. "That's amazing! Who does it belong to?"

"No idea. It's totally abandoned, as far as I can see."

"Look at all those brambles and things. It's like Sleeping Beauty's castle. However could you get into it?"

"Probably round the other side. There's a yard, I think. But it all looks more or less disused."

"But it must be prime real estate, worth millions. They can't just *leave* it."

"There could be stuff stored in there, maybe. The roof looks fairly watertight."

"Let's have a look! There's nobody about. It's too intriguing to resist — don't you think? We need a magic sword to cut through all these prickly things."

"We can't, Joss. People know who I am. They'll report me to Tabitha Ibbotson and Gladwin."

"Don't be so wet. Come on." Jocelyn was already trotting around the long side of the building, searching for an entry point. Thea was transported back thirty years or more, when her younger sister would fearlessly lead them into one pickle after another. Even in their respectable Wiltshire home, there was more than enough scope for trouble, if you looked hard enough. She had little choice but to follow, while muttering darkly to herself.

"People always say I'm nosy, but I'm nothing compared to you. And you're always the one who falls

189

over or disturbs the guard dog, leaving me to take the blame."

"Can't hear you," her sister sang out, over her shoulder.

"Keep quiet, can't you? Somebody's liable to come out and shoot us." It felt all too horribly likely, just at that moment.

But Jocelyn had forged ahead, and was rounding the furthest corner, pushing through a half-closed gate in the process. Thea looked all around fearfully. They could be seen from several upstairs windows, if anyone had troubled to look. They were definitely trespassing, once through the gate. "Listen, Joss, will you? Come back." Memories of other finds in other barns were filling her head, and she began to feel sick. "Let's just leave it all alone, okay?"

"Stop fussing. Come and see what I've found."

There was nothing in the voice to suggest another murder victim, or even a pile of illegal tiger skins. That, Thea realised, had been one of the things she had half-expected to discover. Or perhaps a cage filled with desperate immigrants — probably Chinese adolescents shipped over in a metal box. "What, then? What is it?" From Jocelyn's tone, she was entertaining images of a litter of kittens.

At first there was nothing to see. The interior was very dark, accessed through an open section that was only partly blocked by nettles. Jocelyn was standing a few feet away, gazing raptly at an arrangement that looked very like a church altar. But Thea's eyes were still struggling to adjust to the gloom. How Jocelyn's

190

sight could have adjusted so quickly was a mystery. "I can hardly see anything," Thea complained.

"You'll be fine in a minute. It's really not all that dark in here. Move right in, and you'll see better."

"We shouldn't be here."

"No, but look. Isn't this amazing!"

Thea's focus rapidly discerned an area of the barn that was much cleaner than the rest. Halfway along one wall stood a table with a bright white cloth and two tall candlesticks on it. Her instinct for history immediately suggested a forbidden religious sect, practising its rituals in secret. Something from a long-past century where people passionately cared about such things, even in rural Gloucestershire.

"What is it?" she said.

Jocelyn had approached the table with no hint of reverence. She reached out to an object placed between the candles. "Is this what I think it is?" she said.

Thea glanced back at their point of entry, still anxious about being discovered. Then she gave Jocelyn's find more of her attention. "It's an ashes urn," she said. "Good grief!"

It was a brick-shaped container made of thick brown plastic. A screw-topped lid capped it. "What a place to keep it," said Jocelyn.

Thea examined the object without touching it. It was much the same as several she'd seen Drew deal with in his line of work. While most of his customers were strongly in favour of burial over cremation, there were occasions where ashes had been interred in his field. "There should be a name label on it somewhere." She tried to think. "But how weird to leave it in this nasty plastic thing. Wouldn't you expect it to be in something more . . . *elegant* . . . more tasteful? If this is a shrine, it's rather a half-hearted one."

"But it's still exciting!" Jocelyn insisted. "I can't see a label." She picked up the urn and turned it round. "Ah, here it is. We'll need more light to read what it says. Here — take it to the door." She held it out to Thea, who stepped back, refusing to take it. "It's much heavier than I would have thought," Jocelyn went on. "What a funny place to put it. Why won't you touch it? I'd have thought you'd be perfectly comfortable with this sort of thing."

"I'm worried someone's going to catch us, that's all."

"It's left right here, for anybody to find."

"It's not really, though, is it?" said Thea slowly. "It's actually hidden away where nobody would expect it to be found. I bet we're the first people to come in here uninvited, probably ever." She recalled the nicely worded sign on the gate to the Barnsley Park mansion. "Proceed By Invitation Only" it had said. She felt the same might well apply to this barn.

Drew had often talked about ashes, and the problems they could present. People would get landed with cremated remains and not know what to do with them. They kept them in cupboards for decades at a time. Then, when someone else in the family died, the opportunity finally arrived for the ashes to go in a new grave along with the new body. "When you think about it, a barn's as good a place as any to put them," she said.

192

"I always thought a barn was for hay and corn and implements and owls and bats. This is odd, even for the Cotswolds." Jocelyn hefted the container again. "Well, let's see what the name is, while we're here." She walked towards the way they'd come in. "It says Gwendoline Phoebe Wheelwright. And a date." She peered closer. "Looks like 5th April 1997. Does that mean anything to you?"

"Not at all. Put it back, will you? We really do have to go."

"What happened to you? When did you get so gutless?"

"I don't know," said Thea helplessly.

"Well, look over there, before you run away." Jocelyn indicated the furthest corner of the barn. There was a large rectangular object sitting on the floor. "That looks like an old trunk."

"We're not going to open it," said Thea firmly.

"Why? Do you think it might be Pandora's Box?"

"I think that's almost possible. I certainly think we'd be laying ourselves open to a charge of unlawful entry, or something of the sort, if we start ferreting inside people's private possessions."

But Jocelyn was unstoppable. She trotted over to the corner and lifted one end of the object. "Heavy!" she announced. "Books, at a guess. Lots of big fat books."

"Or ledgers," said Thea, suddenly capturing an elusive thought. "Or record books. Or lost parish registers. Except they're not lost, just turned to dust by silverfish or something."

"What records?" Jocelyn finally decided to let it alone and turned towards the door. "What are you talking about?"

"It's a long story, and can't have anything to do with anything. Come on, quick, before somebody finds us."

"If this was the Famous Five, there'd be a man with a black beard waiting to grab us as we leave."

Instead there was a middle-sized brown dog, slowly wagging its tail, ears perked in eager enquiry.

CHAPTER
FIFTEEN

"Hello!" said Thea. "Haven't I seen you somewhere before?" The dog cocked its head, checking the words for something familiar. Thea knew instinctively that it was female, and ready to co-operate with any suggestion, however inconvenient. Basically Labrador, there was something of a bull terrier in the set of the shoulders.

"Where's its person?" wondered Jocelyn.

"Jess!" came a man's voice, answering the question.

The dog gave a muffled *woof* and set off towards the road. Man and beast coincided at the corner, where the small road branched off the high street. The man showed no signs of affection or relief, just a curt nod of approval at the instant obedience. The animal clearly knew better than to jump up or show any demonstrations of fidelity.

"Your dog's got the same name as my daughter," said Thea, having followed the dog. "Fancy that."

"I've seen you before," he said, with narrowed suspicious eyes.

"Yes. You were walking Jess on Saturday afternoon, near the business park."

"Business park? Oh, you mean the big house. Funny to hear you call it that." His tone implied that she had made a serious social gaffe.

"It is, though, isn't it? It's got a lot of small businesses in the stables and whatnot. I saw the website."

"Got a business, then, have you? Looking to start something up here in Barnsley?" His manner was every bit as unfriendly as it had been on Saturday. He looked as if a smile would cause him genuine pain.

"Oh no. Not at all. I'm just staying a few days. This is my sister. We've been exploring. This barn's unusual, isn't it? I mean — there aren't many left that haven't been converted into houses."

"Not substantial enough. There are always people sniffing around it, talking about neglect and waste. None of their business, of course."

"Is it yours?" Jocelyn asked him.

"What? No, of course it's not mine. What would I be doing with a barn?"

"All sorts of things," replied Jocelyn robustly. "Keep spare furniture. Breed fancy rabbits. Store potatoes or logs. Loads of things."

Still the man did not manage a smile. His dog stood meekly at his side, with no expectations. Thea felt angry with him for his disagreeable manner. "I'm an accountant," he said. "I do not breed rabbits or grow potatoes."

"Oh, well," Jocelyn shrugged. "We'll be going now."

"Hang on," said Thea. "You didn't see a Chinese woman over near that big house, as you call it, on

Saturday, did you? Black hair, not very tall. I forgot about you when I was telling the police what had happened."

"Police?" There was anger, but no alarm, on his face. "What are you talking about?"

"You must have heard about the murder on Sunday? In the Corner House; the one that belongs to Mrs Ibbotson. I'm the house-sitter. I took the woman back there, and somebody killed her."

"Oh —" A thwarted expression crossed his face, as if he'd lost control of the conversation. "I knew it had to be you, when we heard the news on Sunday. Everybody in the village has been discussing you."

"So, what have they been saying?"

"That there's a lot more to the whole business than we're being told. That you've brought trouble and gossip to a quiet village, just like you've done elsewhere. We know about your reputation, Mrs Thea Osborne." The tone was accusatory, implying a repugnance that Thea found hurtful.

"Well you've got that wrong. My name's Slocombe, not Osborne."

"Ah, yes. Married that peculiar undertaker in Chipping Campden, didn't you?"

"*Broad* Campden," Thea muttered.

"So you didn't see the Chinese woman?" Jocelyn asked, trying to maintain dominance over the conversation.

"Of course I didn't," said the man impatiently. "The general view is that you brought her with you on

Saturday when you arrived, and kept her shut up in the house so nobody would see her."

"The *general view*?" scoffed Jocelyn. "A lot of brainless guesswork, you mean. What a stupid thing to think."

Thea was finding it hard to stand her ground, despite her sister's valiant defence. The interpretation made by the villagers was not so very far from the facts, after all. It was the implication of wholesale suspicion and hostility that undid her. "Do they think I killed her, then?" she asked faintly.

The man stretched himself to maximum height, which was about nine inches higher than Thea. "I prefer not to discuss the subject any further. If the police feel the need to speak to me, then that's a different matter." He put a hand to an inside pocket of his light cotton jacket and withdrew a card. "You're welcome to pass my details onto them, if you see fit. It's all on there. Now, if you'll excuse me. Come on, Jess."

The dog followed at his heel, casting a quick glance back at the woman she had recognised unerringly as a friend.

The sisters watched him go, not daring to meet each other's eye. There was a lurking urge to giggle; the childish sense of adventure not quite quenched. "Well, that wasn't very nice," said Thea, looking at the card in her hand. "His name is James Williams. And he's a *chartered* accountant. How dull." Her voice was shaky, and her insides were quivering.

Jocelyn seemed to feel no matching sense of upset. "Don't forget I'm married to one. They're not all like that."

Privately, Thea had always thought Alex was rather inclined to be humourless, if not actually stuffy. He had other defects, which had brought him close to public acrimony a few years earlier — but had quickly seen his mistake and behaved perfectly ever since, as far as Thea knew. But he had remained forever tainted in her eyes, and she'd done her best to avoid him. She changed the subject slightly, saying, "That poor dog! I don't imagine she gets much affection lavished on her."

Jocelyn was lukewarm about dogs and regarded Thea's enthusiasm for them as unreasonable. "It'll be fine. All it wants is for him to take charge and give it some exercise. Dogs are like doormat wives — they can't do enough to please their beloved master. They're pathetic."

"At least he didn't catch us in the barn. He might have called the cops on us. He couldn't have realised that we'd been in there."

"That wouldn't have mattered. You could have pulled rank and revealed your intimate friendship with a detective superintendent. Actually, I doubt if he would. I think he was rather shaken to come face-to-face with you. He took the offensive because he was worried you'd start asking him awkward questions."

"No," Thea protested. "He can't have any reason to feel worried." Then she hesitated. "Although he *was* there on Saturday, when I found Grace. And he didn't appear to be in a very good mood. Maybe he'd been trying to find her, using his dog as a tracker."

"Mark my words. He's probably rushing off to pack a bag and disappear to the Orkneys as we speak."

Thea stopped to think for a moment. "I didn't get that impression, actually. I thought he was just irritated by all the publicity and disturbance. He didn't have to give me his card, did he?"

"Bluffing," said Jocelyn. "He hopes it'll make you think he's got nothing to contribute, so you won't bother to tell the cops about him."

"In that case, I'll text Gladwin first thing tomorrow and dob him right in it."

And then Jocelyn really did giggle. "It's so nice to see you," she said. "We ought to do this sort of thing more often."

Back at the house, they both faced up to the harsh fact of a recent murder right there, above their heads. "You'd think there'd be a ghost," said Jocelyn with a shiver. "I'm not sure I could stay here on my own."

"I don't have much choice. Besides, it doesn't really bother me. If it had been somebody I knew and liked, that might be different. But she was just a stranger, who might have been telling me outrageous lies, for all I know."

"Like what? You haven't told me anything at all about her."

"Because I've just spent hours telling Clovis the whole thing. I can't go through it all again. Even Drew doesn't know all the details."

"You haven't told me about Clovis, either, for that matter."

"We met him back in May, when his father died. Drew did the funeral."

"And?" demanded Jocelyn impatiently.

"Nothing, really. He's nice."

"Thea, stop it. He's *gorgeous*. You can't be such an old married woman that you can't see that. There you were, standing in the road with him, two of the most attractive people in the country, and nothing was happening. It was unnatural. He's not a long-lost brother of ours, is he? Even then, I doubt if that would stop me."

"I told you — I was quite smitten to start with," Thea said. "Just an automatic hormonal thing, I suppose. At that point I tried to persuade myself he was a rude and possibly violent character with nothing to redeem him, but that didn't last long. It's the way he *looks* at you. Eye contact can be insanely powerful."

"I'll have to take your word for that. I seem to have missed out somewhere. I remember you going on about Mr Lodge at school — the way he looked right into your eyes all the time he was talking to you. He never did it to me, I have to say."

"I was his special favourite," said Thea complacently.

"You were the prettiest girl in the school, that's why. I don't know why I haven't hated you all my life."

"Yes, well, now he wants to play the boy detective and help me solve this murder."

Jocelyn made a sceptical face. "Does he indeed? And why is that, I wonder?"

"I'm not sure. He did sort of hint at ulterior motives. Something to do with rare animals. He's got this high-powered girlfriend called Jennifer, who works for charities. Maybe he wants to impress her somehow."

"By spending time with a married woman?"

"By showing how clever and brave he is. By trying to share in her interests."

"Oh. Right. So can we have some coffee and toast or something and then I'll go. You should phone Drew. Don't let him think you've forgotten about him. And for heaven's sake don't let him find out you're seeing the lovely Clovis while you're here all on your own. I was wrong before — it would only cause trouble if he knew about it."

"I won't. If you don't tell him, nobody else is going to, are they?"

"Let's hope not."

She waited until Jocelyn had been gone for fifteen minutes and then made the call to Drew, having come to the conclusion that he had not really meant it when he told her to skip a day or two, if there was nothing urgent to report. There was too much mystery circling around the Slocombe household for her to stay silent. She used the landline. It was nearly half past eight — a time when the children would normally be in bed, baths and stories all finished with. But if it was still under way, she didn't want his warbling mobile to intrude and lead to a prolonged exchange with Stephanie and Timmy that would probably delay their getting off to sleep. Nor did she want her young stepdaughter to pick up the call.

To her relief, it was Drew himself who answered the phone. "Hello? How can I help you?" he said, sounding just like his normal self.

"It's me. When are we going to get one of those doings that tells you who's calling?"

"Sometime. Are you all right?"

"I'm fine. Had an interesting day. Did my interview with the police this morning. Talked to a nice dog with a nasty man. Jocelyn showed up." She was carefully editing as she spoke, smoothly filling in the lunchtime hole left by the absence of any mention of Clovis. "How about you?"

"One new funeral. Timmy says he's going to be an accountant when he grows up. Your dog found a dead ferret or something and brought it in."

"Ferret? Surely not! It'll be somebody's pet, if so, and she'll be in trouble."

"Weasel, then. Might be a weasel. Pretty little thing."

"I am missing her," Thea sighed. "And you, of course. The time is passing rather slowly. I feel as if I've been here for weeks, instead of three days."

"I can't let him be an accountant, can I?"

"Absolutely not. We'll tie him in chains in the cellar before we can allow that. The nasty man with the dog's an accountant, and he's enough to put anybody off."

"Alex isn't so bad, though."

"That's what Joss said. He is quite dull, though."

"Should I worry about you being murdered by a nasty accountant?" For the first time in this call she heard a repeat of the weariness and something hinting at a deeper malaise that had bothered her the previous day. Something flat and unengaged in his tone.

"No. Not at all. Are you okay? You sound peculiar."

"Tired. I can't get used to the empty bed. I keep waking up in a panic and not getting off again for ages."

"Oh dear." She tried to resist the feelings of guilt, irritation, concern and other negatives. She liked sharing a bed with him, she reminded herself. She almost liked the fact that he couldn't sleep without her. But she also liked having a bed to herself for a little while. And she definitely did *not* like the implication that her rightful place was at his side, day and night. "Well, it won't be for very long."

"Did they solve the murder yet?"

"Not as far as I know. They might have found out the woman's identity by now, with any luck. I haven't heard anything from the police for a bit now. I met two quite nice men from the village," she offered, as an afterthought.

"Two out of three isn't so bad," he said.

"What? Oh — I see. That's right." She was thinking about the Jackson brothers and the way they'd seemed to have time on their hands. And then she began to wonder what she would do the next day. "The police have lent me a car, so I can go for a drive tomorrow," she told her husband. "I'll have a look at Bibury, probably."

"Yes, you told me that. It'll be nice to have some better options."

"Mm. I'm not sure about Bibury, actually. It's always full of Chinese tourists, apparently."

"You told me that as well. What's wrong with Chinese tourists?"

"Nothing, really. I just wonder why they home in on that particular village. It seems a bit brainless, somehow."

"And your murder victim might have been one of them — do you think? Somehow missed her bus and got into a pickle."

"A bit more than a pickle — but yes, there might well be a connection somewhere. Although it wouldn't fit with what she told me." She was hoping he would start to show a genuine interest, asking for details and offering theories, as he had done in the past. Instead, he just mumbled something that sounded like *uh-huh*, and said he should go because he'd got a mug of coffee getting cold.

"Right, then," she said. "I'll phone you again tomorrow evening."

"There's really no need."

"I *want* to, Drew. I need to hear your voice, okay? I'm going to keep phoning every evening whether you like it or not."

"Oh, well, then," he said with a fond little laugh, "I suppose I'll have to let you, if you feel like that about it."

It had all been so *tepid*, she thought sadly. Like people who had been married for fifty years. How had it got to this point so quickly? Was it entirely her fault? She automatically assumed it must be, because Drew was indisputably good. He had no vices. Everybody who met him liked or even loved him. They trusted and respected him. He was principled, sensitive, patient and sweet-tempered. And a whole lot more along the same lines.

She gave an irritable shake. She'd been through all this before, and concluded that nobody could be perfect, and if Drew made a better job of it than she did, then this was a problem for them as a couple. She wanted life to be dangerous now and then, to make mistakes and lose her temper. A couple counsellor might very well say that she was doing all that for two. That between them the Slocombes made a fully rounded person, but that splitting the positive and negative elements of personality between them was not entirely healthy. She knew the theory, but saw no way of changing the way she and Drew were implementing it in practice.

And then, inevitably, images of Clovis Biddulph began to sneak into her head. *He* wasn't tepid. He was smouldering and brave and reckless. He wanted to know all about the murder, and actually get involved in digging for clues. If she allowed him to participate, that too would be reckless. Whatever he might say about his beloved Jennifer, there would be definite danger in spending time with him. While her own turbulent hormones seemed to have gone off the boil somewhat, there was no guarantee that they wouldn't fire up again. She had no doubt that she could seduce him if she set her mind to it. He had delicately indicated that she was safe from attack, if that was how she wanted it. The ball was in her court, and the way she was feeling about Drew just now, she might well decide to lob it back with an invitation pinned to it.

206

She went to bed with a milky drink and a paperback. Just above her head, the attic seemed to exude mystery and long lists of questions. There was no ghost; nothing fearsome or macabre — just an insistent need to find an explanation for what she had realised immediately, on Sunday morning, was the strangest death she had yet encountered.

CHAPTER
SIXTEEN

And then it was Wednesday, and Dave and Sid showed up bright and early. They were installing worktops and cupboards, drilling through the walls and sorting through the stack of flat-pack boxes out in the back garden. Again, Thea was impressed at the lack of ostentation. When the first batch of appliances was in place, the doors opening and closing smoothly, everything straight and true, it looked like any ordinary kitchen she'd seen. "That's the easy bit," said Dave, standing back to admire his work. "It gets a lot noisier now." He indicated the black space on the wall. "I suggest you leave us to it for a couple of hours, if you've got anywhere to go. We'll be tiling this afternoon, so that'll be quieter."

It was ten-thirty, and she had been content to sit with her coffee and the radio, and not make any plans for the day. "I suppose I should go to Bibury," she said, with scant enthusiasm. "I might take my sketchpad and see if I can find an unusual angle for a picture."

"Ooh — an artist, are you?" said Sid.

"No, not at all. But I did used to like drawing, when I was about sixteen. It might be a bit embarrassing, though, if the place is very busy."

"It's always busy," said Sid.

It was not what she really wanted to do, but however much she urged herself to make something more exciting happen, there didn't seem to be very much opportunity. Without a companion — in which category she very much included her dog — she could not think of a pretext to go knocking on doors or questioning random people walking across the fields. Making sketches felt like the sort of thing under-occupied elderly ladies did, at least in the eyes of the world. If she wanted to have something to show for her time in Barnsley, she should probably just take a few photos with her phone. But where would be the satisfaction in that? To make her own original drawing would surely be more worthwhile.

But she could not motivate herself right away. She spent half an hour tidying the living room and then skirting the garden looking for a few flowers to bring into the house. There was some crocosmia left, and a bed of neglected hollyhocks that were valiantly flowering regardless of their crooked stems and weedy competition. Thea didn't have the heart to cut them, but found some white daisies and orange day lilies to make a halfway decent display.

As she carried them back, again navigating around all the building materials, she came face-to-face with Caz Barkley.

"Oh!" she yelped. "I didn't hear you."

"Sorry. I did ring the bell, and one of the builders showed me where you were. This must have been a nice garden at one time." The young detective gazed over the patchy lawn to the apple trees and dilapidated shed at the far end. The garden was roughly square, and probably a quarter of an acre in extent.

"Yes," said Thea. "And will be again, I expect."

"If you say so."

"Do you want coffee? We can probably get into a corner of the kitchen to boil water. They're doing wall cupboards and tiling today."

Barkley nodded carelessly. "I'll wait for you in the front room, shall I? I can't stop long."

Thea had the coffee made in four minutes, and Caz launched directly into business. "We can't find any trace of your woman. She didn't land at Manchester Airport on Saturday morning, or any time on the two days before that. She must have told you a pack of lies from start to finish."

"She didn't actually say it was the airport. She hardly said anything about what she was doing there, or how she got there. Maybe that was where she lived. Or maybe she got there on a train — or a ferry. Do ferries arrive in Manchester?"

"No. Liverpool."

"Well, that's not far away, is it?"

Barkley sighed. "It's too vague. We have no idea where she was this time last week. It could be anywhere in the world. There's no way we can start searching every database and camera for her."

"Didn't the pathologist find anything useful? Vaccinations? What about labels on her clothes?" She was ransacking her memory for details of forensic examinations she'd read about in Jeffery Deaver books and others. "Exotic seeds lodged in her gut?"

This time Barkley lost patience. "Stop it," she ordered. "We don't have the manpower, right? She died of strangulation. The person who did it seemed to know exactly how to kill someone quickly. I had a quick read up on it last night," she admitted. "Did you know it can take less than twenty seconds for the victim to lose consciousness, if the jugular is constricted?"

"I did not," said Thea, fingering her own neck. "I suppose that's actually quite a long time to keep a tight grip on somebody."

"Not really." They fell silent for a moment, trying to imagine the whole process.

"Anyway," Caz went on, with a little shake. "The killer — or killers — had to have been lurking around here on Sunday, waiting for you to leave the house, even though that's difficult to believe. Had you told anybody you were going out? Did you phone anyone? Despite what people think, it's fantastically unusual for baddies to hide in the undergrowth waiting for their chance to kill somebody."

"I know," said Thea. "I've spent my life telling people that. But these days, they can keep an eye on people electronically. I mean, with secret cameras and that sort of thing. They might even have planted some sort of tracker on Grace." She was well aware that she was quoting Clovis, and equally aware that she had never entirely believed what he'd said.

Caz closed her eyes, and appeared to be counting. "We'd have found it on the body," she grated. "And where do you think these cameras would have been hidden? Apart from anything else, it's illegal to watch people surreptitiously. All cameras have to be clearly visible."

"Well, I don't imagine they'd be worried about legality, would they — if they were planning to murder somebody? That's illegal as well, isn't it?"

"Okay. I'll admit it's technically possible."

"And it was you who said he — they — must have been watching for me to leave," Thea reminded the detective. "How did you think they were doing it?"

Caz shook her head. "We're agreeing, then, aren't we. And we both probably think it's more likely it was just luck that you were out at the time. If you'd been there you might have been killed as well. Have you thought of that?"

"Not very seriously. I've been assuming that Grace was very much the target, for some very specific reason."

"There's not much evidence for that."

"Yes, there is." It felt important to Thea to argue this point. "She was scared of being found. She'd left all her personal possessions somewhere, in case she could be traced through her phone. She was tired out. Any other scenario implies a homicidal lunatic, just randomly killing women in houses for the fun of it."

Barkley shook her head. "That's not what I said. I agree that Grace was the target — but if you'd got in the way, you might have been collateral damage. The phone thing doesn't cut much ice. Ordinary citizens can't trace a person through their phone. You've got to get a warrant and wait for the provider to co-operate."

"Oh."

"No, the problem is there's absolutely nothing to go on. There's no useful footage from the business park, either. There are plenty of blind spots where a car could park and somebody get out and run off without being caught by the cameras. Again, we haven't got the resources to check the owner of every single car coming in and out on Saturday morning. It's possible in theory, but much too labour-intensive."

Thea frowned sceptically. "Surely it's not that hard? There can't have been so very many, after all. Check the registration numbers against the DVLA records, and flag up anything that doesn't belong to anybody who works or lives there." She paused. "Well, I guess there are various sorts of customers as well. I can see it would take some work. But the camera shows the people inside the car as well, doesn't it? Check the ones with small dark females in them. There might only be one or two."

"They don't show the people inside," said Barkley tiredly. "You get a glimpse of the driver, usually in profile, but not much more than that."

"Well, I still think there's a whole lot of evidence you could find. Somebody who lives or works in one of the businesses must have taken Grace there in a car on Saturday. I bet there's some nasty illicit business going on behind an innocent front. That's not impossible, is it? She was very obviously oriental, even if her father was British. She must have stood out."

"What are you saying? That she's been dealing in illegal ivory? Smuggling tiger cubs? And it's not true that she'd stand out. You must have noticed that this is a very popular spot for Chinese tourists. It's famous for it."

"I forgot," Thea admitted. "That's got to be significant, don't you think?"

"I don't see how. At least — I can think of about ten possible theories that might fit the few facts we've got."

"Can the pathologist say whether she was only half-Chinese? She told me her father was British. It might not be true, of course. But she did speak very good English and said she'd lived here for twenty years."

"And she had an English name," Barkley added. "He did think she was mixed race, yes. Without a DNA test it's mostly guesswork. And we're not asking for a test at the moment."

"Because it costs money," Thea nodded. "I'm getting the point."

"It's crept up on us, somehow. Year on year, there's less money for any forensic examination. As well as a smaller workforce. We're always chasing our tails these days. And now there's this huge trafficking case, everybody's been diverted into that. The media aren't helping, needless to say."

"Really?"

"Haven't you seen it all? Everybody's screaming about bloody pangolins. Headline news everywhere you look. The BBC News Channel have dug out every bit of film they've got with the things in, and seem to be showing them in a loop, twenty-four hours a day. There's a new charitable campaign raising money specifically to protect them. It's gone insane."

"I missed all that," said Thea. "I had a visitor yesterday — and went out for lunch before that. The telly doesn't work and I've only heard a few minutes of radio."

Barkley blinked in disbelief. "Amazing," she muttered. "I didn't think it was possible to drop out that much. Don't you go online at all?"

"Not very often," said Thea. "Although I did play a game of online Scrabble the other day."

The detective rolled her eyes and actually groaned. "That doesn't count," she said.

"So — basically you've come to tell me it's all bad news, you'll never find who killed Grace, and I'm probably still the chief suspect. Right?"

"Nobody thinks you did it. But the Big Boss is going to want us to keep a close eye on you, once he's read all the reports. It looks bad to have a murder left unsolved."

"Should I be worried he'll have me charged, just because there's nobody else? Isn't that what happens in America?"

"No chance. Not with the superintendent on your side. But you might get interviewed again. You seem to keep remembering new bits of information."

"Do I? Like what?"

"The woman having a British father — I haven't seen that anywhere in the notes."

"Well, I told your Cirencester man yesterday. I'm fairly sure I told him absolutely everything. Oh — except for the accountant man. I did forget all about him."

215

Barkley flipped open her standard-issue notepad and dug a pen from a pocket. "Go on, then." There was a faint hint of excitement in her voice.

"He was walking towards me on Saturday afternoon, just about level with the big house at the business park. He's got a nice Labrador bitch called Jess, who isn't loved half as much as she should be. He's a boot-faced boring accountant called James Williams. He lives somewhere hereabouts. He told me the whole village was talking about me and they think I'm a highly suspicious character."

"And you forgot to mention him? Sounds as if you know practically his whole life history."

"I met him again yesterday, with my sister. He gave me his card." She took it from the side table where she'd placed it the previous day. "He seems to think he might be questioned by the police, when I tell you he was out there on Saturday." She felt proud of her efforts, but Barkley looked doubtful.

"You think he might have seen something?"

"It's possible, isn't it?"

"Not possible enough to justify questioning him. The timing's not right, is it? We already know the woman was hiding in the bushes when you were on your walk."

"But he might have seen her coming from another direction — or somebody chasing her. She could have only been there for ten minutes, and not all day as she told me."

"Too many variables," Caz asserted firmly. "We need to focus on her identity. You noticed, of course, that she wasn't wearing a wedding ring?"

"I did, actually. And she never said anything about a husband."

"Well, she did have a ring after all, on a string round her neck. Eighteen-carat gold, beautifully made. With initials engraved inside. English characters, not Chinese."

"Please tell me there's a G."

Barkley smiled. "There's a G." She glanced at her notepad. "It's G. B. and K. A. W. Look." She showed Thea the exact rendering. "And do *not* suggest we look through every marriage record for the past thirty years involving a half-Chinese bride with the initials G. B. Even with the search engines we've got now, that would take weeks."

"I don't think marriage certificates record people's ethnicity anyway," said Thea. She had a thought. "Did the pathologist say whether she'd ever had children?"

"He says she didn't. Not normally, and not by C-section."

"Oh."

"And before you ask, there are no missing persons reports that come remotely close, either. It's all one big blank, unless we call in every cop, every minute of CCTV and some impossibly brilliant forensic team — and even then, we might not find her. If everything she told you was a lie, then there's virtually nothing to go on."

"There has to be something," Thea insisted. "We can't just let it go. What'll happen to her body? What would have happened if I hadn't found her on Saturday?" This was a new thought, bringing

217

disagreeable implications. "Maybe she would still be alive. She might have walked along that awful jungly path to Bibury, in the dark, and stowed away on one of those tourist coaches and got clean away."

"The superintendent always says it's futile to ask 'What if . . .?' questions. What's happened, happened and you have to take it from there."

"I know, but . . . So, why exactly have you come to see me, anyway? Just to tell me you haven't got the manpower or whatever to carry on this investigation? Or what?"

"The investigation will carry on indefinitely. I really came to warn you that you might have to be interviewed again. And to tell you to be careful. Don't go making things happen locally. If there's a killer somewhere in this village and he thinks you're getting close to finding who he is, you'll be in real danger. You do see that, don't you?"

"Is that what Gladwin told you to say?"

"More or less. It's common sense, basically."

"How exactly am I supposed to be careful? Avoid isolated spots? Get somebody to stay here with me?"

"Use your common sense," Caz repeated.

The idea of having Clovis staying as her guard and protector vibrated briefly inside her. Totally out of the question, of course. Impossibly transgressive. Jocelyn might be an alternative, but she sounded pretty bogged down at home. "I might phone my daughter and see if she can take a few days off," she said, knowing there was very little chance of that. If police resources were as stretched in Greater Manchester as they were in

Gloucestershire, she would be committed to long shifts and no sudden days off for the foreseeable future. "You knew she was in the police, didn't you?" she added.

"No. Where?"

"Greater Manchester."

"Where your woman said she'd come from on Saturday?"

"As it happens, yes."

"Maybe we could persuade them to lend her to us for a bit. She could get seconded, as a liaison officer."

"Really? Could it be done quickly? I'm only here for the rest of this week. Once the kitchen's done, they've got the bathroom, and then I can go."

"It wouldn't hurt to ask," said Barkley.

"Will you do it — or should I?"

"It's got to be official. But you could give her a heads-up and see what she thinks. You're close, then, are you?" There was a wistfulness in her voice, and Thea remembered once again that Caz Barkley had grown up in the care system, presumably not at all close to her mother.

"Fairly. We like each other, if that's what you mean. I don't see her terribly often. But my sister's girl, Toni, has just been to visit and seems a bit worried. Something's not entirely right, apparently. I ought to see if there's anything I can do about it."

"I'll get onto it this morning. She could be here tomorrow with any luck. She'd have to be properly briefed and given a complete set of assignments to justify bringing her here."

"Amazing. Are you sure?"

"Obviously I can't be sure they'll let her go. But it must be worth a try."

The prospect of having someone to share the nights with was embarrassingly welcome. But there were difficulties. "Where would she sleep? I can't put her in the attic and we're not allowed to use Tabitha's room. There aren't any beds anywhere else." And if Jessica was going to be there, that put paid to any hope of having Clovis turn up to help with the detective work.

"Tell her to bring an air bed, then."

"Good thinking."

"It won't help the investigation," said Barkley with pessimistic certainty. "It's been three days now. Whoever killed your woman could be on the other side of the world by this time."

"More likely he's just carrying on as normal, and nobody suspects a thing."

"You sound as if you believe it's a local."

"Do I? I suppose nothing else makes much sense. The way I see it, somebody fetched her from somewhere — maybe Manchester — and drove her here, for a reason. There's a Barnsley connection somewhere, I bet you."

"But it's such a small place. Hardly any people live here permanently."

"Just over two hundred," said Thea. "I looked it up."

"Pity they didn't find any fingerprints, then." She looked at the ceiling. "Up there, I mean."

"None at all?"

"Yours and the dead woman's on the door and light switch, that's all."

220

"Not the builders'? Or Tabitha's? Well, you wouldn't have hers for comparison, would you? She must surely have gone up there sometimes."

"Yes, but not in the past three days. Fingerprint traces fade with time, you know. You can easily tell which are the fresh ones."

"Well, I never. I didn't know that." She thought about it for a moment. "I suppose it's obvious, really. If they all remained intact for years, you'd have to eliminate hundreds of people."

"Right."

Barkley got to her feet. "I'm going. Tell me your daughter's name, rank, home station, and I'll see if I can wangle a transfer. You never know — she might actually turn out to be useful."

CHAPTER
SEVENTEEN

Thea sent a text to Jessica, five minutes after Barkley left. "Have suggested you be sent here to help with murder investigation. Hope that's okay? All a bit sudden, I know. You'd stay with me in a village called Barnsley. Phone me when you're free."

It seemed only fair to give as much information as she could — not that Jess would have much say in the matter, from the sound of it. She might even be seriously annoyed, if it clashed with things she wanted to do.

There was still more than half of Wednesday to get through. The plan of driving to Bibury remained her best option, as far as she could see. The day was dry, if not especially sunny, and she realised that she might find a spot to park in, from which she could discreetly make a drawing. A vague notion persisted that if she could show Drew some artwork made during her absence, she would thereby demonstrate her innocence of any secretive behaviour. "It took me *hours*," she would say, proffering the sheet of A4 covered in pencilled detail.

It would also work as a calming process, or so she hoped. The restlessness and suppressed anxiety were starting to increase. Unsolved murders were unsettling at best. Surely everybody in the village must be feeling the same way? If they were, there was little sign of it. As usual, there was nothing to observe in the street — nobody walked along the narrow pavements, or gathered outside the pub for a sociable chat. Those who did walk, headed off along the footpaths with their dogs. Even the theoretical permanent residents probably had little flats in Chelsea they spent half their time in. Money was even more evident in this eastern side of the Cotswolds, where property values were routinely in seven figures. But there were still ordinary family homes, passed down the generations, with old-fashioned accoutrements and unpretentious occupants. When, eventually, an aged widow died and her offspring leapt like vultures to dismantle and sell the old place, another little piece of local history would disappear. And if the aged widow was in fact a spinster, with no immediate descendants, as had happened with the Corner House, then some lucky friend or distant cousin reaped the rewards instead.

So she made herself a minimal lunch and set out in the unfamiliar car. It took barely five minutes to reach Bibury, where there were alarming numbers of people walking along the roads and paths, filling the tables at the little café by the fish farm shop, and patronising the handful of other shops. It was quite a shock to see so many other humans after the deserted villages of Barnsley and Broad Campden. There was nowhere to park the car. She drove over the bridge and turned right towards the famous row of ancient cottages. The whole road was densely packed with vehicles, including camper vans and minibuses. The wider area was full of coaches and the larger motorhomes. And sure enough, a good proportion of the trippers were of Asian appearance. Twice Thea saw women who could have been sisters to Grace, which sent her thoughts back yet again to the poor woman. Was nobody looking for her? Where was the husband with the initials K. A. W.? Should the police not be making far greater effort to track down more details about her than they were doing?

She turned the car round awkwardly in a gateway and went through Bibury again. There really wasn't a single space to park, so after a few hundred yards she randomly took a small country road to the left and miraculously found a small lay-by, where she stopped. But it was not in view of the river or the handsome old Swan Inn, and certainly not the renowned Arlington Row, which had been her intended subject for a picture. All she could see was fields, and stone walls and some well-concealed houses. But at least she could sit unobserved if she did decide to get out and do a drawing. She had the Ordnance Survey map with her, which told her she was on the junction with the old Arlington Pike road, which gave her a pleasing sense of history. Perhaps she should draw a drover with his herd of fat cattle on their way to market in Cirencester? She was rather good at drawing cows, and he could have a nice, big, rangy dog as well.

She also had her phone with her, turned on and fully charged as Clovis had instructed. And just as she opened the car door, having decided to get out and find a quiet corner to sit, it started to warble. *Jessica* said the screen.

"Hi, Jess. You got my text, then?"

"It nearly gave me a heart attack. What are you thinking? You can't just move me around the country like a chess piece. I'm totally involved here. There's no way they can spare me. It'll cause terrible ructions to even ask." The voice was breathless with anger.

"Okay. Calm down. It just seemed worth a try. They're really short-handed down here, and there's been this murder —"

"Isn't there always? I did hear a bit about it, actually. Do you want to explain exactly what happened?"

"Not now. It's a long story. If you're not coming, then you don't need to know."

"You're not in *danger*, are you? If you were, they'd provide some protection. Or you could just go home. Why not do that?"

"I might leave early," said Thea vaguely, struggling with a strong feeling of disappointment. "So, you're short of staff there as well, are you?"

"You could say so. Everybody wants to be on holiday, which doesn't help. The ones with kids, that is — which is most of them."

"I'm sorry to startle you, then. It just seemed like a good idea, that's all. When will I see you, do you think?"

"We've got the Bank Holiday weekend in the diary, haven't we? If nothing kicks off here, I'll be free then. I had to stake a claim to it nearly a year ago."

"Good. That's not long now."

"So — what's with all this wild animal trafficking down your way? The news is full of it. Cheltenham, for heaven's sake! You must be just up the road from there."

"Not far," Thea agreed. "But I almost never go there. I can never find anywhere to park." Which was beginning to feel like a theme for the day. "I heard about it, and Gladwin's immersed in the whole business, but I don't know any details."

"It's *huge*, and getting bigger by the day. Your murder isn't linked to it, is it?"

"Not that anybody can see. It could be, of course. The victim *was* Chinese."

"Well done, Mama. Trust you to get yourself right in the middle of something like that."

"Gladwin put me here," Thea snapped. "The whole thing was her idea from the start. I'm looking after a house belonging to one of her friends."

"She ought to know better, then. Look — I'll have to go. Sorry I can't join you, but it was always a daft suggestion. See if you can stop anything going through officially. It'll only cause ructions for me otherwise."

"Probably too late. Sorry about that. See you soon, then, kiddo. You are all right, aren't you? I forgot to ask."

"Yes, I'm all right. Bye, Ma."

Somehow the notion of sitting in a field with a sketchbook felt a lot less appealing after that. It was too obviously a means of killing time or worse — evading several issues that demanded her attention. There was Drew, and Clovis, Jessica, Grace, Jocelyn and sundry briefly encountered locals, all worthy of due consideration. If she ignored them, with their hidden agendas and hinted-at mysteries, she would become sidelined and no longer integral to their lives. You had to work at relationships; everybody said that. You had to anticipate their wishes and put them before yourself. Unless they were beautiful single men like Clovis, of course. And Jocelyn didn't seem to have any problems at the moment. In fact, Jocelyn had been modelling a good sister and friend, by making the effort to share her concern for Jessica.

Who but the most unfeeling monster could set all that aside while she sat in a field with a sketchbook?

So she fingered her phone and asked herself where she should begin. Barkley, probably — in the hope of averting the request for Constable Osborne to be seconded to Gloucestershire. Then who? It was all too difficult, so she put the phone away again. Barkley was quite capable of dealing with it herself, and would probably tell Thea as much.

Which left her feeling restless and ruffled and thwarted. She could do no good by phoning anybody, especially as most of them seemed to be annoyed with her. So it seemed she was going back to Barnsley, without having made any sketches or spoken to anybody in Bibury. She got up with a sigh, wondering how she was going to fill the remains of the day.

At the car were two people, staring at it with profound disapproval. "Oh — sorry," she said, approaching them from the field. "Is it in your way?"

"This is private property," said a man holding a clipboard.

"Is it? It looks like an ordinary lay-by to me."

Wordlessly he pointed to a sign set into the hedge and barely visible for overgrown vegetation. "No Parking" it said.

"Ah."

The second person was female, about Thea's age, holding a mobile phone and looking impatient. "It's easily missed," she said. "Now — can we get on?"

Thea made no move to get into her car. Instead she eyed the couple inquisitively, trying to work out what they were doing. The woman noticed her expression and smiled. "He's an estate agent and he's showing me this house." She pointed over the little road to a building behind another overgrown hedge. "Except we haven't started yet. I was checking whether or not this land belongs to the property."

"It definitely does," said the young man. "There's no question about it."

Thea was trying to see the actual house. "It looks rather neglected," she said.

"It's been empty for eight years," the woman explained. "Some great legal wrangle over who owns it, and whether it could be sold. Apparently, it's only just been resolved and they've finally put it on the market. I can't wait to see inside it," she concluded, with another impatient look at the agent.

"What a waste," said Thea. "When there's such a housing shortage."

"No shortage of places like this," said the woman. "When you start looking, you find there's one in nearly every village standing empty for one reason or another."

"It's a scandal." For some reason, both women glared at the agent, as if the whole thing was his fault. In response he sprang into action, leading his client through the rickety gates and up to the front door of the house.

Driving back, Thea mused on the complexities of families, inheritances, legalities and disagreements. It must be keeping solicitors nicely feather-bedded, she supposed. But you could hardly blame them, if families were daft enough to throw away their money and peace of mind on wrangles over a house.

It was after three o'clock, which was good news. She had reached the point when she wanted to leave Barnsley and go home as soon as she could. The coming evening felt prickly with unfinished theories, unfulfilled obligations, unpredictable turns of events. She was severely lacking in information or understanding, unable to trust much of what people told her.

She drove back to the Corner House and sat for a minute in the car. Sid and Dave were out of sight at the back, and there was no sign of life anywhere along the village street. How strangely silent these Cotswold villages were. She remembered Frampton Mansell and Daglingworth and how rare it was to see anyone in the lanes, or even in the front gardens. And now her attention had been drawn to the fact that some of the houses were permanently unoccupied — not just kept as country retreats for rich City bankers. When a murder took place in their midst, the ripples were almost invisible, too. The residents' real lives were nearly all conducted somewhere else.

Thea's sense of history would often contrast these empty scenes with those of a century or two ago. Children would be bowling hoops, horses and dogs on all sides, the Monday washing flapping in the breeze. And here in Barnsley, there'd be the added thrill of sporadic flocks of sheep or herds of cattle being driven from place to place, along the road selected long ago for that very purpose. She sat there imagining the piles of steaming manure left behind, perhaps a few torn ears from scraps between local and drovers' dogs. Perhaps, too, a few new litters of puppies conceived on the sly, adding useful new blood to the gene pool. If the village served as a resting place, there must have been some kind of compound close to the inn where the animals could be corralled for a few hours. At busy times, there could well be two distinct sets of drovers, needing to keep their beasts separate. Where, Thea wondered, were the first-hand accounts of this utterly forgotten way of life? There must be many people alive who had known drovers — had them for grandparents or elderly neighbours, and surely listened to their stories. Not for the first time, she resolved to see if she could discover more about the details of this specific settlement. Some googling would pass a contented hour or two, if nothing else. And the not-quite-abandoned barn continued to intrigue her, at the back of her mind. She could stroll down for another little look at it, perhaps. And she might even do a little search for Gwendoline Phoebe Wheelwright, whose mortal remains were sitting in a dark corner of a dusty old barn.

The googling was dramatically more productive than she'd imagined. Following one link after another, she found herself in an online history for the Wheelwright family where various relatives blogged, drawing the connections between them and asking questions. The very openness of it was refreshing. No secrets here, concluded Thea. If a younger son got sent off to Australia for stealing a hogget, then that appeared to be more of a source of pride than of shame. The focus was on the nineteenth century and earlier, where recriminations and grievances could be assumed to have long ago evaporated. The family had lived in the heart of Barnsley for generations. Pages from the census were reproduced, to show the quantity of children and servants — both at their height in the 1870s. Life was good, as one present-day contributor remarked.

But while access to the site was open, it was not permitted to add to it without due registration having taken place. There was a care for privacy that had not at first been apparent. Few surnames were used, and most people employed usernames that concealed their identity. There was nothing concerning anyone in the family still living, which Thea gradually realised was rather odd. Surely the whole venture could not be satisfactorily pursued if this was all there was? There had to be a much less accessible website, only open to certain individuals. Hazily, she wondered just how such a thing might work. But the older information was sufficiently interesting for this to be a minor concern. It was full of anecdotes and side notes from diligent researchers who had contacted cousins and lateral branches, and sometimes unearthed diaries and old pictures. One central figure had to be co-ordinating it all, gathering it together and inspiring prodigious efforts. Any archivist would surely salivate at the notion of handling the original material, wherever it was.

It carried Thea through to six o'clock, when she realised she was hungry and thirsty, and in need of human contact. Sid and Dave had tapped on the window beside her at five, and waved goodbye for the day. They showed no sign of wanting to consult her on anything.

She switched on the radio and tuned it to the early evening news. The pips confirmed her timing, and then the top headline seemed to be directed straight at her. "Police raids overnight in the area of Cheltenham and South Gloucestershire have significantly extended the investigation into the trade in rare animal products. There is thought to be a firm link with gangs in China, with a great deal of money involved. A statement is expected later this week."

"Oh!" said Thea aloud. For a moment it felt as if the whole matter of Grace's death was on the verge of solution. Wasn't it self-evident that she had been somehow connected to one of these Chinese gangs? Didn't that fit perfectly with the few remarks she had made? The fear, the need to stay hidden, the deception she'd experienced, the underlying confidence and even subtle hint of affluence. Unfair as it undoubtedly was, there was a stereotype that insisted that a rich Chinese person, like a rich Russian, was unlikely to have acquired the money by ordinary legal means.

Grace had, it seemed, been driven to an area where pangolin scales had been discovered, by people who had first frightened and then murdered her. Somewhere along the way she must have understood that the truth behind her visit was not what she had believed. And that truth carried a serious threat, the most serious there could be. She had very probably known her life was in danger, from that moment, and gone to considerable lengths to remain safe. And her captors had been clever and persistent and within hours had tracked her down and killed her. This too fitted with the usual image of wicked Chinese gangs. They would have sophisticated electronic devices, surveillance systems, perhaps local agents disguised as ordinary Cotswolds folk. So, did Grace accidentally stumble into the clutches of a rival gang? Or did she possess skills that were needed by the criminals and was lured here under a wholly false pretext? Perhaps she understood

Chinese medicine or futuristic methods of preserving body parts. She could have been brought in as a consultant, under the assumption that when she learnt the true nature of those who wanted her, the promise of money would be enough to ensure her co-operation. Or perhaps they'd skipped any sort of enticement, and simply threatened her with death if she didn't do as they asked. It all made enough sense for Thea to believe her own hypothesis carried quite a healthy proportion of credibility. The quick and skilful method of killing gave it added force. If Grace had simply made her way to Barnsley to visit a penfriend or see at first-hand the famous Arlington Row, almost every detail of Thea's encounter with her would have been different.

The radio repeated almost the same words, later in the programme, with a barely relevant clip from a distraught animal rights spokeswoman, about the cruelty and general wickedness of those who trafficked in poor innocent pangolins. For good measure, she added a rant about rhino horn, despairing of the sheer stupidity of thinking it held any magical qualities. Dimly, Thea understood that the woman was missing the point. All magical qualities existed thanks to human belief in them, and humans could steadfastly believe a vast range of extremely stupid things. In most cases, you really weren't supposed to judge or criticise, because that would hurt their feelings.

It would be a real satisfaction if the murder could be neatly tied to the trafficking, with additional punishment for the perpetrators. They'd get much longer spells in prison if they could be shown to be killers as well. It gave Thea a new surge of purpose. Somehow she was going to nail these people, in the few days she still had left in Barnsley.

CHAPTER
EIGHTEEN

The Wednesday evening call to Drew began as most of the others had, with Thea using the landline yet again. Stephanie picked up the phone yet again. "God, Steph — what's happening? Why is it always you that answers? Is there something wrong?"

The child took a sharp breath. "No!" she gasped. "Everything's all right."

"I don't believe you. You sound so odd, darling. What's the matter?"

"It's a *secret*. You mustn't ask me. I'll go and find Dad. He didn't think you'd phone today. He says he asked you not to."

"But I want to talk to him. I told him that last night. Where is he?"

"Oh . . . somewhere. Wait a minute."

"I can end this call and start again on the mobile, if you like. Would that help?"

"Oh yes! That would be great. Do that, then. I'll put this one back."

"Okay, then."

Thea gave it twenty seconds, and then keyed the shortcut for Drew's mobile. Had Stephanie really said there was a secret? The idea was just as startling as it had been when it first occurred earlier in the week. Thea felt angry, then hurt at being excluded. It had not sounded like a *nice* secret, as she had hoped. She didn't have a birthday coming up. Drew knew better than to plan a surprise holiday, party or unannounced visitor. But half those twenty seconds were spent coming to see that she could not ask him. Stephanie would be blamed for her failure to stay quiet. And if it *was* something nice, she would ruin an elaborate plan that had her gratification as its main purpose. She would do a lot to avoid that.

Even if it was something sinister, a dark and dangerous threat that had to be kept away from her, she had no choice but to wait until her husband was ready to reveal it.

Drew answered, in a quiet voice. "Sorry about that," he said. "I could have come to the phone quite easily, you know."

"So you're not lying in bed with your leg in traction, then?" said Thea lightly, with no knowledge of where that idea had sprung from.

"What? No, of course I'm not. What's Stephanie been telling you?" His laugh was so forced, she could feel the effort down the line.

"She didn't tell me anything. I'm joking, you idiot. I could have said you were at the end of the garden, burying my dog." Her heart stopped. "You weren't, were you? She's okay, isn't she?"

"She's absolutely fine." He sighed. "Don't have any more fanciful ideas, okay? Once you start, I'll never be able to stop you. Tell me about your day. Has Gladwin been to see you? Have you used the car?"

"I drove to Bibury this afternoon. I was going to do a drawing, but I couldn't get anywhere near the picturesque part. It was heaving with tourists, most of them Chinese, as everybody said it would be. Some of them look as if they've actually settled there permanently, but mostly they just hop off coaches to take photos and then whizz off somewhere else."

"So no picture to show me?"

"Not yet. But I have done a tiny bit more of my needlepoint picture. And Barkley came this morning, quite early. She didn't have anything new to say, really. Gladwin's still totally embroiled in this illegal animal trade. Sounds as if they're tightening the net, with raids and so forth. Did you see any of it on the telly? I've only caught bits on the radio."

"No. We haven't had the telly on all week."

"Congratulations." How many weary parents could claim the same at this stage of the summer holidays? Certainly, never a one in Thea's time. But it was different now, she remembered. "I suppose they've been on their gadgets instead," she accused.

"They have a bit. As a reward when they've been good, mostly. And when they've got a bit noisy. There hasn't been too much of that." Stephanie and Timmy were not especially noisy children anyway — something Thea felt grateful for. There was less of the mindless rampaging that she remembered from her two sisters' children in years gone by.

She found herself lost for something to say. Desperately she racked her brain for a joke that wouldn't annoy him, an anecdote that wouldn't worry him, a promise that wouldn't be broken. She couldn't mention Clovis, and rather hoped to stay off any detailed references to murder. "They've just about finished the kitchen here," she said at last. "Up to the bathroom tomorrow. They're wonderfully fast workers."

"It's all modular these days, I suppose," he said vaguely. "Just slot it all together like Lego."

"Must be," she agreed, thinking that would surely not be possible in the case of a new bathroom. Tabitha was having new facilities installed — bath, shower, lavatory and washbasin — but all except the shower in much the same positions as the old ones. The shower was being fitted into a space in a corner, and would obviously require considerable new pipework as a result. "So everything's all right with you, then, is it?"

"More or less," he said. "Only two funerals scheduled for next week. Andrew wants to go away at the end of September, and I've told him that'll be all right. He hasn't had any time off all year."

"Hasn't he?" Thea paid less attention to Drew's colleague than she probably should. He worked as required, which could mean a run of three days or more during the week in which there was virtually nothing to do. Such an undemanding workload seemed to her to scarcely justify any actual holiday. But she guessed she was being unfairly Victorian about it, and his union, if he had one, would take exception to such views. "More than he got when he was farming, anyway," she couldn't resist saying.

"One reason he quit farming was to reduce the levels of stress he was under."

"I know. It's none of my business, anyway."

"So, when are you coming home?" He sounded like a small boy asking when his mother would come and rescue him from boarding school. "Do you know yet?"

"I can't see any reason to be here after Friday. I'm going to try and contact Tabitha directly and see if it's all right with her for me to go then. It was all left a bit vague."

"That's good. Friday, I mean. And will we have to come and fetch you? What about that borrowed car?"

"I don't know. I'll find that out tomorrow. Why? Would it be a problem to collect me? Friday evening, or maybe Saturday morning."

He was quiet, then said, "It might be. We haven't decided about Saturday yet."

That sounded extremely odd to Thea. She began to demand an explanation when she heard Timmy shouting not far from wherever Drew was. "Hey! Dad!" the little boy yelled, much louder than seemed to be called for. "Come quick."

"Sorry, better go," said Drew, superfluously. "Sounds as if it's important. Thanks for calling, love. Use the mobile first next time, okay? I *did* say that before."

"So you did. I hope Timmy's all right. He sounds pretty desperate."

"Bye," said Drew and ended the call.

240

The thing was, she reflected, Timmy had sounded much more like a boy overdoing a part in a school play than a child in genuine distress. He was just shouting the words, with little real feeling behind them. He had actually not sounded desperate at all. He had sounded rehearsed and insincere.

So, something unusual was being planned for Saturday, was it? Something that might prevent Drew from driving the short distance down to Barnsley and back. At least all three of them were alive — and she hoped he hadn't been lying about Hepzie. Never again, she vowed, would she allow herself to be separated from the devoted dog. Whatever nonsense Drew might be hatching, it was less immediately concerning than the prolonged separation from her pet. But the plot that was hatching could be something special to welcome her home, perhaps? She tested the theory against the evidence, and concluded it was untenable. Anything she could think of was untenable, in fact. All she could do was wait patiently for the revelation when it finally came. If it was something disagreeable, she ought not to be in any hurry to discover it.

Thursday was a rerun of Wednesday, at least in the first hour or two. She woke gradually, missing the spaniel, reviewing the day past and the day ahead, and then welcoming the builders on their early arrival. "Gotta get upstairs today," said Dave. "You'll need to have everything out of the bathroom."

"Already done," said Thea.

"Did you see the kitchen?" Sid prompted her, his face expectant.

"Oh — yes. Lovely," she did her best to gush. "You've done it all so quickly. Tabitha's going to be thrilled." She could not bring herself to pretend that a beautiful kitchen did anything to stir her own soul.

"Bathroom should be done by the end of tomorrow," Dave boasted. "Provided the doings get delivered as promised. Should be here any time now."

"A new bath? And loo?"

"And the rest," Dave nodded. "We need to get the old stuff out by dinnertime, and the new vinyl down. All organised on paper." He waved a clipboard at her. "There's a plumber coming at two. We can get the shower in with him, first."

"You got somewhere to go?" Sid asked her. Her response to the kitchen had clearly disappointed him, and lowered his expectations of her. She was sorry, but also irritated.

"Not really. I've no idea what I'm going to do, to be honest. What's the weather like?" She peered past him to the sky outside. It looked more or less clear.

"Nice day, they say. Warmer. How about a bit of shopping? Plenty to explore in Cirencester."

"It's a thought. Pity we're so far from the sea. It'd be nice on a beach, by the sound of it." Both men gave helpless shrugs at that. "Well, I might play on my computer for a bit. It's still very early. Do you think I'll be able to leave on Saturday, then? You'll have done all the indoor stuff by then, won't you?"

242

"Thought you were leaving Friday," said Dave. "That's what we were told — get everything done and dusted by end of Friday, because after that there'd be nobody to supervise."

"We've got another job Monday, anyway," said Sid.

"Right. Just checking." The truth was, as the two men doubtless understood as well as she did, that she had not really been needed at all. Builders could get on just as well without supervision — especially ones like these, who clearly had plenty of responsibility and a decent work ethic. The whole exercise had been pointless, or worse. Without her, Grace might still be alive. But Gladwin had meant well. It wasn't her fault the original purpose of giving Thea some space and time to herself, a little holiday from the demands of her stepchildren, had turned to ashes. Some people might even think that was a kind of divine justice.

The computer researches of the day before had been diverting, she remembered. Right here on the doorstep was a rambling family stretching back three hundred years and more, all meticulously documented and shared amongst descendants across the world. Thea regarded herself as still rather too young for the obsessive delvings that so many people engaged in, at a time of life when they felt their own place on the tree becoming more pivotal. Once you had grandchildren, it seemed, you took the whole business more seriously. And if you were retired, with time on your hands, what better use for it than to burrow through old records and newspaper stories, in search of the fullest possible picture of the people who came before? People dead for centuries, who had the exact same ears as yours, and the same peculiar passion for apricots. It made you hopeful for your own great-great-grandchildren, and how they might even one day find you interesting.

But she could not escape the feeling that she was simply putting off a much more serious and potentially unpleasant activity, and should give the laptop a miss. Her usual motto of *Make something happen* had let her down over the past few days. Wandering at random around Barnsley and Bibury did not constitute proactively searching for clues as to who murdered Grace. Even though she had gone over the same footpaths, and explored a suspicious-looking abandoned barn, she had not behaved remotely like a keen amateur detective looking for clues — for the perfectly good reason that there simply *were* no clues. The police must surely have crawled all over the business park by now, checked every scrap of CCTV footage, asked a thousand questions, and apparently come up with nothing. And that meant Grace must have lied in almost everything she'd told Thea. In the face of implacable lying, most people were helpless. The rules of ordinary communication were so comprehensively broken that you had nowhere to stand. Her name wasn't Grace. She wasn't Chinese. She hadn't been forcibly driven to Barnsley. But she *had* been killed. Where the story would have made more sense if she had merely died of natural causes — heart failure for preference — the fact of a deliberate murder intensified every crucial second of Thea's encounter with her. There absolutely had to be a clue there somewhere.

244

And did the police not realise that? Were they just waiting for some tiny forgotten word or look to surface, which would then give them the thread they needed to follow? If so, Thea should be persistently hypnotising herself into total recollection — and with every passing day that was going to be more difficult.

On top of all that, Clovis Biddulph could not be ignored. Here was a man who wanted to participate in the search for answers, and seemed to have the time and the brains to make a decent job of it. *Seemed*, however, was the operative word. Could it all be one great bluff, designed to weaken her defences and allow him to get closer to her? Surely not. Hadn't they emerged on a calmer and more adult footing now? Respect and consideration for Drew had become the driving force, and very little harm had been done. Or so she hoped. Hoping and believing might not be enough to protect her now, if Clovis had ulterior intentions. He had delicately left the next move up to her, and three times that Thursday morning her thumb had hovered over the little numbers that would bring his voice into her ear.

The only person left was Caz Barkley, forgetting the impossibly preoccupied Gladwin. And even Caz should not be called without some seriously good reason for doing so. Only if she, Thea, had a brilliant idea, or walked into a thrilling new piece of evidence, could such an interruption be justified. This latter notion took root, suggesting that there could well yet be something to discover at the business park, especially if she approached it from the official direction, instead of staring over hedges at the back.

"I'm going for a long walk," she told the builders.

"What do we tell anybody that comes looking for you?" asked Dave.

"You can say I've gone for a look at the business park," she said, after a brief hesitation. She couldn't see that it mattered if she told the truth.

"Private road, that," said Sid.

"Oh well — I don't suppose they'll mind. I'm not going to do any damage."

He shrugged and raised his eyebrows, as if to say *On your head be it.*

So she gathered up her map, purse and phone, shouted a cheerful goodbye to the builders and went out with a sense of high adventure. She went on foot and made for the front entrance of Barnsley Park, where small businesses were conducted in lovely old stone barns and cottages, and nothing was plainly visible. Here, if anywhere, the truth must lie.

She had to walk an inconveniently long way along a crooked road with more traffic than was comfortable. There was no pavement, and a very variable verge. Sometimes it was quite wide and grassy, before narrowing and turning prickly with thistles and other weeds. This, she remembered, was why she'd opted for the footpath previously. But the footpath gave the businesses a wide berth, leaving them on the far side of walls and fences that gave no obvious access to them. This way, she would walk boldly into the yard, seeing the big house from the other side, and working out just how many people lived and worked there.

She felt small but conspicuous as she entered the driveway. For a while all she could see was a wall on one side, with big beech trees beyond it, and a fenced field containing sheep on the other. Then she rounded a bend and found herself face-to-face with a stone tower she had not seen previously. She could still not see the mansion, which must lie beyond the woodland. Still there was a long stretch of driveway before reaching any buildings. Keeping well to the left, where she hoped she would be less visible against the backdrop of wall and greenery, she walked on until finally within a few yards of a collection of single-storey stone buildings. Her historian's eye noted changes and additions to an estate that went back centuries. Originally the curtilage of the manor house, with a big kitchen garden, paddocks for livestock, humble dwellings for the staff, it had mutated effortlessly into a twenty-first-century working collective that looked barely altered at first glance. There were no lurid signs in primary colours, no obtrusive floodlights; just a sense of quiet enterprise taking place behind the tasteful oak doors and stone facades. But a more modern wall of glass revealed recent changes, along with a sign warning that CCTV was operating on the premises.

It was quickly apparent that casual visitors were not encouraged or expected. If you wanted a picture framed or a piece of harness repaired, you came to the appropriate unit and dealt with the person working there. Using her habitual imaginative guesswork, she ran through other likely goods and services that might be available. Private detective, goldsmith, poodle parlour, potter, garden designer, genealogist, masseur, manicurist — the list flowed readily through her active mind. All entirely likely in the affluent materialistic Cotswolds. People wanted quality handmade goods, provided by skilled individuals, and services that made them feel special. They were always short of time, too, which meant they couldn't possibly create their own garden or trim their own poodle. Or trace their own ancestors. Probably, she concluded, the genealogist and private detective would be the same person, perhaps vaguely described as a "researcher" with impressive computer skills.

It was all her own fantasy, she reminded herself. The problem was, the reality was not easy to ascertain. There was no evidence of any artisan handicrafts. Nobody proclaimed their line of work with any clarity. There were small boards beside some of the doors, which she scanned self-consciously. The word "Solutions" appeared twice, but nobody seemed to offer "Logistics". She was gradually aware of faces peering out at her, from windows on all sides of the yard, one woman standing just inside the big glass windows, arms folded. At any moment, someone would emerge with a frosty, "Can I help you?" and she would have to invent a reason for being there. And that would carry a degree of risk. She wanted to say, "I gather there's a furrier here," and watch the effect. Illegal tiger skins or fox furs could so easily be tucked away in back rooms. But the

248

police had already performed a thorough investigation into all these businesses — or so she assumed. They could hardly have failed to pursue the flimsy story told by Grace, however implausible it was proving to be.

So she turned round and began to walk away again. Anybody watching would, with luck, conclude that she had come here in error, looking for a non-existent footpath, perhaps. Or seeking a lost dog. She began to mime behaviour that would fit such an explanation. Craning her neck to look over the hedges, turning round every few steps, and trying to maintain a worried expression. She hoped that her demeanour had not been too different as she'd walked up the driveway initially. There was something increasingly unsettling about the whole place, with nobody outside, no comings and goings, only a few faint voices that she suspected came from a radio somewhere. A summer weekday morning, with reasonable weather, should surely bring at least a few people outdoors. Could they not sit in the fresh air with their crafts or Dictaphones or laptops? She had read on the website that families lived in the ancient cottages — so where were the children on holiday from school? And didn't anybody own a dog?

And still nobody accosted her. She knew she was being watched, but presumed that so long as she kept walking, causing no trouble, she would be left alone. It was a creepy sensation, like something from a horror film. Her vivid imagination flipped into notions of lurking monsters — huge slimy creatures that had disguised themselves as human beings. If she offended them, they would throw off their false skin and come slavering after her. There had always been this unsettling aspect to villages in the Cotswolds: the suspicion that hidden eyes were watching from the silent stone cottages. The loosening of the usual boundaries that kept you firmly in time and place. In a Cotswolds village you might carelessly step through a portal into an earlier century — or even perhaps a *later* one, which would be even more terrifying. They so often felt like a film set, or something fiercely preserved for the sake of permanence. Nothing was allowed to change — that was how the tourists liked it, and the tourist was king. Especially here, just down the road from historic Bibury. The beauty was so extreme that there was a wholesale fear that it might crumble and vanish if constant vigilance was relaxed. This had all become plain to Thea years ago, and had developed into an unexamined given now she lived here permanently. Only when forced to confront the paradoxical reality did she revert to thinking about it.

Feeling the eyes on her back as she returned down the driveway, she was slow to notice that a car was pulling up beside her and a surprising face was glaring at her from the open driver's window.

CHAPTER
NINETEEN

It was Caz Barkley. "Here you are," she shouted. "The builders said you'd come up here, but I've driven up and down twice without seeing you."

Thea frowned. "I should have been easy to spot. Why didn't you phone me?" She checked that she had her phone in her pocket. "Look — I've got my mobile, for a change."

"Yes, but it's not switched on, is it?" The tone was of an exasperated parent. Barkley was a good fifteen years younger than Thea, which made her flinch at the role reversal.

"Ah," she said, with a sigh. "So why do you want me?"

"I've been told to watch out for you. Make sure you're okay. See if you've made any useful discoveries." Caz stared hard at Thea's face. "But *why?* Why are you here? Didn't it occur to you that it might not be safe, if anything that woman told you is true?"

Thea blinked. "What's going to happen? It's broad daylight. And I don't see how anyone can see me as a threat. I don't know anything, do I?"

Caz sighed. "I haven't got time to explain it to you. Just get in and let's get out of here."

"I'm not stupid, you know," Thea insisted. "It makes sense to have a better look around. Nobody here's going to know who I am, are they?"

"Get in," said Barkley again.

Thea got into the car, and Barkley turned it round, driving over an immaculate grass verge in the process. Thea had a question. "Just how closely involved are you in this investigation?"

"I think they call it free-floating. I go where I'm needed. They seem to think there's not a lot more they can follow up on where your woman is concerned. Until they get a firm identity for her, it's all pretty much stuck. I haven't even seen the whole file."

"That's weird, when you've got the post-mortem report."

"They'd let me see it if I asked. But essentially, we're leaving most of it to Cirencester. If there's a link to the pangolins, then we'll have to work more closely with them. So far, we can't see that there is. Somebody's meant to be trying to track down the K. A. W. person. Remember? The initials on the wedding ring?"

"I remember," said Thea. She sighed. "Isn't it obvious that somebody around here does know who she is — was? They didn't just kill her at random, did they?" She was musing aloud, going over old ground, not making much sense even to herself.

"Jessica," said Caz sternly. "We need to talk about Jessica."

"What about her?"

"Well, Gladwin thinks you ought to know they've got a few concerns about her, up there in Manchester."

252

"Is this about her drinking too much? My sister said the same thing. I don't know what *I* can do about it. She's old enough to be responsible for her own actions."

"You're her mother," said Barkley mildly. "You're supposed to worry."

"I know I am. I will if you think it'll help. But I've never found that worry does much good. It might make the worrier feel virtuous, but beyond that, it seems rather futile to me."

"I'm not sure it's possible to control it, is it? You're either worried or you're not. You can't deliberately worry — can you?"

"You can a bit. But worriers don't seem capable of switching it off, so you got that part right. I'm just not a worrier. Jess knows that. She even claims to like it that way. It's not very nice to be worried over, after all."

"Isn't it?" There was a distinct wistfulness in her voice. "Anyway, that's not the point. The *team* are worried about her. They think somebody ought to be informed that she might need some help. She's on her own up there — no family or boyfriend or anyone. She's not very old, is she? When did you last see her?"

Thea felt rather as she had on Tuesday when Jocelyn had said the same things. "A while ago. Listen, I texted her and she called me yesterday, and she sounded fine. She doesn't want me dashing up there to cross-examine her about drinking, or whatever it is. What good could I do? I know it sounds bad — but that's the sort of family we are. We're not very demonstrative. No gushing or sentimentality."

Barkley was driving, and couldn't give Thea the long questioning look she'd have liked to. But ten seconds later they were at the Corner House, and the car stopped. The younger woman turned sideways and said nothing for a moment. Then, "Don't you understand about *support?* Just being there, ready to listen to her, taking an interest. Not just leaving her to sort herself out, and taking her word for it that she's okay. You know quite well she's not, because people have been telling you. You don't have to solve anything, or tell her what to do. But she sounds to me to be struggling. I've never even met her, and *I'm* worried."

Thea sat back in her seat, disliking herself with a vengeance. "You're right," she said. "I'm such an awful person. Everything that happened this week just makes that more obvious. Forgetting the anniversary. Making Grace sleep on the floor. Agreeing to meet bloody Clovis —"

"Who? Surely not that man whose dad died? The one with the fancy clothes and expensive scent?"

Thea nodded. "He's got a girlfriend now. First really serious one ever, apparently."

"Bully for him. What's that to do with you?"

"Nothing. But he fancies himself as an amateur detective — probably after what happened when his dad died. I got the impression he's trying to impress his woman — she works for conservation charities, apparently. I told him all about Grace being killed and he wants to help with the investigation. That's okay, isn't it?" Belatedly, she realised that it was generally frowned upon by the police for details of a case to be

254

shared with members of the public. "I didn't tell him anything sensitive." At least, she hoped she didn't.

"It's not ideal. There are plenty of senior people who don't like the way we tell *you* things. Any more rank amateurs will really annoy them."

"I don't think he's going to cause any trouble."

"You mean he's going to get into a cosy huddle with you one evening and go through all the guesses and hunches and fantasy scenarios that the two of you can come up with?"

"Probably."

"That's another thing, then," said Barkley obscurely.

"Pardon?"

"You being a less-than-perfect wife to your really nice husband."

"Exactly. That's what I said. I'm a horrible person."

"Shut up. That's not the point."

"Isn't it?"

"Look — I'm not a couple counsellor. But even I know nobody's perfect, and hardly anybody's really horrible. Your girl's opted not to tell you what's happening with her, for whatever reason. So you weren't to know until your sister told you. And then you agreed that it would be good if she could come down here, to help while we're overstretched. If that hasn't worked out, it's not your fault. But now you've got a new situation. That's why I was looking for you, to tell you about it. Her secret's out now, and you know she's got a problem. I'm not saying it'll be easy, but if you care about her, I think you need to do something. Okay?"

"She's coming to see us for the Bank Holiday weekend. That's not far off now. I'll make sure I take her out, just us two, and see if she'll talk. I don't see how I can do more than that. I can't leave Drew any longer, once I'm finished here. Stephanie says there's something secret going on at home, and I have absolutely no idea what it can be."

"And meanwhile, you try to ignore all this family crap by seeing the most beautiful man in England."

"Right. And that makes me a horrible person."

"No it doesn't. It makes you the envy of every woman who sees you — and possibly a bit of a fool. But we all give in to temptation from time to time."

"Right," said Thea again, feeling very slightly better. "So, can we just crack on with this murder case, so I can get back to being a halfway decent wife and mother?"

"Feel free," invited Caz Barkley. "All contributions gratefully received."

"At least they let me get involved," said Thea.

"No they don't." Barkley was forceful. "They just haven't worked out how to stop you."

Thea laughed, but the other woman was clearly not amused. Thea defended herself. "I've been quite useful at times."

"Against everyone's better judgement, believe me. But with everything stretched as it is, you've got to be a bit of an asset. We're all having to be in three places at once — this month especially, with so many people on leave."

Thea merely smiled forbearingly. She'd heard much the same before. Even Jessica had complained about depleted numbers.

"Anyway," Barkley went on. "Just don't get into trouble. Nothing that's going to require a team of police rescuers, right?"

"I promise," said Thea rashly.

"Now please get out, so I can go back to work. We're still searching lock-ups for animal parts, and logging hundreds of calls from the public, all sure they've seen suspicious Asians carrying bags of pangolin scales. The problem — one of many problems, actually — is that the trafficking has spread to Africa now, which makes it all much more complicated. And the wretched things are so easy to catch. They're like hedgehogs — they just roll into a ball and sit there when anything scares them. Any ten-year-old can pick one up and sell it to a dealer. The whole thing's hopeless, really. But now the media have got their teeth into it, we've got to be seen to be making an effort."

"Surely it won't go on much longer? The story's sure to die down, and you can get on with other cases."

"Eventually." Barkley sighed. "Of course, the best outcome would be if your woman turned out to be working with the traffickers. That would kill two birds with one stone, and get everybody a brownie point."

"And we do want them to stop killing pangolins," Thea said. "I really hope you can catch some of the ringleaders and make an example of them."

Barkley sighed again. "We're never going to get the top people — and even if we did, they'd get nowhere near what they deserve."

"Oh, well," said Thea helplessly. Then she straightened up. "I've got to find something to do for the rest of today, haven't I? Any suggestions?"

"I'd like to tell you to get yourself back home to that husband, but that would probably be a waste of breath. And there's always the slight chance that you'll turn something up here, most likely by accident. But it's not for me to say. You'll think of something."

"Right," said Thea, feeling small and silly. Other people always seemed so much more focused and purposeful than she ever did.

"I've really got to go," the detective said. "I've been much longer than I should already. Have fun — and don't get yourself killed, okay?"

Thea went back into the house in a chastened frame of mind. However you looked at it, she'd been rounded up and returned to base like a runaway sheep. Barkley hadn't said anything of any significance to her — merely told her off for being a bad mother and worse wife. The whole day so far had been a complete waste, and there was little prospect of any improvement that she could see.

Dave and Sid were banging in the bathroom, taking out the old fittings. A dust sheet covered the floor from the foot of the stairs to the back door, but the stairs themselves were unprotected. Small grains of old

258

plaster were scattered here and there. She decided to go up and have a look at it all.

The old bath was standing on end on the landing outside the bedrooms, looking pathetic. When she peered round the door, she saw Sid hacking off the tiles that had covered the wall beside the bath. "You'll have to do a lot of retiling," she said, making him jump. "Have you got the new ones?" She liked tiles, the more colourful the better. "What are they like?"

Dave was kneeling on the floor doing something with pipes. "They're there, look." He ducked his chin at a pair of boxes standing in a corner. "Came yesterday."

"Can I look?" Without waiting for permission, she tiptoed across the gritty floor and pulled open the upper box. The tiles were tightly packed, only their edges showing. She extracted one and examined it. "Bit boring," she judged. It was pale blue, with ripples of white and a darker blue. "Are there any jazzy ones to intersperse with these?"

"Nope," said Dave. "They'll look great when they're up. Soothing. Who wants a jazzy bathroom?"

"Me," said Thea. "I did our bathroom in red and black when we moved."

"Lovely," said Dave, with undisguised irony.

"Well, it's up to Tabitha, obviously," Thea conceded. "I'll get out of your way now."

"Going out again?" asked Sid. "That woman found you, I presume."

"She did, thanks. And she drove me back here. It's at least half a mile to the entrance to the business park."

"So it is," said Sid, as if he'd already told her that.

"I'm not going out again just yet. I might go for some shopping later on."

She went downstairs, once again feeling disgusted with herself. What was the matter with her, that she was always so self-obsessed and judgemental? No wonder she had hardly any friends and that people kept secrets from her. She was in her mid-forties, and what did she have to show for her life? All she did was upset people and ignore their suffering. For the hundredth time, she yearned for her dog. Hepzie would cuddle up to her and reassure her that she was at least loved by one living creature. The unswerving loyalty of a spaniel was cheaply won, she knew, but it felt no less wonderful for that. And Drew still loved her, she supposed. He'd known what she was like when he married her, and seemed to find it perfectly acceptable. They'd weathered a crisis a few months earlier, when it had seemed for a while that they might be irrevocably headed in different directions, and since then life had been quite calm — at least on the surface. Now he, like Jessica, had a secret from her. Something that Stephanie and Timmy knew about, which made it worse.

Detective Constable Caz Barkley was like an all-seeing recording angel, confronting Thea with her shortcomings. "You're her *mother*," she had said, as if that spelt out every duty, every move and thought and feeling that Thea should be acting on. Simple, had been the implication. Just do what you know has to be done and stop being such a prat.

So she texted her daughter again, slowly formulating a message she hoped would sound concerned and supportive without overdoing it. "Good to talk yesterday. You seemed a bit stressed. I'm here if you want to chat." Was there anything more she could say or do? A direct phone call would obviously be better, but Jessica was a working police officer, apparently extremely busy, and would not welcome sentimental conversations with her mother in the middle of a working day. The media had given considerable coverage to the under-resourced state of the police force and the frustrations that resulted. Too many unsolved crimes, piling up case by case, with nobody available to give them due attention. One bold chief constable had complained that the media themselves made it a lot more difficult, by inciting public hysteria over a handful of prominent crimes, which then had to be given an unfair share of police time, to satisfy the baying mob. He didn't say "baying mob", but it was clear that that was what he meant. The current obsession with pangolins was a case in point, with Merseyside one of the hot spots. Shipping containers had to be searched for smuggled animal parts, in all the major ports.

The list of other people she ought to be worrying about had not got any shorter, either. Drew, Grace, Gladwin, the people of Venezuela and whatever population was currently experiencing floods or fires or earthquakes. Caz had seemed to imply that a good person should at least accord a degree of unselfish concern for anybody they knew to be suffering.

Thea chose Grace to take the place at the top of the list. Admittedly, the woman was beyond suffering now — but perhaps she was being missed by a frantic husband or mother somewhere. The mystery of her death must have left a void, a hole in the complex tapestry of life that needed to be filled. Not only should the killer be brought to justice, but an explanation for the act was urgently required. Thea was angry with the unknown person, who could so easily have bumped her off as well, if she'd got in the way.

And Drew — what about Drew? He seemed so reluctant to talk to her; every time she phoned he was distracted somehow. He showed very little real interest in what she was doing and told her virtually nothing about life without her in the Slocombe household. Something was obviously wrong, and Caz Barkley doubtless believed that it was wanton neglect on Thea's part to sit idly by in Barnsley, without going home to see what was going on. Now she had a car, she could easily pop back for an hour, and find out how things were. But what good would that do? She had to see things through for Tabitha Ibbotson, at least until the end of Friday. The bathroom pipes might leak; the builders might stop working; deliveries might go to the wrong house. And Grace's killer might not be caught. And if she went home, to be greeted deliriously by her dog, how cruel to then go away again without her. Similarly, the children would be unsettled. And Drew — she tried to guess at his reaction. "Checking up on me?" he might say. Or, "We weren't expecting you for another two days or so." There could be no satisfactory excuse for a flying visit, and every reason why it was a bad idea.

So, she wasn't going to do that, then.

She would, however, go out again. The house was noisy and dusty and boring. Barnsley was also quite boring, but the air was fresh and there was always a chance of meeting someone. She'd have a quick walk around the triangular block, before perhaps going into Cirencester for a look at the shops and museum. The exercise would be beneficial, if nothing else.

She walked briskly along the main street, past the back-to-front Barnsley House (Hotel and Spa, as it said in large letters), as well as the church and the pub and the village hall, and then turned right, into the country lane that led northwards in a Roman-straight trajectory. There were no other pedestrians in sight.

As she approached the next junction, where a second right turn would take her back to the Corner House, she was strongly reminded of her walk with Grace. They had been coming the other way, but once into the next road, it was the exact same route as the two of them had taken. Thea recalled the painful shoulder, the naked fear every time a car went past, the total lack of any personal effects. Whatever the truth of the matter, those details were indisputable. If the post-mortem showed no significant damage to Grace's shoulder, that didn't prove that she was pretending. A wrench or strain would be difficult to detect without a far closer examination than the average pathologist had time for these days. If it bore no relation to the cause of death, then it was hardly significant anyway.

263

She kept walking briskly, her thoughts working in pace with her steps. But they merely went around in the same old circuit as before, the scraps of information refusing to fit together in anything like a coherent picture.

It was only twenty minutes later that she arrived back at the house, having learnt nothing new, and failing to make any further deductions. It was still well short of midday and she had no desire for any more coffee. She was on the brink of deciding to do a second loop around the village when she noticed someone standing just inside the Corner House gateway.

"Are you waiting for me?" she asked, hurrying forward. The woman was familiar, but it took a moment to place her.

"I am, actually. Remember we met on Monday?"

It was the friendly person with the camera, who had been recording wording from the headstones. "Oh — yes. In the churchyard. What can I do for you?"

"Nothing. I just thought you might like to go for lunch or something. You seemed interesting, and when I realised you were still here, even after that awful business, it occurred to me you might like some company."

Thea had learnt from hard experience that human motives were seldom as pure and straightforward as this sounded. But that was no reason to repel this cordial advance. If anything, it gave the whole encounter added spice. "How nice of you," she gushed. "I was just wondering how to pass the afternoon. My name's Thea Slocombe, by the way." She held out her hand.

The woman took it in a firm grip. "Norma Chadwick. Pleased to meet you."

"Oh — not Jackson?" said Thea. "I thought you were Richard's wife."

"Whatever gave you that idea?"

Thea reran the scene from Monday morning. "I don't know. You looked like a team, I suppose. How embarrassing — especially these days. Just a quick assumption, on the basis of almost nothing."

"Well, we *have* known each other all our lives. I suppose there's some sort of chemistry between us — body language. That kind of thing. But I have a husband called Bernie, and Richard's got a disabled wife. We do a lot of family history together. Actually, we're cousins, after a fashion. We share an ancestor — beyond that it all gets very complicated. But it's not unusual, even now. There's still a lot of old families here, and they're all connected."

"Yes," said Thea. "You told me."

"Did we?"

Thea realised she'd made a second blunder in two minutes. She was conflating the information she'd found on the computer with what had been said face-to-face. "I think you did," she said. "At least I got that impression, the way you were all so knowledgeable about the names on the headstones."

"Mm." Norma Chadwick was eyeing the house behind them with considerable interest. "How can you stay here after what happened?" she burst out. "Aren't you absolutely terrified?"

"Not really. There's no reason why they should come back for me, as far as I can see. And I can lock the doors now. Whoever it was must be long gone by this time, anyway."

"Mm," said the woman again. Then she turned to look over her shoulder. "You've got more visitors," she remarked.

Two men were walking along the road towards the house. Thea and Norma were standing just inside the gateway, on the small area of gravel left unoccupied. The builders' van and Thea's borrowed car took almost all the parking space — which had been reduced by the cement mixer and skip that were part of the building work. The men were fifty or sixty yards away, their faces quite easy to recognise. But Thea was sure she had only seen one of them before. And he was smiling broadly.

"Clovis," murmured Thea.

CHAPTER
TWENTY

"Glad we caught you. This is Ben. He's from Cumbria or somewhere," Clovis introduced his companion. "We got chatting up by the village hall. I could see there was no hope of parking here, with all this lot in the way."

Thea merely blinked and waited for enlightenment. Norma Chadwick bounced slightly on the balls of her feet, like a teenager.

"I'm Norma," she said. "Hello, Ben. Come to see what you can find out about the murder, have you? We were thinking you might not be able to resist."

"Auntie," said the young man, who appeared to be little more than a boy, when Thea gave him a closer look. "You don't mind, do you?"

"It's not up to me. You've come all this way again because you heard there was a murder, so it wouldn't be very kind to try to stop you, would it?" She turned to Thea. "He's a very keen amateur detective, I'm afraid. Where he lives, there've been quite a few nasty crimes, which he's been involved in. He actually *witnessed* one death, if you can believe that."

"Oh?" Thea tried to decide whether she felt intrigued or hassled. Another amateur detective probably wasn't

267

going to be very good news, she concluded. If you counted Clovis, that made quite a little gang.

"I did," the youth assured her. "And I've got some free time before going up to uni. I'm doing forensic archaeology, you see. Any experience I can get will be hugely useful. This man"   he indicated Clovis — "has been telling me a bit about what happened here. Sounds as if there's a real mystery." His eyes were shining. "Poor old Uncle Dick didn't really want me to come back — it's a bit crowded at his house at the moment — but I've promised not to be a nuisance."

Thea nodded absently, working out the relationships and still wondering what the appearance of this Ben implied for her personally. If nothing else, it looked as if he'd be getting between her and Clovis. "How can she be your aunt?" she demanded. "She's just told me she's not married to either of the Jackson brothers."

"Oh — she's not exactly an aunt. Dick's not altogether my uncle either, come to that. But we are all related. I've been coming down here since I was a baby, and I've always known Auntie Norma. She was the first person to show me how to do a spreadsheet, when I was about six."

"And he's always been a very rewarding pupil," the woman said fondly. "I've taken a lot of interest in his progress over the years." She addressed the young man. "I came here to suggest lunch, as it happens. I thought this lady might be feeling a bit lonely."

"Thea. She's called Thea," said Clovis, with a proprietorial air. "And I think I've got a prior claim in that respect."

There followed a comical interlude in which everyone looked at everyone else, trying to assess the underlying realities. Thea felt a mild embarrassment, combined with a girlish glow at Clovis's claim on her. "Well . . ." she said. "We could probably *all* go somewhere."

"No, no." Norma backed off, her hands held up vertically. "I can see I'd be surplus to requirements. And if you're all going to talk about gruesome murder details, I'd rather not be there, anyway."

"It was very nice of you to think of me," said Thea. "Honestly, I wasn't expecting anyone to turn up." Hearing herself contradicting Clovis, she added quickly, "At least, I wasn't sure we'd made a firm arrangement."

"No problem. If you do need somebody to talk to, here's my number." She proffered a small business card, which Thea glanced at before putting it in her pocket. "You're welcome to come over and have a drink with me and Bernie one evening."

"That's very kind," said Thea, wishing this had all happened three days ago.

"There's a pub in Ampney Crucis," said Clovis. "Do you know it?"

"No, but I'm more than happy to give it a try. That whole area's still a mystery to me. Have you got time for us to do a bit of exploring?"

"All day," he said airily. "There's a church that's worth a look, and we could even walk along to Poulton or somewhere. You know it, do you, Ben? The Crown of Crucis, they call it."

"Not very well. I do know that my grandfather was born in Poulton, unlike all his brothers, because Great-Grandma had gone for a ride when she was eight months pregnant, and went into labour before she could get home. It's a family legend. He was her sixth child, and she dropped him right by Betty's Grave. Luckily it was a June afternoon, and there were haymakers close by. Mother and baby were both perfectly well within an hour or so. Oh — and Great-Granddad is buried in Ampney Crucis. He's the one we're all descended from."

"Betty's Grave?" echoed Thea, in complete bewilderment.

"It's a local point of interest. I've always wanted to know the truth of it, but there are so many different theories, it would be impossible to find the true one now. It goes back centuries."

"Hey — another mystery," said Clovis inanely.

"Well, let's hope we solve this one before the century's out," said Thea, feeling slightly sour. "Because there's nothing happening as far as the murder is concerned. The whole business is absolutely stuck."

"Great!" Ben was practically rubbing his hands in anticipation. "You'll have to tell me every single detail." He looked from one to the other. "And I need you to explain the situation with you two, as well. If you see what I mean."

Thea felt her hackles rise. Such impertinence! " 'Need to explain'?" she repeated. "Who says we need to do anything?"

270

"Sorry." He put up his hands. "That came out wrong. I meant —"

"We know what you meant," said Clovis kindly. "And it's a fair question. I'm sure Thea's been wondering the same thing, in fact, about my reasons for getting involved. All I can say is that I might have found a connection with the woman who was killed, and I want to see if I can check it out before saying anything to the cops."

"No progress since Tuesday, then?" said Thea.

"Nothing concrete. Jennifer should be here — she's the one with the ideas. But she had to be at a meeting this morning. I've barely even spoken to her today."

"Jennifer?" queried Ben.

"My fiancée. She's marginally linked to the pangolin business, and is convinced the murder has to do with that. But she's too busy to do much about it."

"So she's sent you," Ben nodded. "I get it. At least — pangolins? Those funny Asian things that people use in Chinese medicine?"

"Haven't you been following the news?" Thea demanded. "Even I haven't been able to miss it."

The boy shrugged. "Can't say I've taken much notice. Are you telling me this murdered woman was in a gang of smugglers?"

"It's one theory, yes. It fits some of what we know." Thea turned to Clovis. "So you really don't have to be anywhere else?"

He gave a self-consciously Gallic gesture. "My time is my own," he said. "I could make two or three phone calls, if I get a moment. Otherwise, I'm all yours."

271

Except he'd be sharing her with this Ben person, who showed every sign of sticking with them for the rest of the day. He carried a backpack over one shoulder, and wore sturdy-looking trainers. As if reading her mind, he said, "And I don't have to be anywhere, either."

"Okay, then," said Thea. "Thanks, both of you."

"Don't thank *us*," said Clovis. "You're the one doing the favour. We're both intent on hearing the latest about the murder, and any thoughts you've got on the matter. We're nothing more than bloodsuckers."

"Leeches," confirmed Ben with a cheerful grin.

"Whose car are we taking?" Thea asked. "I should pop in and tell the builders I'll be out. And I need to get my phone. What else? Money, I suppose."

"We'll go in mine," said Clovis firmly. "It's up at the village hall."

Everything was quickly accomplished, and they set off down a minor road that took them southwards out of Barnsley. Thea found the geography confusing, as they passed through two Ampneys in rapid succession, with a third only half a mile distant. The distraction of the undulating landscape, old stone walls, sudden beauties in the shape of houses, churches and gardens, only muddled her more. "I lied," said Clovis gaily. "It's Ampney St Peter that's closest to Poulton. I do tend to get them confused."

"Let's start with the pub. Where did you say that was?" said Thea.

"Ampney Crucis."

"Betty's Grave's a bit past Poulton," said Ben. "Do you want to go and see that as well?"

"After lunch," decreed Clovis. "If we leave it any later, all the best food will have gone. We could leave the car and walk there and back. It'll take forty minutes or so."

"I won't walk for forty minutes," said Thea mulishly, suspecting that she had lost the thread at some point. "And I still don't really understand who you are, Ben. Are you the young relative that Richard Jackson was talking about on Monday?"

"Er . . . probably. There's Edward as well. We're connected through my mother."

"Lunch!" said Clovis loudly. "We're almost there now. We can get all the family history out of the way once we've ordered some food. Although I was rather hoping we might stick to the subject of the murder."

"Don't worry," said Ben. "I'm with you. Murder, not ancestors. Definitely."

They settled at an outside table and waited for food to arrive. Clovis effortlessly took the role of Chair, showing no sign of wanting to be alone with Thea. That, she realised, was the source of her bewilderment. He had apparently deliberately recruited this young Ben, after a random encounter in Barnsley's car park. That also puzzled her. "Exactly how did you two find each other?" she asked.

Between them, the two men delivered an account in which Ben had asked Clovis if he knew which house was the scene of a recent killing. Clovis had laughingly offered to walk him there, since it was his own precise destination. "Pure luck," said Ben, with a small frown. "There was absolutely nobody else in sight to ask. I saw him parking his car and coming down the steps into the street, and waited for him."

"We swopped names, and that was about all we had time for, before we got to the Corner House. We saw you standing there with that woman, and you know the rest," Clovis explained.

"Hm," said Thea, turning to Ben. "So why were you so interested, anyway? Had you heard of me before?"

"What? Haven't we said all that? I'm always keen to follow murder investigations, because of my studies. And no, I hadn't heard of you. Why? Should I have?"

"She's quite famous around here," said Clovis. "The house-sitter who stumbles over bodies and somehow manages to find the killer, nine times out of ten. Only a few months ago, she fingered the person who —" He stopped, the details of that recent homicide still rather too sensitive for a careless summary. "Well, that's not relevant now."

"And I didn't," protested Thea. "It was Caz Barkley who got there first."

Clovis sighed at the memories he'd evoked. "Nasty business all round," he said.

"Okay — so this Chinese woman," urged Ben. "Do they know who she was? How was she killed exactly? Where were you at the time?" He was rummaging in his backpack, and to Thea's wonderment he produced a notebook and pencil. "It seems remarkably mysterious," he added with relish.

274

"They still don't have an identity for her. I found her on Saturday afternoon and took her back to the Corner House, where she stayed the night. On Sunday morning, after I'd been out for a little walk, I came back and found her dead. The police weren't sure whether it was murder or natural causes until they did a post-mortem. Turns out she was strangled. She told me she'd been driven to Barnsley from Manchester, and had to escape from the people who'd brought her there. She was genuinely terrified when I found her." She stopped for breath, wondering whether the summary had made any sense.

Ben was busy making notes. "Manchester?" he echoed. "Driven from Manchester?"

Clovis answered. "Right. Which is another reason for linking it all to the pangolins. They've found a hoard of dead ones up there somewhere, according to the news."

A waitress carrying a laden tray interrupted them, and they settled to their food with everything hanging in the air for a full minute.

Then Ben repeated Thea's account back to her, almost verbatim. Then he said, "So who was she?"

"Nobody knows. There don't seem to be any real clues. They can't find any record of her at the airport. The only thing they've found is that she had a wedding ring round her neck with initials inside. When I found her, she didn't have anything with her at all. She said she'd left everything in the car. She was hiding under some bushes."

"So why Barnsley?" He tapped his teeth with his pen. "Must be something dodgy going on at that business park. Uncle Edward worked there at one time — helped get it set up, in fact."

"But he's retired now, isn't he?"

"Long since. Spends all his time in his garden these days."

"Not doing family history like his brother?"

"Not as far as I know. That's all got rather bogged down last I heard, anyway."

"You told me you couldn't be sure the woman wasn't lying about everything," Clovis reminded Thea.

"I know. There was something very unconvincing about her. I mean — the story is pretty crazy, when you think about it. But she obviously had good reason to be scared, as it turned out. And she said, 'We fear those we hurt' as if that explained a lot. It's pretty obvious that she'd said or done something that *really* upset somebody."

"Enough for them to kill her. Right," nodded Ben.

"Another big part of the mystery is how they knew where she was," put in Clovis. "Were they watching the house all night, waiting for a chance to get in?" He looked at Thea.

"It's a horrible thought. It makes it more or less my fault — going out like I did, leaving the front door unlocked. I really made it easy for them, didn't I?"

"You keep saying 'them'," Ben observed. "Do the cops think there was more than one person?"

"They haven't said. I guess I mean it just as a blanket word for 'he/she/they'. For all I know, a woman on her own might easily have done it. Apparently, it's just a matter of knowing where to press, and keeping hold for

276

a few seconds." She shivered. "The poor woman might never have known what was happening."

"I think it takes long enough for the victim to realise they're in trouble," said Ben, with a ghoulish expression. "And to kick and scratch and shout a bit, as well."

"So — for maximum efficacy, you'd want two people," said Clovis. "Don't you think?"

"Ideally, yes," said Ben, adopting the air of an expert. "But not necessarily."

Clovis spoke up. "Of course, if there was a whole gang of them after her, that wouldn't be a problem."

"Come on!" Thea protested. "Even in Barnsley, people would notice a gang of Chinese traffickers marching into that house and out again, ten minutes later. Don't let's get silly about it."

Before Clovis said any more, Thea noticed Ben's expression. He was watching the older man with great attention, as if trying to read his thoughts. Clovis was obviously not happy at the way she'd spoken to him, but when she reran his words, she was even more certain she'd been right to challenge him. For the first time, she questioned why he was there at all, and how seriously he was taking their discussion. If she was reading Ben Harkness's face correctly, he was wondering much the same thing.

"Okay," said Ben, after a few moments. "I think I've got it now. Just — where's the incident room? Who's the SIO?"

"I think it's all being run from Cirencester. That's where they interviewed me. But they're so short-staffed it's not being given very high priority. There's probably just one detective constable on a computer, trying to track down who she was. That could take ages."

Thea looked around at the people sitting at other tables, nervous of being overheard. They were only three miles from Barnsley, after all. There could be locals listening in. From what she was beginning to understand, most residents of these villages were related to each other. She spoke in a low voice, answering the young man's questions as thoroughly as she could, all the while surprised at her own willingness to co-operate with him. There was something magnetic in his intense interest, that simply drew information forth. An underlying competence gave her a sense of reassurance. He did not waste breath on emotional outbursts or peripheral remarks. He made Clovis look amateurish, in fact.

Clovis coughed and they both looked at him. "I don't think I'm being silly," he said. "I'm only saying what the police probably think. They'll be hoping there's a direct link to the animal traffickers, and when they solve that, they'll get someone to admit to killing Grace at the same time. So they won't waste too much effort from this end, if you follow me."

"All that could well be true," said Ben. "But it's no way to conduct a murder investigation, all the same." He grinned. "So it's down to us, then."

Now *he* was being silly, Thea thought. Just a boy detective with too much time on his hands. But Ben was still speaking. "We have to be *methodical*. Timing,

278

distances, evidence. How much have the police actually told you?"

"They couldn't find anything wrong with her shoulder. She had a wedding ring round her neck. It had initials engraved on the inside. G. B. and K. A. W. We're guessing the G stands for Grace, and the K. A. W. is her husband."

Ben nodded and made a note. "What else?"

"I told you — not a thing. They can't find any trace of her on a flight into Manchester at the end of last week. But what if she was lying to me about her name? Then all they've got is what she looks like. It must be a big job to analyse every face on every flight."

Again the young man nodded. "Possible, but timeconsuming. I'm surprised they even attempted it." He thought for a moment. "So we don't even know her nationality for sure? Did she have an accent?"

Thea shook her head. "She sounded like an ordinary English person."

Ben blew out his cheeks. "She was certainly good at keeping a secret. Now let's go back to Clovis's point about how the killer or killers knew where to find her." He waved a hand invitingly at Clovis.

"Well," the man responded. "As I said before, they could have set up a remote camera in a car, that would show them the minute Thea left the house."

"Blimey!" said Ben, admiringly. "That's right. Did you notice a car or van parked nearby?" he asked Thea.

She shook her head doubtfully. "There's a bit of a lay-by just across the road, where there's often something parked. That would be the obvious place. I don't remember about Sunday, though. I wasn't taking any notice of that sort of thing."

"The police should question all the neighbours, then," the youth decreed.

"Except one of the neighbours might be the killer," objected Clovis.

"That would be a big coincidence," said Ben. "After all, nobody knew Thea would take the woman back to her house."

"It's not *my* house," Thea corrected him. "Remember?"

"Ah! Can we go back over that, then? Whose house is it?"

"A woman called Tabitha Ibbotson. She's a professional pianist — quite famous, apparently. She knows Detective Superintendent Gladwin, who's a friend of mine. She set this whole thing up, thinking I could do with a break from domestic duties."

Ben frowned. "Isn't house-sitting rather domestic?"

She laughed. "In a way. But I don't have to do any cooking, or entertaining children, or answering the phone, or deadheading the roses. I can just slob about with a book."

"Ha!" snorted Clovis. "Some chance of that. If I know you, Thea Slocombe, you don't do very much of that."

You don't know me, though, do you? she wanted to say. "I'm actually very lazy by nature," she told him.

"Okay," said Ben, very businesslike. "So how long were you out? Where did you go? Did you see anybody?"

280

She gave him the wearily familiar report, feeling even more rehearsed than she had suspected Grace of being. "It was the next day I met your relations in the churchyard. I was very glad to chat to nice normal people."

"Yes, yes," said Ben impatiently. "Let's stick to Sunday, shall we? Here you are, in a nice ordinary little Cotswold village on a Sunday morning. That doesn't really suggest violent killing, does it? And yet it happened. And we have to find out why it did."

The others just looked at him. "Okay — so we're finished here, are we?" All their plates had been cleared and glasses drained. Ben checked his watch. "Listen — while we're here, can we go and have a quick look at the churchyard? I think I should go and check out my great-granddad. My mum said she thought the headstone might need attention."

"No problem," said Clovis. "We can leave the car and walk. It'll take about three minutes."

Thea sat back and gave him a long look. His face was as gorgeous as ever, his attitude relaxed, his wallet clearly well filled. They all took it for granted that he was paying for the meal. But why was he really here? His contributions had been minimal, his engagement tepid. Did he care about Grace at all? Was he just passing the time? And how extensive was his local knowledge? They were three people who scarcely knew each other at all, discussing a horrible crime as if it was an intriguing puzzle and nothing more.

"What?" he said, aware of her scrutiny.

"Nothing, really. Just a bit puzzled as to what the three of us think we're doing, I suppose."

Ben gave a melodramatic groan. "It's me," he said. "It's all me. This is what I do — I've done it umpteen times back where I live. I get everybody fixating on clues and evidence and motives and so forth, just by asking a few questions. I don't understand how it happens, quite honestly, but it seems to work every time."

"Same as me, then," said Thea. "Welcome to my world."

CHAPTER
TWENTY-ONE

Clovis once again took the role of leader. "We can go to the churchyard first, and then how about looking at Betty's Grave? And Ready Token? That's a village, by the way. And wait till you see the amazing place just over the churchyard wall."

In spite of herself, Thea had to ask, "Ready Token? You can't be serious."

"Honestly. We can go back that way, and you'll see for yourself."

They trooped up the quiet road to the church, glimpsing the tower ahead. Clovis continued with his history lesson. "The cross in the churchyard is extremely ancient. Fifteenth century at least. The church is called The Holy Rood, because of it."

They let him prattle on, until they were standing around the object itself, which did indeed look old. A long slender stone stem supported a four-sided carving with religious images in remarkably good condition on all sides. "Nice," said Thea, before gazing all round at the graves. "Plenty of space for more," she remarked.

"My great-granddad is over here," said Ben. "He died aged thirty-three in eighteen ninety-seven, leaving a wife and a lot of kids. I've got a very complicated family," he announced proudly. "So complicated that there's a whole farm that's been standing empty since the late 1990s not far from here because nobody can decide who should inherit it. The trouble is, there were no obvious claimants amongst my mother's relations — . I mean they all seem to have an equally valid claim. It's bonkers, basically."

Thea was reminded of the empty house she'd seen at Bibury. "Surely they can rent out the fields?" she queried. "Won't it all get overrun with thistles and brambles otherwise?"

"Maybe," Ben shrugged. "I just know they've been spending big money on legal fees for umpteen years, and not getting anywhere."

"Your grandfather must have been pretty old when your mother was born," said Thea, having performed one of her habitual calculations. "If he was born in the nineteenth century. Which he must have been if his father died in 1897."

He gave her an approving look. "Right. My mother was born in nineteen fifty-five, when he was sixty. Not so unusual, really. But don't ask me to give you a full family tree. I can only do it if I've got something to write it all down on, and then I always forget about eight of them. Everybody two generations back had at least five children, and then they all seemed to run out of steam, apart from my mother. I'm the only one who comes from a big family now."

They roamed amongst the graves until Ben called, "Here he is! Look — Samuel Thomas Wheelwright. You can only just read it. My mum was right — the stone needs straightening. Another year or two and it'll fall over completely."

"Wheelwright," Thea repeated slowly. "I've seen that name just recently." Before she could snag the exact memory, her phone began to jingle in her bag. "Sounds as if I left it on for once," she said, as she fished it out. "Oh — it's my sister."

It transpired that Jocelyn was calling to check that Thea had contacted Jessica, and to ask whether she'd seen any more of the delectable Clovis. "Can't talk to you now," said Thea firmly. "I'm standing in a churchyard, with two other people. It's all a bit busy. Jessica sounded fine when I spoke to her. I'll be seeing her in a few weeks anyway. I'll keep you posted . . . yes, Joss, I know. Thanks, but it's not necessary. I'm going, okay?" And she firmly terminated the call before the name of Clovis could be uttered again. Irrationally, she feared that he would hear it and want to know what was being said.

But the call had conveniently reminded her of where she'd seen the surname on the headstone. "We found the cremated remains of a person called Wheelwright in a barn in Barnsley," she said succinctly. "What do you think of that?"

Ben stared at her. "What? In a *barn*?"

"That's right." She paused to think. "I don't suppose it belongs to this family farm you're talking about, does it? Right in the middle of Barnsley?"

"No, it's the other side of Cirencester, I think. I've never actually been there. How do you know they're somebody's ashes?"

Clovis was equally bemused. "You never told me about that," he reproached her.

Ben had lost all interest in the churchyard or walking to Betty's Grave. "Can you take me to see? When was this? Will they still be there? Whose barn is it?"

Thea answered his questions to the best of her ability. "They're in an urn — the sort provided by the crematorium. There's a name label and a date. Gwendoline Phoebe Wheelwright. It was only Tuesday I saw them. Dozy of me to forget the name so quickly. Anyway, I shouldn't think anyone's going to move them."

"Well, let's go and see," urged the youth. Clovis allowed himself to be hustled back to the car and instructed to drive back to Barnsley immediately.

"The thing is," said Ben breathlessly, as they drove, "I remember my mum talking about her Great-Aunt Gwen. If I've got it right, the whole argument about the farm started when she died. Must be more than twenty years ago — I wasn't born, nor Wilf. He's my older brother. Mum always says if she'd been a bit quicker off the mark, she might have inherited the property herself."

"So who else is after it?"

"Pretty much everybody, to start with. It's all gone quiet lately. There are all sorts of descendants staking a claim. Gwen's father was one of Great-Granddad's offspring. Gwen was a childless widow when she died, and everyone thought the place belonged to her. But in fact she was just living there by default, you might say. It was never officially hers — nobody did the necessary

286

paperwork. She had an older brother, Eric, who was killed in the war, which was one reason everything got so muddled. He didn't make a will, and even if he had it might not have been valid. There were cousins who contested his claim on the farm, even back in the nineteen-forties."

"So why not sell it and share the proceeds?" asked Clovis.

"Good question. Stubbornness, I assume, or maybe they couldn't if they didn't know exactly who it belonged to. Anyway, Uncle Dick's been researching into it recently, and he thinks he's got a pretty good case for claiming it. Most of the others are dead by now."

"But they'll have descendants of their own who might be interested," said Thea.

"Dick thinks there's really only one surviving branch that might cause trouble. When I was here a week or so ago, he was talking about getting in touch with them and seeing where things stood."

"Well, just looking at these ashes won't tell you anything," said Thea, who was half-regretting her revelation. A nice afternoon walk would have suited her perfectly.

"It might. Don't you know who owns this barn we're going to?"

"I have no idea. It looks completely abandoned. We had to push through a whole lot of nettles and brambles to get into it. Here, Clovis — this is it, on the right." They were entering Barnsley from the west, and had just passed the big hotel and spa that was the village's chief claim to fame. Clovis pulled off the road and they all got out.

"Romantic," murmured Clovis, gazing at the ivy-covered building.

"How do we get in?" asked Ben.

"With difficulty," Thea repeated. "And we'd be trespassing, I suppose." She looked all round. There wasn't a soul in sight. "But nobody seems to be watching."

"Can't see any cameras, either," Clovis reported.

"Let's get on with it, then." Ben walked up the short lane to the barn. Thea followed him, impressed all over again by the fairy-tale quality of the place. The growth of creeper all over the facing wall was rampant, suggesting years of neglect. Its presence in a tidy little Cotswold settlement made it all the more remarkable.

"Round here," she said. "There's a farmyard on the other side, which might have people."

"Is it a working farm, then?"

"I don't know. The house seems to be uninhabited." It was obviously becoming something of a theme, she realised.

"There'll be somebody managing the land," said Clovis confidently. "The buildings might be scheduled for some sort of conversion. All sorts of stuff is probably going on behind the scenes. It doesn't have to mean it's been abandoned. But I don't think we're being watched, so this is as good a moment as any to have a look."

Thea regarded at him wonderingly. A grown man, more or less respectable, showing no hesitation in taking part in a madcap adventure involving nettles and spiders and unambiguous trespass. Perhaps he was much less respectable than he liked to appear. She remembered again his unconventional mother.

Ben was charging ahead, examining the same barely passable way in that Thea and Jocelyn had found two days ago.

Two minutes later they were all standing inside the barn, getting used to the gloom, peering into the shadows. "It was just here," said Thea, staring at the homemade shrine, which was now devoid of any adornment. "And it's gone," she announced.

It was five minutes or more before the others believed her. They walked the whole length of all four walls, peering into shadowy corners, before admitting that she must be right. Apart from the locked trunk at the back, there was nothing else inside the building. There was no upper storey, no musty hay bales providing opportunities for hiding anything. "It's gone," Thea repeated, three times. "Somebody's taken it."

They gave up then and pushed through the prickles back to the car. "It must be that Williams man," Thea decided. "He was here when Joss and I emerged from the barn. I didn't think he'd seen us, but he must've done."

"Who?" asked Ben and Clovis together.

Thea explained. "I think he must be local," she concluded. "He walks his dog around here."

"It is very bizarre indeed," said Clovis. Thea sighed at this statement of the obvious. Was it possible she was going off the man? Was he revealing hidden shallows, as Barkley would certainly believe, if she knew what was going on?

"Ashes," mused Ben, his gaze on the ground. "What do we know about ashes?"

"They're heavier than they look. Sterile. Hopeless as fertiliser. Usually in very fine pellets rather than dust, but it does vary. Eighty per cent of people dying these days are turned into them." Thea rattled off these facts with complete confidence.

Ben stared at her. "Urn . . .?" he said.

"Oh — didn't we tell you? I'm married to an undertaker," she said blithely. "I just assumed you'd know that."

"Wow! You *are* an interesting person, aren't you! Wow!" He was pink with admiration. Then he gave himself a shake. "So — you must know whether it's possible to extract DNA from them. Ashes, I mean."

"It obviously isn't," she said, feeling slightly less confident than before. "They're *cremated*. Burnt at very high temperatures. Totally dead. That's why they're no good as fertiliser, even though people will insist on burying them under roses, poor things."

"The people or the roses?" asked Clovis, with a fatuous grin.

"That's what I thought," said Ben, ignoring him. "And is it true they really do give you back your actual person? Or is it all just chucked in together and everybody gets a shovelful?"

"According to Drew, they're scrupulous about that. They wait until the furnace has cooled down after every

290

cremation, and scrape out the ashes, one person at a time. All carefully labelled and any instructions followed to the letter."

"That's reassuring," said Clovis. "But I'm still glad my dad was buried in your field, without the fiery furnace being involved."

"So what do we do now?" asked Thea, having waited in vain for Ben to say it.

They had gone back to the car, but made no move to get into it. "No idea," said Ben. "Except I should probably try and get hold of Uncle Dick, to tell him I'm here." He pulled a face. "Something's not right, is it? Something to do with my family, I mean."

"It's a red herring," said Clovis. "Nothing to do with Thea's murder."

"Obviously. But we can't just ignore it, can we? I mean — why were Gwen's ashes in that barn in the first place?" He stared hard at Thea, as if trying to read the answers in her face.

"Well, if she's the cause of all this family disagreement, then perhaps it made sense to keep her remains in a neutral place," she suggested slowly. "Perhaps some members of the family remember her fondly, and set up the little altar to her. It's rather a nice idea, in a way."

"So why move them now?" asked Clovis.

"Why now?" Ben repeated. "That's always a useful question. Maybe something has shifted in the legal wrangling. And maybe . . ." his face brightened, "maybe somebody does think you can get DNA from ashes, and they're trying to prove a relationship. I bet that's it," he concluded cheerfully.

"Have you any relatives called Williams?" Thea wondered, still convinced the accountant was the culprit.

"Not to my knowledge. I'll need to have a proper look at the whole family tree to be sure."

"Hang on," Clovis objected. "This definitely doesn't connect to the murder at all, does it? We've got completely sidetracked. Shouldn't all this wait until we've finished discussing the Grace woman?"

"Well, yes," said Ben dubiously. "Except I thought we *had* finished. What else did you want to talk about?"

Clovis wriggled his shoulders. "Just . . . what about those initials on the ring, for example?"

"Yeah," said Ben, with no sign of enthusiasm. "We could have a think about that — but this feels more urgent, to be honest. If I can just sit down with my phone and notebook for a minute, I'll be able to get my thoughts straight. We could use the house on the corner, for preference."

"Yes!" said Thea. "Come on, then."

"I'll have to move the car," said Clovis. "I'll catch you up."

For the third time, Thea paused to scrutinise him. Something wasn't right. It was akin to the feeling she had about Drew. Both men were withholding something from her. Both were behaving oddly. Or was it her, imagining things? Was she suspecting secrets where they did not exist? In contrast, the boy Ben was wonderfully refreshing. He said what he was thinking, he had no inhibitions about casting accusations right and left, and his mind had all the sharpness of a healthy young genius.

"It can't possibly connect, though, can it?" she said, as they walked briskly through the village, past the Village Pub, the church and a handful of old stone houses. "The murder, and your family feud, and Barnsley Park and the ashes. How could they possibly all be part of the same thing?"

"We should accept that it's not impossible," he said sententiously. "We'll know more when I've checked out a few things." He looked up at the building in front of him, as Thea steered him through the lopsided gate. "Nice old house. What's being done to it?"

"Just updating the kitchen and bathroom, basically. Nothing's been touched for seventy years, or something. Forty years, more likely, in the kitchen, I suppose. They're not doing anything structural, apart from a new piece of wall at the back. That part isn't so old, anyway."

"How do you get on with the builders?"

"Fine. They're really nice chaps."

"My mother's an architect. I get to hear a lot about builders. Mostly good, funnily enough — but there's a few she'd quite like to slaughter."

"Sid and Dave work fast as well." She was speaking quietly, unsure whether the men could hear her. "They'll be knocking off soon. Early start, early finish seems to be the pattern."

She unlocked the front door, and ushered the young man into the hallway. "We can leave it open for Clovis," she said.

"I'm not sure he'll be coming," came the startling response.

"What? What do you mean? Of course he's coming."

"How well do you know him?"

"Well enough." She felt defensive and utterly confused. "Why?"

"Have you got a phone number for him? Address? Employment record?"

"His number is in my phone. He called me a time or two. And my husband will have an address for him. We did his father's funeral . . . oh!" She flushed with embarrassment. "Maybe he hasn't got it, after all. It was all very complicated. But I could easily find him if I wanted to."

"I might be wrong, but I don't think so. He hasn't seemed genuine to me from the first moment I met him."

"Gosh!" she said weakly. "So what are you thinking? That he murdered Grace?"

"No, no. I'm not saying that. But he does obviously have an unhealthy interest in the whole business. Luckily, I don't think he's very clever. Are you sure he actually likes you, by the way? Because I caught one or two looks that suggested otherwise."

"I don't know. At the moment, I don't really know anything at all. The ground's just given way under my feet. But I was starting to wonder about him, believe it or not. You're right — there was something secretive and a bit . . . withdrawn about him today. And maybe he thinks he has reason to be angry with me. He can get very angry." She blinked away a sudden rush of self-pity. "The first time I spoke to him, he was shouting and making threats."

"Well, he's not here, is he? I think he was beginning to feel out of his depth around the point where we started eating our lunch, and it just kept on getting worse. So he's baled out, the first chance he got."

"So that just leaves you and me," she said, with a brave smile.

CHAPTER
TWENTY-TWO

They sat at Tabitha Ibbotson's dining table, using Thea's sketch pad for the flow chart that Ben insisted on constructing. "It's the way I do things," he told her firmly. "Can we start with everyone we know in the village?"

She blew out her cheeks. "That must be a lot of people. Don't tell me you know them *all*?"

"Actually, no. Just the relatives, basically. Right — let's do it. Start with the Jacksons, Richard and Edward." He put the two names at the top of the page. "Then Auntie Laura. She's married to Richard, but she's got awful arthritis and hardly ever goes out. Edward's wife is dead. Then Norma — her mother was Gwen's sister, I think. Or possibly aunt. Who else?" Again he tapped his front teeth with the pen.

"What about the other people I met in the churchyard? A woman with a very straight fringe, and another man I haven't seen again. Your Uncle Richard and Auntie Norma were there as well. Norma had a camera. I recognised Richard from his limp, when I saw him again. He says it's his knee."

"Right. He hurt it somehow at the weekend. Some sort of tendon damage. Not very serious, or so he says."

Ben was speaking carelessly, most of his attention on the names he'd recorded.

"So who's the woman with the fringe?"

"What sort of age?"

"Probably fifties. Seemed very businesslike. I haven't seen her again."

"Sounds like Julia. She's Auntie Laura's sister. Their father had a farm at Poulton, I think. She's on the parish council."

"So not a Wheelwright or a Williams or a Jackson?"

"Nope. If they're related at all, it'll be via a second marriage with step-siblings. Something like that. Listen" — he gave her a severe look — "don't ask me to construct a complete family tree. I told you — even my mother gets confused, and she's a lot more clued up about it than I am."

"Okay. Point taken. So what's Julia's interest in the headstones in Barnsley?"

"Keeping an eye on things, probably. I don't really know her, but they always say how socially committed she is, whatever that means. I'm surprised she hasn't marched in here and demanded to know all the details about the dead woman, as representative of the parish."

"Well she hasn't. And the other man?"

"Describe him."

She found this difficult. "Very ordinary. Grey hair. Didn't say much. Looked a bit like a vicar."

He laughed. "That's not ringing any bells. I've never met the vicar here — probably covers about six churches in the area, anyway."

"Oh, I came across that when I was googling. I think it might be seven, if I remember rightly."

"He — or she — is probably a bit too busy to be deciphering headstones on a Monday morning, then." He nibbled his pencil in deep thought, then made a few more notes. "Those initials on the wedding ring," he said. "Remind me."

"G. B. and K. A. W."

He wrote them down. "In that order, were they?"

"I suppose so. I didn't see them myself. Barkley told me."

"Because, wouldn't you expect the person wearing the ring to put themselves second, not first? I mean, if both parties had the same thing, they'd reverse the initials and wear the one with the beloved first. Get me?"

"I think so. And you're right. It's obvious, when you think about it. Can you possibly be saying my woman was K. A. W.? That would change everything." She stared at him, trying to process the implications.

"Just a suggestion. If it's right, it could mean that she invented the name Grace and the G initial is George or Graham."

"Or something Chinese."

He shook his head. "I don't think there's much of a Chinese element here. I suspect that's nothing more than a red herring. I hate red herrings!" he snapped. "And there always seem to be some. It comes of not knowing any of the background. We just grab at the most obvious things."

298

Thea was still distracted by the outrageous disappearance of Clovis, her thoughts wandering repeatedly in his direction. Ben's explanation was entirely unsatisfactory. People didn't just go off like that, without a word of apology. What had happened to change his mind so drastically? He'd been keen enough at the beginning, seeking her out and listening intently to her story. "I can't stop thinking about Clovis," she admitted, when Ben gave her an enquiring look.

"Well try, because he's a separate issue."

"How can you be sure?"

"I just can." He put his pen down and leant back. "Don't ask me to show my workings, okay? Not for side issues. It'll take all night."

She looked at her watch. "Gosh, it's past four. Shouldn't you call Richard?"

"In a minute. We can't stop now. Help me to *think*, will you?"

She stared at his jottings. "You've left out Gwendoline Phoebe Wheelwright and her inheritance. And don't we need some sort of family tree?" Suddenly implications began to dawn. "Oh — Ben. These are your *relations*, or most of them. What if . . .? I mean, aren't we . . .?"

"We have to follow the evidence, wherever it leads," he said like a much older man. Or like somebody reading from a book. "And I'm not too worried at the moment, because I can't see anything that leads anywhere. We're missing about twenty connecting links. We need more *facts*."

"All I can see are the holes. How did anybody know Grace was here in this house, for a start? I keep coming back to that. Were they — whoever they are — still searching for her when I brought her here? And what on earth had she *done* to deserve being killed?"

"We need help," he decided suddenly, reaching for his phone. "It shouldn't take long to find out about K. A. W." He was already thumbing and swiping. "What if the W is Wheelwright? It's worth looking at the Electoral Register." There followed three minutes of silence before he reported, "Karen Alison Wheelwright, with an address in Banbury. That's the only one."

"And you think that's her? The dead woman?"

"It could be."

"How can we find out for sure? Would there be a picture of her somewhere?"

"Hang on. Let's check marriages. See if she married a G. B." He went quiet again, giving Thea time to ponder the implications. She was afraid she would never catch up, but it proved easier than she'd thought, as she peered at the small screen over Ben's shoulder. The story was, bit by bit, starting to take shape. "It all hinges on the motive," she murmured. "Doesn't it?"

"Mm," said Ben.

Then Thea's own phone emitted a musical *ping* to announce a text. "Good Lord — listen to this. 'Sorry to disappear like that. The truth is I was getting in too deep, and feeling like a fool. I was only trying to impress Jennifer, anyway, proving it was all down to the Chinese. That would have been a perfect solution — blame everything on them. After all, they're responsible

300

for most that's wrong with the world. Might not be seeing you. Sorry again. Clovis.' "

"The man's a racist," said Ben in disgust. "You're well out of that."

"Yes, but —" She sighed. *But he's so terribly handsome*, she thought with regret, before firmly banishing the man from her mind. "Getting anywhere?" she asked.

"Maybe so. There's something here, look. A newspaper report about Karen Alison. She entered into a civil partnership, three years ago, with a woman called Grace Berensen. G. B. In Banbury. Apparently, she's a successful entrepreneur, with her own consultancy business. That could mean anything, of course. Grace Berensen is a respected social worker, who specialises in elder care." He looked up with a grin. "I always think that sounds like somebody who looks after trees and picks elderberries. Anyway, the people of Banbury evidently value them as pillars of the community."

"I don't believe you could possibly have found all that so quickly. It's a miracle."

"Not really. I checked the Oxfordshire newspapers first and there it is. A photo as well. Is this your woman?"

Thea peered excitedly at the tiny image. "I can't see it properly." Ben expanded it for her, and she squealed with amazement. "That's her! The one on the left. So she wasn't called Grace, after all."

"She took the name of her partner — wife, I suppose. Probably the first thing that popped into her head."

"The real Grace looks nice," Thea said wistfully. "Poor woman. Presumably she's got no idea what's happened." She sat there, open-mouthed, trying to process this disconcerting discovery. She reviewed the brief time she'd spent with the dead woman — who she had to start calling Karen instead of Grace. She had lived only twenty miles away. She had no discernible links with any sort of trafficking. And yet — she had been deliberately killed, here in this very house. Her fear had been real and entirely justified. The dramatic story that Thea had constructed from the snippets Grace/Karen had given her suddenly felt more ordinary, but at the same time more terrible. "But she must have told me *some* lies," she concluded. "What about all that stuff about Manchester and people in a car. I believed that part of the story."

"We don't know that she was lying," said Ben. "This doesn't disprove the basic story. But it *does* establish an identity for her and that's the main thing. Plus, of course, this murder victim, Ms Karen Alison Wheelwright, is almost certainly some relation to me, and my mum, even if she does look Chinese. Did you say she told you she had an English father? Then he's got to be a Wheelwright. I wonder if I can find his first name somewhere?"

"Oh, Ben. Stop being so calm about it. This is linking the whole business to your *family*, for heaven's sake. What if . . . what if one of them killed her?"

He shivered, as if throwing off a dowsing of cold water. "It's all speculation at the moment. We haven't got a shred of evidence against anybody."

302

"Yet," she muttered darkly. The picture was still coalescing inside her head. The main obstruction was the inclusion of the city of Manchester — nothing she could imagine explained how that could fit.

"We need to locate this Grace Berensen," Ben said. "In fact, we ought to let the police know what we've found, before we do anything else. If we don't, they'll have us for obstructing the course of justice. You know who to call, I assume?"

"Normally, I'd go straight to Gladwin. She's a detective superintendent. But she's up to her eyes in this pangolin business, and I haven't seen her all week. I suppose it'll have to be Cirencester, and I don't know them there. Not very well, anyhow."

"Call them," he said. "If I've learnt anything in the past year or two, it's when to stop acting unilaterally and let the professionals take over."

"I'm not sure I ever quite got the hang of that," she admitted with a laugh.

"And this time it's all a bit too close to home for comfort. It never even crossed my *mind*," he burst out. "What's my mother going to say if I turn out to be the one who landed one of my uncles with a murder rap?"

"Still jumping ahead," she cautioned him. "We're not there yet, by a long way."

They spent the next ten minutes on their respective mobiles. Thea called Cirencester and left a message with a person who sounded about fifteen, for whoever was in charge of the Barnsley murder enquiry. "The identity of the victim is Karen Alison Wheelwright," she said unambiguously. "She has a partner called Grace

Berensen, living in Banbury." There followed a string of bemused questions, which she did her best to answer, until she heard herself saying, "It's all there on the computer! Find it for yourself," and cutting the call. "There! I called them," she told Ben. "Satisfied?"

"Send a text to your Gladwin person as well," he advised. "Belt and braces."

"And Barkley. Don't forget Barkley."

"I don't know who that is."

"She's a very bright detective sergeant. You'd like her."

"Good," he said, without looking up.

Thea went into the shiny new kitchen and made two mugs of tea. Her brain was whirling with theories, names, images, while her emotions were equally tangled. Guilt towards Drew combined with embarrassed bewilderment about Clovis, and minor nagging worries about Jessica and Hepzie. There was still no clear path through any of it.

But Ben was miraculous in his capabilities. He was making it all look so easy, and yet the police clearly had been dragging far behind him. Something as simple as transposing the two sets of initials on the wedding ring had unlocked the mystery within moments. Thea was tempted to simply sit back and enjoy watching him at work.

As he sipped his tea, he shared his latest findings. "I went onto the Wheelwright family website — the one that's only open to family members. I've found Karen's dad — he was called Simon and he died six months ago. That could be the answer to the 'Why now?'

304

question, actually. I'm very much afraid it does all hinge on this inheritance business. If I've followed it properly, then Karen's grandfather must have been Gwen's brother. The whole gang of them are descended from Great-Granddad, including this Karen, my mother, even Auntie Norma, through her mother somehow." Again he chewed the pencil. "She's always been around, in and out of the Jacksons' houses. But if I remember rightly, they've been neighbours for ever, very tight-knit. There was some sort of disgrace somewhere in her background. Something that was hushed up."

"And that's not on the website?"

"Definitely not. She'd never have allowed that."

Again, Thea's mind began to whirr. Did Karen know about the "disgrace"? Had she been threatening to make it public? Or what? She wanted to ask Ben, but he looked as if he could do with a break. "Should we pack it in for now?" she asked him. "Let the police take it from here."

"I don't know." He looked anguished. "What if the solution to the whole thing is just a few more taps away? I'll feel really stupid if I miss it now, having got this far."

"Well, it's driving me crazy," she grumbled. "I just wish we could speak to Gladwin. We should put the radio on and see whether there's any more news about the pangolins. If that's been sorted, she'll have some time for this."

"I can check the news on here," he said, in a mildly scornful tone. Again he tapped and swiped, before announcing, "News blackout. That means it's all kicking off as we speak. You won't get any sense out of her if she's on that case."

"Well, I'll try Caz, then."

"Isn't she part of it as well?"

Thea explained the free-floating role of the detective sergeant, as well as she could, and Ben absorbed every piece of information as if he were a sponge. "You know what?" he said at the end. "You've been completely on your own through all this, haven't you? Where I come from, there's a proper little gang of us. Three, usually. My girlfriend and her boss are always right there, so we bounce everything off each other. It makes things a lot easier."

"Sounds great. I've usually got my dog with me," Thea said idiotically.

"What about your undertaker husband?"

"Sometimes he gets involved," she said vaguely. "The first time I met him, he'd just found a body. But he's not a natural detective, really."

"Not many people are. I'm not sure that *you* are, when it comes to it."

"I'm very nosy, and I'm good at getting people talking. I'm not always very sympathetic, though." She sighed. "And I think my brain's past its peak."

He drained his tea, but did not return to his computer searches. "We need more than I can get, sitting here. Who can we go and talk to, I wonder?"

"I'm sure your relatives are wondering where you are by now." The prospect of him disappearing back to his aunts and uncles or cousins or whatever they were was not a happy one. Clovis had deserted her, leaving her feeling foolish and puzzled. Ahead lay several hours of evening, with nothing to do but phone her husband and try to pretend she'd had a nice ordinary day.

"I could ask who the other man was — in the churchyard on Monday. I don't expect he's important, though. And I could pick some brains about the Wheelwrights. Stuff they haven't put on the website."

"You don't think, then —" She stopped, unsure as to how much she dared say. "I mean, hasn't the whole thing got alarmingly close to home? Will you tell them what you've just found out?"

"Whoa," he protested. "Slow down. It's not that urgent. I think we ought to sleep on it, and see if it looks clearer in the morning. I'm not going home till Sunday. And no — I won't tell my people anything yet. It's all too murky still."

"Tomorrow might be my last day here. I need to get home — something's going on there that I don't understand. I should never have come. The whole thing was a stupid idea from the start."

"Was it yours? The idea, I mean."

"Actually no — that was all thanks to Gladwin. She meant well — and she couldn't have known how preoccupied she was going to be. We thought she'd be able to drop in once or twice, and we could go exploring or something."

"And now she's under so much pressure, she's forgotten all about you."

"I don't expect she has. She's really nice, you know. I liked her from the start. That was ages ago now — I

307

was doing a house-sit in Temple Guiting. I think. They tend to blur after a while."

"That's a very smart piano," he remarked, peering into the living room on the way out. "Must be worth a bit."

"She's a professional pianist. I suppose she has to have a good one. It's part of my job this week to keep guard over it. Not that much was likely to happen to it."

"Other than fire or flood — and I don't expect you can prevent anything like that."

"No."

They hovered on the doorstep, acutely aware that nothing had actually been solved, despite their best efforts. "I'll give you my number, in case something happens," he said. "And what's yours?"

She handed him her phone. "Put yours in." Then she recited her own number, which had taken her about three years to memorise.

"Good," said Ben.

"Where do they live?" she asked, as he began to walk away.

"Who?"

"Dick Jackson and his wife. The ones you're staying with."

"Oh — right here in the village. Just the other side of the big hotel. Five minutes away, at most."

She let him go then. Perhaps she was projecting her own feelings onto him, but he did seem to droop as he walked away. There was so much she didn't know about him, things she wanted to discover. A sharp pang of anxiety shot through her: what if she never saw him again? What if he suffered the same fate as Grace/Karen? What if somebody murdered this remarkable youth, afraid that he was getting too close to the truth? His own relatives were not above suspicion. He was there, under their roof, impossibly vulnerable to attack during the night. Then common sense took charge. Ben Harkness was clearly no fool. He would ensure his own safety in all sorts of clever ways. It was probably more sensible to worry about her own well-being. Not only was she alone in a large house, but she was in a very unstable mood. Frustrated, guilty, anxious — all the same feelings that had been lurking for days were coming to a painful climax.

When in doubt make something happen, she told herself again. It had been her motto for several of her dramatic house-sitting experiences. Force things along, call someone's bluff, ask the searching questions. There were several options open to her. Firstly, she could drive to Cirencester and make sure her report on all the discoveries of the day had reached somebody in authority. Or she could go out and knock on doors, just for the sake of it. Or she could have a go at continuing Ben's researches on her laptop, while she considered the coming evening. The last was the easiest and the most appealing. But Ben had swept through so many references and websites and archives on his phone that she had not managed to catch a proper sight of anything. She might know a bit of the theory, but in practice she didn't think she could even manage to successfully log in to anything useful. So she gave it up, and went back into the kitchen for another mug of tea. What she really wanted was wine, and a nice steak or freshly caught trout. And a congenial companion to chat to. And a dog who worshipped her.

Outside it was warm, but overcast, which had been the default condition for most of the month. Since Jessica had grown up, the month of August had lost much of that bitter-sweet urgency, where it was regarded as the entire summer, the only time a family could get away for a holiday. She and Carl had enjoyed only one self-indulgent fortnight at the end of June, when Jessica was seventeen. They'd gone to Brittany, feeling like fugitives from every responsibility. After that, Carl had died and Thea found herself swamped with house-sitting work all summer. Jessica left home, Hepzibah was acquired, and holidays seemed like something other people did. And now she was back several steps, frantically trying to give two children a good summer while preserving her own sanity.

Feeling sorry for herself on every level, she drifted around the house. She should be concentrating on the murder — the resolution felt so close, along with a vague sense of danger. The police were nowhere in sight; nobody really cared what became of her in this strange old village. Awful things were going on behind the bland exteriors — nothing was as it seemed. Nobody was telling the truth.

It was after six. Outside it was still light, the day far from finished, but everyone had deserted her. It was all very well for Ben to preach about knowing when to stop playing amateur detective, but just walking off and leaving her in limbo began to feel unfair. After all, he was amongst individuals who could turn out to be active players in the investigation. While he probably wasn't actually in any danger, he was at least quite likely to be in line for some excitement.

Make something happen! her inner voice shouted at her again. But what? Still she drifted and dithered and hesitated. Anything she did now could make matters worse. She might blunderingly ruin a delicate plan that clever Caz Barkley was unfolding without Thea's knowledge. All around her were people she did not know or understand. Even Ben Harkness could well have an agenda that he'd kept to himself.

When the doorbell rang, she went limp with relief. Even if it was a gang of murderous men with guns, it would be better than this paralysis.

It wasn't a gang of men. It was a single woman, with nothing in her hands at all.

CHAPTER
TWENTY-THREE

Norma Whatever-her-name-was stood there, faintly smiling. "All on your own?" she asked, with a lift of the eyebrows.

"As usual." The bitterness surprised even Thea herself.

"Well, that's not good. Come round to mine for the evening. We can play cards or something. Have some wine. Have you eaten yet?"

"I had a big lunch, so I'm not very hungry."

"I find hunger isn't very relevant, though. Don't you?"

Thea laughed. "I suppose that's true. Well, it's a very kind thought, but . . ." She could find no excuse that would sound remotely convincing. She couldn't even convince herself. Why was she hesitating? What did this immediate instinct to refuse the offer really mean? The woman was perfectly ordinary and friendly. She was only following up on her earlier attempt to make a connection. Perhaps that was it. Why was she so persistent? "I need to phone my husband," Thea finished lamely. "He'll expect a call from me any time now."

"Bring your phone. Call him from my place. I'm literally one minute away from here."

The house was indeed virtually next door to Tabitha's. It stood "kitty corner" as the Americans would say, diagonally opposite and then about fifty yards along towards the centre of the village. Thea had passed it several times without taking any particular notice. A nice-enough stone building, detached, with a low hedge in front, it was just one of hundreds of similar Cotswolds homes. It had no close neighbours. Norma opened the front door without the use of a key, which prompted Thea to ask, "Is your husband at home?"

"He's not, actually. The fact is, he's in Bulgaria at the moment — or is it Romania? One of those places. He's a bit younger than me — still working up the career ladder, as they say. He's doing well in the property business, and whatever's going on politically, the Brits never get tired of buying somewhere cheap in the sun, even if the infrastructure's impossible. He does try to warn them," she added defensively. "They always think it'll be fine in their particular case. Sometimes it is, of course."

"Does he go to Poland?" Thea asked, suddenly put in mind of Clovis and his innovative musicians. Clovis was still prodding and poking somewhere deep inside her skin.

"A bit. It's a much better country to live in than most of the others, but not so cheap any more."

"It's nice that you leave the door unlocked," Thea said.

313

"Oh, yes. Most people have got so paranoid about security, haven't they? I've got nothing worth stealing, and you don't get many burglaries these days anyway, do you?"

"Don't you?"

"Oh no. The crimes are all done on computers now." Thea recollected that the woman had taught Ben how to work a spreadsheet — which implied she knew her way around a computer.

Thea was looking around the house. The hallway was lined with pictures in handsome old frames. There was a long narrow rug running the length of the hall floor that looked handmade. The stairs were carpeted in a rich crimson and the banisters were made of ornately turned wood that looked like oak. "I know — it's like a museum," Norma said. "All old stuff from our parents. These are family photos, look." She indicated the pictures. One showed a large Edwardian wedding group, the bride and five bridesmaids all clothed in something white and highly attractive.

"Pity they make the bridesmaids wear such hideous clothes these days," Thea remarked idly.

Norma did not reply directly. "Those girls are all sisters, cousins of the bride. It's a lovely picture, don't you think? And see that house behind them? It belonged to the bride's mother, and then went out of the family. It's a complicated story — just one of many, really."

Thea's spine began to tingle. There was something going on, a code or a hidden revelation. "Do you know who Gwendoline Wheelwright was?" she asked.

"I do, yes. Yet another of the Wheelwright relations. This couple here were her parents, in fact. Why do you ask?"

"Um . . . I just saw the name somewhere." *Norma was a nice person*, she repeated frantically to herself. There was nothing to worry about.

"It all connects, you see," the woman was saying, in a friendly tone, rather proud, if anything, of the big, solid, middle-class family she belonged to. "Even young Ben has his roots here. We've been trying to persuade him to come back and live here, you know. But he seems wedded to the Lake District."

"He's a bit young, isn't he, for that sort of decision?"

"You might think so, I suppose. But such a clever boy is an asset to the family. We don't want to lose touch with him."

"Is he an only child?"

"Oh, no!" laughed Norma. "Ben's the second in a family of five. But he's the only one who ever showed any interest in his mother's relatives, and even he gets very confused by it all."

There was something meaningful in the constant repetition of the word *family*, Thea realised. And something even more meaningful in the fact that the woman who had died in the Corner House was connected to this self-important collection of people, who evidently placed great significance on genes and inheritances and errant branches who went off to places like Cumbria and even presumably China. But it couldn't possibly lead to a person being murdered. Here, she decided, was the moment of truth, crunch time. Assuming Norma really was here on her own, it was as safe a moment as she could hope for to reveal something of what she knew, and to ask a whole lot of questions.

"You know what?" she said. "I think that woman who was killed at the weekend was another member of your family. I suppose you must have known her. She only lived in Banbury. Not far away at all."

Norma was slow to react. Then she simply shook her head and said, "No, no. You've got that totally wrong. From what I heard, the woman was *Chinese*. She must have got on the wrong side of somebody in a tour group. Things can get terribly heated on those buses, you know. The same people squashed up together day after day, all kinds of arguments can break out, and then get completely exaggerated."

"Enough to lead to murder?"

"I don't see why not."

Despite Ben's discoveries and her own suspicions, Thea was half persuaded. It did fit with the few fragile facts she knew. "Is that what everybody in the village thinks?"

Norma shrugged. "We haven't really discussed it. And honestly — she can't possibly be a relative. We'd *know*, if she was." Her manner was disarmingly transparent, the eyebrows raised again in sincere denial.

"Well, her name was Wheelwright. Could it be that some of the others knew, but not you?"

Norma went quiet and rather pale. She swallowed down her obvious shock and smiled. "I hardly think so. You've got hold of the wrong end of the stick there.

316

Who told you that, anyway? It's impossible. We've all been beavering away at the whole ancestry thing for years now, sharing our findings. Listen — let me phone Richard and see what he says about it. If you're right, then there's something very secretive going on, and I want to find what it is."

Again the spine tingled. "Oh — I expect Ben will have told him the whole thing by now. He found a whole lot about Karen on the Internet. It was amazing."

"Karen? But I heard that her name was Grace."

"I know. Ben's found the whole thing on the Internet."

"I see. We might have known he would. He's such a clever boy, isn't he. And he does love anything to do with murder. You should hear his poor mother on the subject. So my guess is he's been digging away on that smartphone thing of his, and come up with some idea that looks convincing — but it can't possibly be right. You know, you can't believe everything you read. There's an awful lot of disinformation."

"I don't think that can be the case here," Thea began to argue. "I mean — why would anybody go to so much trouble? I think we can at least be certain of her identity now. And that's all the police will need to get to the bottom of the story. They can question Grace Berensen — that's her partner — who's sure to shed a whole lot of light on the matter."

Norma flashed another quick smile, and then sighed. "Best leave it all to them, then. Listen — I've got a cottage pie all ready to be warmed up. What do you say? Shall we have some supper first, and then see about all this other stuff? I can show you my husband's collection of beer mats." She laughed. "He's terribly proud of them. They come from all over the world. And we could sit out on the patio to eat. Don't you feel you have to make the best of any dry evening, at this time of year?"

Could she possibly be as blithely innocent as she seemed? Nothing appeared to worry her, even startling revelations about her family. Did it not occur to her that if the fact of Grace's identity had been kept a secret, there had to be a reason for that? Something nasty, guilty and ultimately violent. Apparently, she could just carry on as normal, regardless of any implications. Perhaps this was the way most people behaved in the real world, and it was only Thea who saw killers behind every rural hedge. With an inner sigh of resignation, she accepted the offer of cottage pie and a large glass of red wine to drink while it heated up. Norma led her outside to a wrought-iron table and chairs on her patio at the back of the house. There were about eighteen plant containers ranged all around the area, full of red geraniums and hectic impatiens. Begonias and violas, too. Unimaginative but undeniably colourful.

It would soon be time to phone Drew. His image had hovered at the back of her mind all day, curiously tinged with trepidation. She found she was in no rush to speak to him, especially given his repeated discouragement of her making nightly phone calls anyway. There were going to be more hard decisions about how much to tell him, how closely to question him, and how much of her unhappy sense of distance she ought to try to convey. He would imply that it was all her own doing, that he was being the model husband in tolerating her absence without complaint. He would say he was happy to go along with whatever programme she had for the weekend, and express satisfaction that she was alive and well. She had no right to demand any more than that, which only made her more unhappy.

"I'll just put some peas on," said Norma, getting up. "Ready in about seven minutes, okay?"

"Lovely," said Thea, just as her phone pinged to announce a text.

"Got your message — extraordinary! Where are you now? Can I phone you? Not sure I should, if you're into something delicate. For God's sake be careful. C. B."

It struck Thea that nobody knew where she was. Not Gladwin, or Ben or Drew or Clovis. The phone was a false friend, useless unless she employed it to inform somebody of her whereabouts. And she did not know the name of the house. Suddenly it hit her that everything was wrong. She was yet again idling about when out there was every kind of wickedness, urgently requiring attention. What was that line about evil flourishing when good people did nothing to stop it? It was after seven, and here she was hiding away from everybody with a nice woman who was making cottage pie, of all things.

Norma had not come back, and in a fit of eager cooperation Thea texted back, "Chadwick house having supper. Probably best not to phone, though not in any danger." Despite the adjurations of Stephanie, Jessica and others, Thea still felt impelled to use telegrammese for her texts. And this time, she wanted it done before Norma caught her and started asking questions.

As it was, the mobile was back on the table when the woman returned. "Shouldn't you be calling your husband?" she asked brightly.

"Not yet. He won't have got the kids to bed yet. Another hour or so should be fine."

"Well, supper's ready, just about. More wine?"

"Why not?" said Thea, against her better judgement.

"And after that, I'd better call Richard. I can't rest until I've had all this out with him. He's sure to be able to explain it to us."

"He's the expert, is he?"

"You could say that. He's been obsessed this last few months. There's that property, you see, standing empty. He says it can't go on like that, not now that Simon's dead —" She stopped herself, eyes widening. "Well, you won't understand any of that. I'm just prattling as usual."

Thea nodded. "The farm that Gwendoline left," she said. "Yes, I know about that."

"Ben again, I suppose." The tone was a lot less admiring this time. "I don't know what the older generation would think of him splurging all the family secrets the way he does."

"I don't think he realises it's meant to be secret." Thea aimed for a mild lack of concern, while her pulse was accelerating. Somewhere just down the village

320

street Ben might be facing an irate old man — or two — who were not taking at all kindly to his relentless researches. The air around Barnsley seemed to prickle with imminent drama. *At least Barkley knows where I am now*, she thought.

She made herself eat the delicious homemade fare in the rays of the lowering sun, which had finally succeeded in breaking through clouds in the closing hours of the day. Occasional cars went by, on the other side of the house, and a plane growled its way across the sky. "Peaceful," she said, wistfully.

Before Norma could agree, there was a musical peal that could only be her front doorbell. The patio was at the back of the house, a door opening onto it from the kitchen. Rather than go through the house to the front, it was much quicker to trot around the side and see who might be standing there. And even quicker than that to call a welcoming "Hello-o-o?" and invite the newcomer to join the little party. Which Norma did, in a loud but wavering voice.

But instead of a single person, there were two. Caz Barkley led the way, square-shouldered and professional, closely followed by a woman Thea had just seen in a newspaper photograph. "Mrs Chadwick?" said Barkley. "I'm sorry to intrude, but I was hoping for a word with Mrs Slocombe. I'm Detective Sergeant Barkley and this is Ms Berensen."

"What on earth . . .?" squealed Norma, getting to her feet, fork still in hand. Nice Norma. Nice *normal* Norma was clearly very perturbed by this turn of events. Thea's mind was working slowly, with no instant realisations or implications bubbling up. Norma was still uttering shrill half-sentences. "How did you know . . .? Who told you . . .?"

Grace Berensen stood back, her eyes red and blurred after what had obviously been a prolonged spell of crying. Thea tried in vain to meet her gaze with a comforting smile. She tried to remember what time she had phoned Cirencester with the dead woman's name. How long would it have taken the police to work out where Grace lived, go to find her, break the news and suggest she go with Barkley to the scene of her partner's murder? It all felt remarkably quick.

Caz addressed Thea directly. "Could we go to the Ibbotson house, do you think? Ms Berensen wants to see the place — you know what I mean. And she'd like to talk to you about what happened." Then she turned to Norma. "It's all right, Mrs Chadwick. That is, we *will* want a word with you at some point. I'd appreciate it if you could stay here until somebody arrives to speak to you."

"Me?" Norma's voice rose even higher. "What on earth for? I had the police round here on Sunday, asking me whether I'd seen anything suspicious at the Corner House. What more do you want to know?"

Caz glanced at Thea. "Just routine," she said blandly. "Nothing to worry about."

Questions began to stir sluggishly in Thea's mind. How much did Caz know? Had she spoken to Ben Harkness? Was she here all on her own, or were there people from Cirencester swarming all over quiet little Barnsley?

322

The cooling cottage pie called to her, the few forkfuls she'd managed thus far only increasing her hunger. "Can I just finish this, do you think?" she asked. "Are you in a tearing hurry?"

"Only Thea Slocombe," murmured Caz, rolling her eyes. "Hurry up, then."

Norma Chadwick watched her in undisguised amazement, as she finished the food. Thea knew she was behaving strangely, ignoring the clear request of a police detective, as well as the evident needs of the suffering Berensen person. But she was giving herself time to think; wanting to test the dawning theories that were nudging at her. She was aware of Grace Berensen finally giving her a close scrutiny, trying to understand this apparent callousness. "I'll just be a minute," she said, with her mouth full. "It would be a shame to waste it, you must admit." She beamed at Norma. "It really is very delicious."

Norma was making no attempt to eat her own meal. She was jittering about on the patio, alternately trying to look relaxed and demonstrating confusion and alarm at the presence of a police detective. Unlike Thea, she was steadfastly averting her gaze from Grace Berensen. "This is awful," she was muttering. "I don't know what to think."

"Just relax," Caz urged her. "We'll soon have everything sorted out."

But that was quickly shown to be over-optimistic. A man's voice was heard approaching, calling as he went, "Norma! Are you there?" Before she could respond, Richard Jackson came into view, his limp as

323

pronounced as ever. In his wake was young Ben Harkness, looking rather pale.

Thea tried to watch all the faces at once, wondering where the deepest significance lay. She was the only person sitting down, which seemed to give her a useful cloak of invisibility.

Richard stopped dead at the sight of the four women. He glared round as if suspecting a conspiracy, pausing with Caz Barkley. "Are you a police officer?" he demanded.

"I am, sir, yes. This is Ms Berensen, and I think you know Mrs Slocombe." She put a gentle hand on Grace Berensen's arm. "I believe this must be one of the Mr Jacksons," she said. "Your partner's relative."

"They're probably *all* her relatives." The woman spoke for the first time.

"Don't you know?" Ben's mind was obviously working at top speed. "Have you not been here with Karen to meet them?"

She looked at him, as if calculating how to take his words. Then she appeared to decide to take him at face value. After a deep breath, she started to explain. "She had no idea they were here. We have only lived in Banbury for a short time. As far as we could see, there is nobody in this area who carries the name of Wheelwright. All we knew was that it had once been a very large family, and that there was a valuable property being contested. Six months ago, Karen began to make enquiries — and this is the result." She dissolved into quiet weeping. Thea recalled Karen/Grace's remarks

324

about greed, and finally realised that light was dawning on the story.

The real Grace sniffed back her tears and spoke again to Ben. "And you? You're another cousin, are you?"

"I am as it happens. I'm as surprised as you are — more so, probably. You hadn't reported her missing, then?"

His youth protected him, of course. Where older heads and hearts would quail before confronting someone so very newly bereaved, Ben stepped in and treated her exactly as he treated everybody else. Grace seemed to appreciate his directness. "What would have been the point?" She spoke with a despair that struck Thea as utterly tragic. "The police don't worry very much about healthy sane adults who drop out of sight for a few days. Besides, Karen would have been furious with me if I did that."

"And yet — it would have made everything so much easier if her identity had been established sooner," the young man continued.

"She would still have been dead," Grace Berensen pointed out.

Everyone fell silent at that unarguable fact. But then Ben went back to his entirely unauthorised questioning. Thea wondered why Barkley or even Richard Jackson didn't stop him. "You didn't hear anything at all about it on the news?"

"No, I don't bother much with the news. I find it only makes me angry."

"That'll be because you're a social worker," he nodded. "Makes sense."

Thea abandoned any further pretence to be eating, and spoke to Caz. "What's happening now? Are we still going over to the Corner House?" The detective merely shook her head, as if to say *Just wait a minute*.

"Richard?" It was Norma who faced her distant cousin, with a puzzled expression. "Why are you here?"

"So this young man can repeat to you what he's been saying to me. You need to hear it for yourself, and tell him what absolute tripe it all is."

Everybody looked at Ben, who lifted his chin, and said in a voice full of absolute conviction, "It was Uncle Richard who killed Karen Wheelwright."

CHAPTER
TWENTY-FOUR

"There!" trumpeted the older man. "What do you make of that? The boy's obviously lost his wits."

"You did, though," said Ben calmly. "Perhaps you should tell us how you hurt your knee. And how you've been in touch with a solicitor in Manchester who's taken on your application to inherit the family farm, left by Gwendoline. How the only serious rival for it was Karen Wheelwright, whose father died this year, leaving her free to pursue her claim. Simon wasn't interested, was he? But Karen most certainly was."

Richard stared furiously at him. "You little snoop! Where have you got all this from?"

"I admit I got into your computer and read the messages from Brock, Clinton and Dannington. Why go to a Manchester firm, I wonder? My guess is that any solicitor around here is either a relative of yours, or knows someone who is. It wouldn't be safe to put anyone on the alert, would it?"

Richard turned to Norma, who was looking very pale. "So there you have it. Wild accusations without a shred of evidence. What do you make of it, eh?"

It seemed to Thea that the man was genuinely outraged. She had seen the way a murderer generally

327

behaved when confronted with his crime. Mostly they went quiet, or began to tell a string of unconvincing lies. Sometimes they turned violent or tried to run away. She couldn't remember one who had maintained such a dignified stance.

"You should probably try to explain yourself, then," Norma said tightly. "Because I can testify to the fact that you were in that house on Sunday morning. I saw you from my bedroom window."

"Uh-oh," said Ben, slightly shakily. "We weren't expecting that, were we?" He looked at Caz and then Thea.

Thea was straining every nerve to make everything fit neatly into a coherent picture. The family inheritance . . . Gwendoline Wheelwright . . . Manchester . . . the business park . . . "Um . . ." she said. "Shouldn't you have mentioned that before? When the police questioned you on Sunday, for instance?"

"He's my cousin," shrilled Norma. "I wasn't going to betray him if I didn't have to, was I?"

Thea's voice gained in confidence. "But I don't think it was him you saw, was it? I think it was much more likely to have been his brother Edward. He's the elder of the two, after all. Wouldn't he have a better claim to the inheritance?"

"Shut up. You've no idea what you're talking about."

"And who moved the ashes from the barn?" Thea threw in, almost at random. The frustration and embarrassment of the afternoon still remained with her. "The ashes of the woman who started this whole business, as far as I can see."

"Thea." Caz Barkley spoke with unmistakeable authority. "Back off, will you? You're not helping."

"She could be right, though," said Ben slowly. "Edward might have a stronger motive."

Richard's face grew redder than ever, but he remained silent. There were too many people, Thea realised. It was sure to turn into a chaotic mess at any moment, unless somebody made a decisive move. She hadn't expected it to be Grace Berensen.

"Karen went to Manchester last week," she said. "She had a letter from those solicitors, asking her to go and see them. She told me she wasn't sure when she'd get home, because there might be reasons why she'd stay there over the weekend."

"Didn't you wonder why she hadn't phoned you? What did you think she was doing all this time?"

"I thought she must be working on her case. We don't live in each other's pockets," she said. "I was working all weekend, anyway. I had a bit of a crisis of my own, as it happens."

She hadn't noticed herself still using the present tense about her partner, Thea observed. The reality still hadn't sunk in very far.

"But she believed she'd got a strong claim to the family property?"

Grace nodded. "Her father was Gwen's favourite. He was always good to her. She knew it was going to be a hard battle, but she was confident she'd win eventually."

"All very stupid," grated Richard. "By the time the solicitors took their fees, as well as courts and barristers and all the rest of it, the value of the farm would be eaten up, anyway." He spoke to Ben. "Which is why I decided not to take it any further. Those emails you saw were out of date, laddie."

A squeal from Norma alerted everyone to the inevitable descent into something much less civilised. "Liar!" she accused. "Bloody rotten liar."

Barkley acted quickly. "All right. That's enough. Thea, please come with me. And Ms Berensen. As for the rest of you, there will have to be formal interviews to get to the bottom of all this. There will be a team of officers from Cirencester shortly on their way. Please ensure that you all make yourselves available for questioning. I suggest you go indoors and sit down. It's getting chilly out here."

Ben opened his mouth to protest, and then closed it again. Then made a fresh attempt. "What about me? Do I have to stay here with these two? And aren't you worried they'll concoct some sort of story together while you've gone?"

She gave him a very adult look. "Seems to me they're more likely to do the opposite. But you can come with us if you're not comfortable here. Just please don't make any more accusations." She turned to Thea. "Exactly who *is* this boy?" she asked. "And where did he spring from?"

"I think he might be an alien," Thea replied. "He seems to have superhuman powers, anyway."

"Well, I'm glad he's on our side," said Caz.

★ ★ ★

Thea felt very awkward ushering Caz, Ben and the real Grace into Tabitha Ibbotson's house. It was even worse having to take Grace up to the attic, leaving the others downstairs. "But there's not even a bed in here," was the first response.

"No. There were blankets and cushions, but the police have taken them all away now. She wanted to be up here. She thought she'd be safe."

"Huh!"

"I know." Thea was feeling more and more wretched, as she saw herself through this sad woman's eyes. "The whole thing's so dreadful."

They stood there for another half-minute, saying nothing. Then, as they turned to go, Thea burst out, "So who did she hurt?"

"What?"

"She said to me, 'We fear those we hurt' and she *was* frightened. She expected somebody to be after her. So who was it? What did she do?"

"I have no idea," said Grace flatly. "It all feels like being in a ghastly nightmare, where nothing is even slightly rational. Karen could be very determined, and outspoken, but she would never *hurt* anybody."

When they got back to the living room, Ben and Caz were both leaning over his smartphone, unaware of anything other than the little screen. "What?" asked Thea, aware of a rising tension in the air above their heads.

"The solicitor's website. There's an out-of-hours number. We're going to call it," said Ben. And he did, there and then, apparently with Barkley's blessing. He asked a few questions, clearly unsatisfied with the replies. "It's a police matter," he repeated.

Thea met Caz's eyes — and whispered, "So why isn't it you talking to them?" Caz waved a silencing finger, shaking her head at the same time.

"Could you give me his number, then?" the boy was insisting. "That can't do any harm, can it?"

Apparently, he was triumphant, since he scribbled down some digits on his ever-present notepad.

He waved the phone at Caz — "You or me?" he asked.

"Best be you. I'm well outside the rules already. And — though it pains me to say it — you seem to be more across the details than I am."

But Ben hesitated. "We need to talk it over first," he said. "If you're not sure . . ."

"I think I know who she hurt." Grace's voice was low and slightly choked. "Karen — you said she must have hurt someone. I think I know who that must be."

They gathered round her, eager and solicitous. "Sit down," said Thea. "In your own time," said Caz. Ben was holding his notepad and pencil.

Grace took the upright chair that Thea urged her towards, and leant her head on one hand, elbow on the table beside her. "It started with Simon — Karen's father," she began haltingly. "He was a very committed socialist. Communist, really, at least in the old days. Remember he was married to a Chinese woman. He was a devoted follower of Chairman Mao, back in the sixties. Anyway — that meant that he never approved of private property. When Gwendoline died leaving the farm, Simon was the one with the best claim on it. But he refused to have anything to do with it. So that meant the Jackson brothers and a few cousins all scrambled over each other to get it. All those years of wrangling, endless legal fees and false hopes. Karen would talk about it now and then, but there was nothing she could do while her father was alive."

"But then he died," said Ben. "And she could do what she liked."

"So who did she hurt?" Thea demanded impatiently.

Caz flapped a hand at her, and Grace ignored her. "She went back on a promise. Simon made her promise never to make a claim on the estate. He made her sign an agreement, and sent copies to the relatives. But she broke it. She said it wasn't valid after he died. So she went up to Manchester last week to see the solicitor handling the whole business, to tell him she wanted to apply for the inheritance."

"And ran into the other claimants who drove her back here, trying to talk her out of it, and when she refused to co-operate, they killed her," Ben summarised.

Grace heaved a heartfelt sigh. "That's what it looks like, doesn't it?" Tears were trickling down her face. "But who would ever imagine they would *kill* her for it."

"So — the Jackson brothers did it, did they?" asked Thea, with a frown. "And Richard twisted his knee on these stairs, when rushing to get away afterwards."

She tried to assemble all the new facts into a better picture. "But who took those ashes out of the barn?" That had been nagging at her all afternoon.

"My guess would be Norma," said Ben. "But I don't think it matters much now. The main thing is that somebody's gone to the trouble to make her a little memorial, and think about her. That's quite nice, whoever it was."

Thea remembered that Gwendoline was also a relative of Ben's, even if she died before he was born. She still hadn't got the family relationships straight, and wondered whether she ever would.

"We'd better go back over the road and talk to them," said Barkley.

After a stunned silence, Thea said, "But . . . won't that be a bit risky? I mean, you won't want all of us tagging along, will you?"

"We need to know whose car brought her back here from Manchester," said Ben, tapping his notebook with a finger.

"That's an easy one," said Caz. "Edward Jackson's vehicle was caught on the CCTV camera at the business park on Saturday morning. But of course he was dismissed as a local who had property there, so nothing was made of it. We can check cameras between here and Manchester to confirm it was the same car that brought her here."

"Norma says she saw Richard leaving this house on Sunday," Thea reminded them.

"But Norma was lying," said Ben, on a sudden thought. "Because Richard's wife told me this afternoon that he spent most of Sunday morning at the A&E in Cirencester, after twisting his knee. He fell down some steps in their garden and landed awkwardly.

I've only just remembered — she talks so much, you tune her out after a bit. But you can check that, can't you?"

"We can check everything," said Caz, slightly uncertainly. "But if that's where he was, why didn't he say so earlier, when Norma claimed to have seen him?"

"He did say she was lying. I think he's the sort of man who doesn't see any need to explain himself. He thinks his probity is self-evident," said Thea. "He knows he'd never kill anyone, and he assumes everybody else knows that as well."

"Norma stands to lose most of all," said Grace. "That's what I've been trying to tell you. Norma Chadwick passionately wants that farm. And Karen just laughed at her. I guess you could say that's the person she really hurt."

Caz then revealed that there had been two uniformed officers from Cirencester sitting in a car outside the Chadwick house for the past hour. It took no time at all to walk over to them, request them to follow her into the house, and arrest Norma as being wanted for questioning. Thea stood in the gateway of the Corner House, and watched as the woman from across the road was slotted onto the back seat of the vehicle. Richard Jackson stood and watched them go. Thea couldn't tell whether he'd seen her, along with Ben and Grace, who were in the driveway, talking quietly. So she called out softly, "Hello! Would you like to come over for a drink?"

He glared at her. In the fading light his expression was hard to read, but she thought it looked every bit as angry as before, "I do not, thank you very much," he snarled.

Ben was suddenly at her side. "He blames you," he said quietly. "You made it so easy for them to kill poor Karen, didn't you?"

She was still trying to complete the picture, filling in gaps and stumbling over loose ends and puzzling questions. "Them?" she repeated.

Ben raised his voice. "Edward and Norma did it together, didn't they? She must have seen you and Karen going into the house on Saturday afternoon, and felt that fate had lent a hand. There was her hated rival, served up on a plate."

"Be quiet!" Richard Jackson thundered. He came limping across the road at top speed. "Do you want the whole village to hear you?"

"Oh, Uncle," sighed Ben. "It's a bit late to worry about that, don't you think?"

Somehow they all found themselves back in the house. Richard Jackson was plainly a broken man, holding himself together by sheer willpower. He accepted a mug of coffee, but made no move to drink it. "There was a meeting up in Manchester for all the claimants to the estate, including Norma. She went with Edward," he mumbled. "I was supposed to go, but Edward said he could speak for both of us. He phoned me on Friday night and said it had gone very badly, and there was almost no chance of us inheriting anything at all. Norma's case was stronger than ours, but this girl of Simon's was almost certain to win. He said we should just cut our losses and forget about it."

"And did you agree with that?" asked Ben.

"For myself, I never much cared. But Norma's been a pal all our lives. More like a sister than a cousin. We hated to see her lose out, just when she'd thought it was in her grasp. The thing is," he raised his head, "that husband of hers, Bernie. He's been borrowing money against the expectation of landing the farm. If they lose it now, he's going to be in quite a mess. He's already got a hopeless credit rating, after getting into trouble in his youth. Norma's spent years trying to live that down."

"Ah!" said Ben and Thea together, fitting another piece into the picture.

"So, Edward backed Norma up when she turned nasty in the car. Karen must have been left in no doubt what they intended to do. No wonder she was so scared when you found her," said Ben to Thea. "That more or less wraps it up, doesn't it?"

Thea had said nothing since the moment when she understood that Richard blamed her directly for everything that had happened. "She saw us from the window?" she said now. "So — what would have happened if I hadn't ever met her? Karen, I mean. If she'd crawled off on her own and somehow got back home to the real Grace with no harm done?" She gazed miserably at Richard. "You're right. It is all my fault."

"Stop it," Ben ordered. "You can't go thinking like that. You thought you were doing her a kindness. You couldn't possibly have known what was going to happen. Besides, Norma didn't have to do what she did, did she?" He turned to Richard. "And you knew all along what had happened, didn't you? You knew and never said a word."

The elderly man nodded slowly. "I thought it best just to let everything settle down without sullying the family name. The woman said her name was Grace. Nobody had the slightest idea who she was. I thought perhaps it would all just remain unresolved for ever."

Thea could see her own feelings of disgust clearly reflected in the faces of the other two.

CHAPTER
TWENTY-FIVE

It was almost eleven when she got back to Broad Campden, having returned the borrowed car and been given a lift by Barkley. Fridays were popular for funerals, but she could not recall Drew saying there was one that day. The family car was in the driveway, which was not conclusive evidence of anything. She quietly opened the front door, eager to surprise him and the children.

But she had reckoned without her dog. Hepzie came flying out of nowhere less than a second after Thea stepped into the hallway. The spaniel's ears flapped and the pink jaws flopped. The dog wriggled and leapt and slavered and wagged, and Thea gathered her clumsily to her chest for a prolonged and guilty hug. Still no sign of human life, she noticed.

They must be outside, she concluded, so she went through to the back door and looked out. A strange little tableau met her gaze.

Stephanie and Timmy were washing the hearse, very seriously and quietly. Soapy water dripped down the headlights, thanks to Timmy's efforts, and Stephanie was giving the long side windows a similar concentrated attention.

Drew was lying on a garden lounger, his head turned away, facing a big straggly rose bush that had boasted four handsome pink blooms in recent weeks. Now the petals had turned limp and brown around the edges. A few lay scattered on the ground. Seeing that Timmy had spotted her, she put a finger to her lips and advanced on her husband. "Oh!" cried Stephanie, as she too realised what was happening.

Drew slowly turned his head, and Thea stopped, aghast. "My God! What happened?" she gasped.

There was a white surgical dressing on one cheek, and as she scanned his whole body, she realised he was wearing a dressing gown. "What . . .? When . . .?" she stammered. Whirling round to the children, she demanded, "What's been going on? Why didn't somebody *tell* me?"

"I fell downstairs, and landed on that bucket we'd left there for the past month or more. Cut my face and broke three ribs. Nothing serious."

But his expression was serious, and Thea knew several long moments of horror; not only at his injuries, but her own desertion and his failure to inform her of the accident. Multiple horrors, in fact. "Oh, Drew," she said. "How absolutely terrible."

"Not really," he argued. "I'll mend."

"Yes, but — I should have *been* here. I could easily have come home to look after you. Why did you keep it secret from me?" *How can I ever forgive you for that?* asked an inner voice that made her shudder.

"I didn't want to make a fuss. There was no need for you to be here. It's not as bad as it looks. I even did a funeral yesterday." He managed a lopsided smile. "Although one of the sons had to help Andrew with the lowering. I'm not supposed to do any heavy lifting."

The horrors just kept multiplying, the more she let the facts sink in. "Stop it!" she ordered brokenly. "Stop being so brave and British, and tell me to my face what a useless creature I am. The worst wife in the world, in fact."

"Come on, Thea," he said, sounding less gentle and forgiving than before. "There's no need for this."

"Yes, there is. You know there is. The truth is, I'm impossibly selfish." She stood back from him, intent on listing all her failings, purging herself of the accumulated guilt from the past week and perhaps longer. "You didn't tell me you were hurt because you thought I'd find it tedious being here with you, playing nurse. You were scared I'd act the martyr. Weren't you?"

Drew tried to sit up straighter, but the lounger would not co-operate. Instead he gasped and clutched his chest. "Stop it," he begged. "I can't defend myself in this position."

She paused, wondering why he thought he needed to defend himself. Then she remembered the secrecy, which she was trying to explain as all her fault, but which just possibly wasn't entirely. "I'm not attacking you," she said, "but it's really not fair that you never even gave me the chance to be here. I can see why — there I was, so self-important with my stupid dashing about after a murderer, and not telling you any of the real story, when all the time you needed me here, but didn't tell me. What sort of a couple are we, if that's the way we behave?" She was weeping, her voice clogged with tears.

A small hand gripped her shoulder. "Don't cry, Thea. We understand. Daddy explained that there are some people who like to stay quietly at home, doing boring things, and some who feel as if they've got to go out and have adventures. It's *good* that there are both sorts. We don't think you're selfish or stupid."

She looked down at the little boy, and forced a watery smile.

"We think you're brave," said Timmy. "And Stephanie's a really good nurse, you know. She's looked after Daddy terribly well."

It wasn't enough, but at least it staunched her tears. She pulled both children to her in a cumbersome hug, while the spaniel retreated to sit under the rose bush. "There's another thing," she said after a little while. "Jessica might be in some sort of trouble. Will you divorce me if I dash up to see her for a day or two?"

"I shouldn't think so," said Drew. "Come to that, I forgot to tell you there was a call last night from a person called Lucy Sinclair. Said you looked after her house in Hampnett —"

Thea was instantly transported to a snowy winter and a dead man in a field. "Yes, I did. Why? She doesn't want me again, does she?"

"She didn't say much, but I got the impression she just wants to meet up for a chat. No hurry, she said."

"She *was* nice," said Thea, hearing echoes of the Hampnett experience and recalling the sudden terror she had felt in that house. "But I wouldn't want to go through that again. Maybe I'll just leave it and see if she calls back."

Drew nodded absently, then said, "Oh — by the way, did you find the Barnsley murderer?"

She flinched. "Sort of. The dreadful thing is, if I hadn't been there in the first place, the murder would probably never have happened. I was a catalyst, of the most malign sort. It just shows I should stay at home from now on and try to mind my own business." She stopped. "No, I won't talk about it any more. It wasn't an adventure, Tim, and I wasn't brave. I was just messing about for no good reason, and did a lot more harm than good. I promise I won't do it again."

Drew and Stephanie gave identically fond snorts. "We don't believe that for a moment," said Drew.

Acknowledgements

Thanks are due to Jennifer Margrave, who, as always, offered generous advice on the legal aspects of the story.